Praise

Heart of D

"Fresh, fun, fast-paced paranormal r... ...ce, spellbinding magic, a wry-humored, gutsy heroine and a sexy-as-sin hero put the charm on this witchy new series from multitalented, always fabulous Lauren Dane!" —Lara Adrian, *New York Times* bestselling author

"Dane always delivers a steamy, exciting ride . . . she leaves me wanting more!" —Larissa Ione, *New York Times* bestselling author

"Unputdownable . . . Great characters, wonderful world-building and, as always, a delicious romance. If you pick this book up, make sure you've cleared the afternoon."
—Ann Aguirre, national bestselling author

Further praise for Lauren Dane and her novels

"[It] just might fry your circuits." —*The Best Reviews*

"Scintillating . . . A roller coaster of emotion, intrigue and sensual delights . . . I was hooked." —Vivi Anna, author of *Glimmer*

"Erotic . . . Sure to keep you reading late into the night."
—Anya Bast, *New York Times* bestselling author

"In a word . . . amazing." —*RT Book Reviews*

TART

LAUREN DANE

HEAT | NEW YORK

THE BERKLEY PUBLISHING GROUP
Published by the Penguin Group
Penguin Group (USA) Inc.
375 Hudson Street, New York, New York 10014, USA
Penguin Group (Canada), 90 Eglinton Avenue East, Suite 700, Toronto, Ontario M4P 2Y3, Canada
(a division of Pearson Penguin Canada Inc.) • Penguin Books Ltd., 80 Strand, London WC2R 0RL,
England • Penguin Group Ireland, 25 St. Stephen's Green, Dublin 2, Ireland (a division of Penguin
Books Ltd.) • Penguin Group (Australia), 250 Camberwell Road, Camberwell, Victoria 3124, Australia
(a division of Pearson Australia Group Pty. Ltd.) • Penguin Books India Pvt. Ltd., 11 Community
Centre, Panchsheel Park, New Delhi—110 017, India • Penguin Group (NZ), 67 Apollo Drive,
Rosedale, Auckland 0632, New Zealand (a division of Pearson New Zealand Ltd.) • Penguin Books
(South Africa) (Pty.) Ltd., 24 Sturdee Avenue, Rosebank, Johannesburg 2196, South Africa

Penguin Books Ltd., Registered Offices: 80 Strand, London WC2R 0RL, England

This book is an original publication of The Berkley Publishing Group.

This is a work of fiction. Names, characters, places, and incidents either are the product of the author's
imagination or are used fictitiously, and any resemblance to actual persons, living or dead, business
establishments, events, or locales is entirely coincidental. The publisher does not have any control over
and does not assume any responsibility for author or third-party websites or their content.

PUBLISHING HISTORY
Heat trade paperback edition / November 2012

Library of Congress Cataloging-in-Publication Data

Dane, Lauren.
Tart : a delicious novel / Lauren Dane. — Heat trade paperback ed.
p. cm.
ISBN 978-0-425-25325-0
1. Man-woman relationships—Fiction.   2. Triangles (Interpersonal relations)—Fiction.   I. Title.
PS3604.A5T37 2012
813'.6—dc23
2012011831

PRINTED IN THE UNITED STATES OF AMERICA

10   9   8   7   6   5   4   3   2

I've been blessed by an abundance of
strong women in my life. This one is for Minnie,
Jewell, Bernice and Linda.

ACKNOWLEDGMENTS

First and foremost, thanks goes to my family. Family is incredibly important, and despite the grumpy times and the trips to the emergency room when my middle child does crazy things like climb bookshelves, they keep me sane and grounded.

My readers—thank you all so much for loving the Brown siblings so much that I'm able to give you Delicious.

People who make me better at what I do: Leis Pederson, thank you so much for your patient and sharp advice. Laura Bradford, thank you for your continuing belief in my work (and for your friendship). Megan Hart, who has read so many IMs, emails and manuscripts, and who has taken the time to talk me off ledges and make me laugh. My beta readers Mary, Fatin and Renee—thank you for all the time and effort you've so freely given me over the years.

My secret illuminati author ninjas, aka TLTSNBN—thank you each and every one for kicking butt and taking names.

1

....

n case anyone ever doubted it, getting up at four in the morning was all sorts of things. Jules Lamprey had been doing it for years so it wasn't so much a matter of *holy crap, it's early* anymore.

What she did like, she thought as she locked her front door and headed to her car, was the way the world held so much anticipation. No dawn yet. But it wasn't the middle of the night anymore either. The promise of a new day was just beginning to manifest itself.

She liked that she pretty much had the road to herself as she made the short trip to Tart. Oh sure, in a while there'd be people waking up to get that first ferry to Seattle, but for now, it felt as if the entire world was all hers.

And for a brief, thrilling moment after she'd parked her car and walked up the block, she stood and looked at her shop.

Tart, in all its glory. Shiny red and chrome with black-and-white tiles on the floor. The place she'd been given so unexpectedly had become her heart. The place she always knew existed because she'd made it so.

Hers. She unlocked the back door and went through to the kitchen, hanging her things up and getting ready to start the day. She figured at least one of her friends would be by in the next hour either to help or seeking tarts and coffee, and that made her nearly as happy as seeing the front of Tart each and every morning.

True to Jules's gut feeling, Gillian came in at six. Gillian Forrester had been Jules's closest friend for well over a decade and a frequent early bird visitor to Tart once she got her son Miles off to school.

Even so, six fifteen was early for Gillian.

"So what? Did you have some hot, early morning nookie with your rock-star fiancé or what?"

Gillian sniffed, but the smile on her lips gave her away. "I really need some coffee."

Jules grinned, leaning in for the hug. Tart had just opened for the morning commuters. She'd already done all her prep and things were baking and her display case was full of delicious treats.

But it was quiet enough for the time being that she could pause a moment to make Gillian a latte and slide a scone her way.

"Adrian was working pretty much the entire night in his new studio. He came home a while ago and told me he'd get Miles to school before he crashed. I sleep poorly when he's working. It's terrible and I should be ashamed of myself for apparently being addicted to him in my bed like some sort of comfort object."

Her best friend had met Adrian Brown the year before in an unlikely way. He was the biological father of her son Miles. They'd had a rough start, but Jules had never seen Gillian happier and the two of them were getting married that summer.

"Ashamed, my ass. You've got love. Love in the form of a tattooed, tall, dark and handsome musician who adores you. Of course you like him in your bed. But it's nice of him to deal with Miles."

Gillian's smile made Jules happy to the tip of her toes. "And we did, you know, get a little early morning—*ahem*—action in. So now I'm awake and he's going to sleep once he gets Miles off to school so I figure I might as well come here, see you, which I don't do often enough of late. And you'll take pity on me and give me caffeine."

It'd been a while since Jules had had early morning action, or action of any kind. Maybe she'd meet some hot rock-star friend of Adrian's at the wedding.

"Well, I'm glad you're here. You're right, I don't see you often enough lately."

"Are you mad at me? You must all feel like I've abandoned you."

She squeezed Gillian's hand. "Heck no. You have a few things going on in your life right now. A kid. A fiancé. A wedding. Your business. A new house. Hanging out with your friends tends to fall to the bottom of the list when you're doing all that other stuff. We don't feel like you've abandoned us. You should know us better than that."

Jules handled a few of her regulars before turning her attention back to Gillian.

"I miss you. There's so much going on."

Jules studied Gillian carefully, worried suddenly that she'd missed something. "Is everything all right? Do you need me to kick anyone for you?"

"This is exactly what I miss. No one you need to kick, though you know how much it pleases me to have my own army of Amazonian warrior women ready to do my bidding and protect me should I need it."

Jules laughed as she worked the counter for a few minutes.

"It's just busy," Gillian said as Jules got back to her. "Wedding stuff, and thank you so much for all your help. And house stuff. We're halfway between my house and the new place and Miles is bouncing off the walls with excitement. Little prat got a D on a big math test last week. I only found out when Adrian had taken out the recycling and found it in the papers."

Jules winced. Gillian loved her son intensely, but she was a tough momma on the big stuff like school.

"Anyway, I figured if I came in here before my first lesson and while my men took care of themselves, we could visit and you could fill me in on how the new arrangement is working."

The new arrangement was the business deal she'd worked out with her friends Mary and Daisy. Mary had moved her catering and dinner club business into Tart's space and had already grown her business by 50 percent. Daisy's art hung on the walls, and she sold it and other local artists' work as well as handling the business and marketing for Tart and Mary's catering business.

A lot of new things happening. So much that Jules found herself juggling her life a lot more lately than she ever had. But she felt like things were really looking up.

"I'm getting used to sharing my space, and it's going well. Profits are up for all three of us. I'm going out to Patrick Carter's farm after I close today. I'm expanding my menu to include locally grown produce."

"He'll love that. I've been worried about him after losing his wife."

"He seemed all right when I spoke to him on the phone. But you know, I can't imagine losing the love of my life after all those decades together. He still comes in here at least once a month though. And I think he's slowly moving forward." The Carters had been one of those couples who seemed to light up at the sight of one another.

"Here, try this one. It's a new recipe." She gave Gillian one of the strawberry buttermilk muffins she'd made earlier.

"If I must." Gillian winked and then tried it, humming her delight. "This is really good. Which pretty much is my answer every time you have me try something new of yours."

"The strawberries were frozen, but once they're in season I have a local supplier. I'm taking some out to Patrick's to give him a sample of what I can do." Along with the cherry turnovers he loved so much. Hey, she wasn't above a little bribery.

"No one is going to complain when you arrive carrying one of your red-and-white bakery boxes." Gillian grinned.

Pride filled Jules at the compliment. She'd worked hard to make the place her own after she'd inherited the building. It pleased her so much that she'd been as successful as she had.

She'd never wake up one day to have her entire life turned upside down and not have a backup plan. Like her mother had.

Jules had been out to Patrick Carter's farm just a few months before. Unfortunately it had been a less-than-happy occasion.

His wife Clara had battled cancer for the better part of the last several years and had finally succumbed to it. The wake had been lovely, filled with friends and family. It had been a tribute to just what an amazing person Clara Carter had been.

Patrick was hale and hearty in that way some men grew into as they hit eighty. Barrel-chested and broad shouldered, he'd spent his entire life on the farm he still worked. He stopped into Tart once a month when he came into town to run errands and she'd sit with him and visit for the better part of an hour or two. He was a terrible flirt, which always made her smile. And he knew about stuff. His stories always entertained her.

But the sadness in his eyes had stuck with Jules. Her friend Daisy, in addition to being an artist and a dancer, had a great mind for business. It was her idea to bring Mary and Jules together to combine their resources. Using locally sourced ingredients in the food Tart put out would add another facet to the business. It was smart and would strengthen her ties and commitment to the community.

So when the idea had come up, Patrick was one of the first names that had come to mind. It was probably a little thing for him, but hopefully it gave her the chance to see him more often and also get him connected to a new and fun project.

The island was small enough that it didn't take long to get out to his place. The curved drive up to the pretty farmhouse was lined with trees. His bees were out in the orchards behind the house. She wanted his fruit *and* his honey.

It wasn't until she'd parked and gotten out of the car, her arms laden with the pastry she'd brought, that she noted Patrick was sitting on his big front porch. But he wasn't alone.

Both men stood as she headed up the steps and she realized the other one was Gideon, Patrick's grandson.

It was an unexpected pleasure to see him. Which was probably why just looking at him sent a little zing through her. That or the fact that he was ridiculously gorgeous. Either way, a zing was a zing and who was she to go looking at any zing askance when she'd been sort of zing-less of late?

"Two Carter men in one place? I'm not sure Bainbridge Island is big enough to handle all this handsome." She winked at Patrick, who kissed her cheek and grabbed the pastry box with a happy sound and a grin.

"If these have cherry turnovers in them, you can have whatever you like, girlie." He indicated Gideon, who stood, smiling at her. "You remember my grandson, don't you?"

Gideon's gold-blond hair was to his shoulders. His beard was neatly groomed and framed a sinfully full mouth. Jeans and boots were part of his job, much like the ones his grandfather had on. But Gideon only made her think, *"hot cowboy."*

"I do," she managed to say instead of drooling. He'd been a cute older boy she'd crushed on growing up. But this Gideon was a man. Damn.

Before she could say anything else, Gideon stepped to her and pulled her into a hug. He smelled like sunshine and hard work and a hint of the shampoo he used.

"It's really good to see you, Jules. Come sit. Granddad has made coffee. I told him we should have offered you food, but he insisted you'd bring it so why bother."

Oh. His accent. Not pronounced or even that noticeable, but it was there. A general slowing of his speech. Sexy.

"Patrick, I brought you some other things in addition to the cherry turnovers." She tipped her head to the boxes, though she didn't bother to hide her flattered smile when she noted he'd already started eating.

He pointed at the box. "You can have one, boy. Just don't get greedy."

Gideon looked to his grandfather. "So says the guy who's shoving one into his face already like a starving man."

Patrick looked over and snorted. "I'm still growing, Gideon. I need it."

She laughed, liking the sight of a far more lighthearted Patrick than she'd seen in some time. It was clear Gideon's presence wasn't just candy for the ladies in the area.

"How long are you in town for, Gideon?" She hoped she didn't sound like a breathless schoolgirl hinting at being asked out. It wasn't as if he was a stranger after all. She'd known him since they were both kids and he came to Bainbridge every summer and over the winter holidays to visit his grandparents.

But the zing? Well, she didn't get any zing when she hung out with Mary's brother Ryan, who was also gorgeous and who she'd known equally as long. Mary's other brother Cal was a whole different story though.

"For good." He handed a mug to Jules. The day was crisp so the coffee was much appreciated. "Granddad and Grandma ran this place my whole life. I figured it wasn't a bad thing to get into the family business."

Patrick gave a wheezy sort of laugh and patted Gideon's knee. "That's a pretty way of saying that since Clara's death I've needed a little help. He's good at saying things in pretty ways."

They had good energy, Gideon and his grandfather. Gideon seemed at ease, his body language relaxed and open. It was a choice he'd made happily, apparently, which Jules was glad of. And not just because if he was around on the regular, she could look into the zing a little closer.

"I'm glad you're back in town. I suppose, then, I need to talk to you both. I'm doing some expansion of Tart and part of that is a new, locally sourced line of baked goods. My partner Mary, she's a caterer and she'd also be interested in local ingredients for her food. We thought it would be nice to have a notation on the menu for the local farms and dairies we buy our ingredients from."

"Really? That's a great idea. Granddad and I were just talking about this earlier in the week. The cattle ranch I ran for years had some relationships with local restaurants. It's win/win for both, and for the locals who are customers."

She liked that he seemed so engaged with the farm already.

"That's a big part of it. I really love the idea of eating and sourcing as much local ingredients and goods as I can. There's so much around here that it's not that difficult to create a menu with at least fifty percent local products. My aim, after a year, is to be up at sixty percent or higher. I like that it gets me in contact with local farmers and ranchers and that it gives my customers a new perspective on the businesses they use without even knowing it."

Gideon leaned closer, his eyes bright, body language engaged with her. She could smell him, which was entirely pleasant when a breeze kicked up from time to time.

"I sure do like the idea of the family farm moving into the future this way. When I took over from my father we took our produce to market in an old truck." Patrick snorted his amusement as he snuck another turnover, winking when he caught her eye.

"We're talking about doing a produce and honey stand from late spring into the fall."

"That's a great idea. Have you thought about the farmer's market?" She was considering it herself, maybe later on. She could work it out with some of her local suppliers to have some of their stuff at her stall so people could check them out too. Hm.

They spent the next hour or so working on schedules for delivery, pricing, talking about the season for each product and those sorts of details. Patrick Carter knew his land. Knew what would be good when, and that helped a lot. Gideon knew these things as well, but he also had new ideas and seemed excited about what he could bring to Carter Farms.

He was smart. Ambitious. Really hot in those jeans he had on. It warmed her to watch him with his granddad. A man who valued family was pretty irresistible.

She really did need to get going. Even so, it took her another twenty minutes until she could finally work up the wherewithal to stand. "I really should head out. I appreciate the company, the coffee and the new business relationship."

Gideon stood as well. "I'll walk you to your car." Gideon hefted the flat of fruit she'd planned to take back to Tart.

"Thanks! You're handy." She bent to kiss Patrick's cheek. "Don't be a stranger."

"Course not. Though I do expect you to bring me sweet things. I need to supervise what's going on with my product, after all." He winked at her and she followed Gideon to her car.

She might have looked at his long legs and perfect ass in those faded jeans a time or six. They were too nice not to look. Like art. It would have been disrespectful, like ignoring a fine painting. Or something. Anyway, he had a nice butt and she wanted to look.

He loaded the tray and closed her rear door before standing straight again. *Man*, he was tall. She looked up and up some more and she wasn't a short woman. Just standing next to him made her feel delicate.

"Thanks for the heavy lifting." Jules cocked her head and shaded her eyes as she looked up into his face. "I've been worrying over him being out here alone. It's good you're back."

"Ah well. He'd have been just fine here without me. He's got a foreman who's been with us for fifteen years. But"—he shrugged—"it was time to come back and do something with my life. I love the farm, I love my granddad and why not?"

"Indeed. Though plenty would have found many reasons not to."

He took her hand. "I'm not them. And maybe they don't have someone like my granddad." He shrugged and she noted the faint blush on his neck and then wondered how his skin would taste. Like the hussy she was.

"You're not them at all. Which is a nice thing. Well, you know where I am if you get a hankering for something sweet. Or want to check out the product." She fought a blush, which in and of itself made her a little giggly inside.

Jules loved men. Most of them anyway. She wasn't shy when she was attracted to someone—and they were available of course. So she wasn't a stranger to flirting, but he made her . . . shy.

He still had her hand in his. She couldn't take her gaze from it. So big, his hand compared to hers. Big and callused, work-worn in places. It was the hand of a man who worked with his hands. Who made and managed things.

It sent a shiver through her and when her gaze returned to his face, he was looking down at her, a hungry look on his features.

Her breath caught a moment as he stood so close. There was something between them. She didn't know what exactly, but certainly attraction. She could work with that.

"I should go."

He let go of her hand before opening her door. "Drive safely, Jules. Maybe I'll stop in to Tart this week."

She nodded after she slid into her seat and got her belt on. "I think you should."

He shut the door and stepped back, leaving her in total silence for a moment before she turned the engine over and The Chemical Brothers poured from the speakers. He stepped back and gave her a small wave and she pulled away.

A new deal and an interesting man who made her warm and sort of, well, tingly. The sweetness of the beginnings of a maybe-something spiced the zing of the attraction between them.

Possibility. She could totally get behind some of that.

Gideon watched her pull away and head back to town. His heart beat a little faster as he caught the subtle scent she wore. Low and sultry. He'd have pegged her for a brighter, more classical scent.

But Jules Lamprey wasn't all that she seemed on the surface.

At first glance, Jules was brilliantly-blonde-girl-next-door beautiful. Sunny hair she wore in a high, sleeked-back ponytail.

Her eyes were large and sky-blue. A wide, open smile. Her clothing flattered. She was friendly, funny, a little flirty. The pretty girl he'd grown up with.

But another layer in? Well, that red-lipped mouth had a little cant up at the left. Like she had a secret. The turtleneck she wore was cashmere. And her perfume was rich and sexy. Like her laugh.

He'd watched the way she drank her coffee. She'd held the cup, cradling it to take its warmth. Her first sip had been with her eyes closed and a happy sigh. She had enjoyed the hell out of the different fruits she'd tried when they'd been working over schedules.

Jules Lamprey was a sensualist. There was something fairly irresistible about a woman who took pleasure in everything around her.

On top of all that, she was articulate, successful and fair in her dealings with his granddad. Independent and intelligent too. The whole package.

Unless he was sorely mistaken—and he didn't think he was—she was attracted to him in equal measure.

Gideon wanted a taste of the rather delicious Ms. Lamprey.

With a pleased sigh, he sat back on the porch with his granddad. "Is she seeing anyone, do you know?"

All around them was land his family had lived on and worked for generations. He'd been away from ranching for a while so it had taken a week or two to really get back into the life of a farmer. He wasn't a stranger to farming, wasn't a stranger to hard work with hands and body. And this was his in a way the Bar M never was.

Even better, he'd done it at Patrick's side, which had filled him with humility and pride. His grandfather trusted him to take Carter Farms into the next generation. It was a weight, but one he'd chosen freely.

Patrick gave him a sly smile and an elbow nudge. "Don't think so. She sure is a pretty one. All that pale hair and those big blue eyes. She's like a soap ad from the old days." Patrick chuckled. "Tart is always busy. She's built it up from nothing. That diner her parents ran did all right, but I never much got the feeling they did it for love of it. You walk into Tart and you know someone who loves the place is running it. And she makes a mean cherry turnover. So really if you get sweet on her, that's a win for me."

Gideon did love his granddad's sense of humor. Such a wily old guy. "One of these days you'll have to tell me how it is you've survived all these years being so shy with your opinions."

"Good to have you around, boy. Your father and your aunt never did indulge me the way your grandmother did. And you do too. Man's got something right when his grandson will laugh at his bad jokes."

Gideon agreed. It was good to *be* around. It fit. He wished his parents had come back to help, but his dad was an engineer, not a farmer. And his mother loved Patrick but she had a life in Oakland. They had offered to move Patrick down there and it had been a genuine offer. His aunt had done the same. But his grandfather belonged here on this land he'd raised children on, the land he and his wife had made into something special.

Speaking of special, Jules had come back into his thoughts. "When I first met her she couldn't have been more than five or so. Still has the freckles, I see. Even in middle school she was a tall, gangly girl. But the woman she's turned into is amazing. Funny how that works with women." Gideon snorted a laugh. "Can't imagine why she hasn't been claimed by someone."

"Jules is the kind of woman who can't be claimed by anyone but the man she thinks is worthy. Everything else is a game. She's smart that way." Patrick pulled another turnover from the box and Gideon considered mentioning it was his third but decided against it.

Patrick peered up at Gideon. "Question is, are *you* ready to date again?"

"I've been divorced three years. It's not like I haven't dated since. I've been over Alana a long time." Probably even before the ink had been dry on the divorce decree. Though it certainly hadn't been any fun to see her with other men. Sadly that had been a fact of life until he'd finally just sold his half of the Bar M to his ex-brother-in-law and gotten the hell out of Wyoming.

The longer he'd been away from Alana, the more he understood his own behavior. The more he knew he'd made the right choice to get away. It had all brought him back here anyway.

Three years of making a new start. It was long overdue. But it had all led him to that very moment and he couldn't help but think it was exactly what he should have been doing.

When Jules arrived back at Tart it was to find Daisy in the kitchen giving orders to a carpenter as he stretched to finish installing shelving on one of the far walls.

"Hey you." Daisy smiled quick and easy as Jules put the flat down on her worktable. "How'd it go?"

"Really well. Patrick was pleased to do it. Oh and hey, did you know Gideon was there? He's going to help Patrick run the place."

"The grandson, right? He's blond like you? He and Cal were tight? I have vague memories of having a crush on him when I was eleven or twelve."

"Join the club." Jules had a vivid memory of the two of them, Cal with his dark hair and olive skin, head back, laughing uproariously at something Gideon had said. They'd been cute teenage boys back in the day. "Yes. He and Cal used to run around a lot."

"Is he still cute?"

Jules put her hands on her hips. "Girl, you have a hot man already. Don't be greedy."

"Ha! Levi is *more* than enough for one woman to handle. But I have several single friends who are all awesome and gorgeous so it helps to know when a new, cute, single dude comes into the mix. Or even for that one gorgeous single friend who also likes boys as well as girls."

Jules tried very hard not to frown. If Cal and Gideon got together, it would suck. Mainly because she was tired of watching Cal date everyone but her over the years. But also because they were both so hot it would suck to know they were together and she wasn't gettin' any of it.

"I really do think you should just make a move on Cal. God, you just frowned at the mere *mention* of him dating. You two should be together."

But they weren't. And it was Cal's choice. "It's not up to me." She muttered this as the carpenter used the drill to get the last screws and brackets in. "It's stupid to even imagine there's going to be anything between us. He kissed me once, back when I was fifteen. And apparently it was so horrible he never tried it again. It's worse when he dates men because while I can work the being-a-woman thing pretty well when I put my mind to it, I can't be a dude. I don't have what he needs."

Now it was Daisy's turn to frown, and of course she looked just as adorable as she did when she smiled. "Just because he likes it doesn't mean he *needs* it. He needs someone who will love him for him, who will understand how close he is to his family, how important all his charity work is to him. So far I've seen him parade around with men and women who don't seem to get it. And it makes me wonder, Jules."

Jules braced herself, knowing Daisy would call it like she saw it. "Wonder what?"

"If he chooses people he'll never end up with permanently because there's one person he's wanted all along but is too shy to just finally make that move and grab your ass and take you to bed and give it to you the way he so clearly wants to."

Jules laughed and hugged Daisy. "You know I love you, right? Thank God you're here today. But I've been amenable to being jumped for years now and he's never made a move. We have a great, close friendship. I have to be happy with it and move on. So Gideon is totally cute and I think I may need to put some of my attention his way. One look at the way he moves, sort of slow and lanky, and you know he'd make a girl all boneless and sweaty between the sheets."

"Always one of my favorite qualities in a man. And it's been a while, if I recall and you know I do, since you've had a man in your bed. So tick tock, time's a running. Grab this Gideon while the getting's good."

They laughed and Jules began to sketch out tomorrow's menu. But Jules thought Daisy's advice was pretty darned good and planned to give it a go. Getting some Gideon sounded like just the thing.

2

. . . .

Just two days later, Jules looked up from wiping her counters down to find Gideon Carter standing in the doorway.

He strolled in as her mouth dried up. He had a way of moving, slow and sensual, his long strides eating up the space between them.

He was like an ad from a magazine, though instead of a cowboy hat, he wore a black wool watch cap and when he pulled it off to stick it in the pocket of his jacket, his hair still managed to look awesomely sexy. But tousled. Like sex tousled. And an image flashed through her brain. Gideon below her, spread out on her bed, naked and sweaty, grinning up at her, that hair of his in disarray around his face.

She swallowed hard and fought the flush at that image. "You really do that cowboy thing justice. Just sayin'. What can I get you?"

He bent a little to look in the cases and she had to stifle her hum of satisfaction at the slice of bare skin that showed at his waist as he did.

"Did I get here too late? I notice you're closing soon."

"I'm closing up now, but you're more than welcome to stay. How about a latte? Are you hungry?" Being alone with him was far better than dealing with customers any day of the week anyway.

He smiled, slow and sexy, and it sent a shiver through her. "You mean I get you all to myself?"

She couldn't help but smile in response. Relief too that he seemed as interested in her as she was in him. "Why yes, is that all right with you?"

"More than all right. Yes on the latte and how about one of those bacon cheddar scones? Please and thank you. That should hit the spot."

Who'd have thought manners could be an aphrodisiac? Damn. If he pulled his hat out and held it in his hands nervously and . . . okay, it was really necessary to stop making up fuck fantasies about him right at that moment. She could go home that night and remember the aw-shucks-ma'am thing when she was alone. Mmmm.

"Nice choice. Go sit and I'll bring it out when I finish." It would enable her to check out his butt too. Win/win.

He pushed a ten across the counter.

"No. Consider it my treat in honor of our new business deal."

He nodded and put the ten in the tip jar anyway before ambling off to a nearby table where he stretched long-as-sin legs and she noticed the boots. Good gracious, when did this cowboy fetish start? Didn't matter 'cause she sure had one now.

She turned to make his latte and took it over a few minutes later. "Hang on, I'm going to lock the front doors or we'll get stragglers." She flipped the closed sign and locked up.

He stood and held a chair out. "Sit with me, Juliet. That is if you have the time. I know sometimes it's busier cleaning up than anything else."

Flattered and surprised, she sat. "I have a few minutes. I'm already done with everything but the espresso machine. Mary often likes to have some when she comes in so I leave it for her."

He bit into the scone and nodded. "Mary is . . . ?"

"Mary Whaley. You remember the Whaleys, right?"

"Ah yes, Cal's little sister?"

Jules nodded. "Yes, that's her. She and I share this space. She has a catering business. She has a party tonight so I know she'll be turning up within the next hour or so."

He nodded. "Nice." He nodded again, toward his plate. "I like this. I was expecting . . . I don't know what. But it's better than I imagined. Did you go to school to learn to cook like this?"

As if he even needed to bother with flattery.

"My grandmother liked to bake. My first real memory of her was that she made me a lemon tart for a tea party. You know, like with dolls?" She smiled at the memory. "So then I asked her to let me help and that was the beginning really. She taught me how to make different kinds of pastry dough. Pastry cream. How to make a lattice-top pie. All that sort of thing. I just love to bake. It's sort of my art, as my friend Daisy says. It makes me happy. So sometimes I take a class here and there. To learn something new. But most of it is from my grandmother and mother."

He ate and she tried not to stare at his mouth. But he had a really nice mouth.

"I like that. This wasn't always a bakery though, right?"

"No. My parents ran this place as a diner. So I worked here. I cooked a lot. Waitressed. Learned how to keep books."

Gideon nodded; his focus on her was so intense she had to swallow back a nervous giggle. It'd been a long time since she'd been so giddy and tingly over a man. It felt good.

"Why'd you change this place from a diner to a bakery?"

She cocked her head. "That's a very long story."

And right as she began to suggest she tell him over dinner, Mary let herself in the doors, her arms full of supplies. Jules and Gideon both jumped up to help.

"Thank you." Mary grinned to Jules and then noticed Gideon. "Gideon Carter, I'd recognize you anywhere."

He smiled, bowing his head slightly. "You still have those curls."

Mary laughed as they brought the supplies into the kitchen. "I've tried everything to get rid of them at some point or other for years. I gave up and let them have their way. What brings you here to Tart today?"

Gideon looked to Jules and then back at Mary. "Jules here does. Man'd have to be a fool to resist something sweet with some coffee and that face to look at."

His gaze moved back to Jules and once he'd caught her attention, his mouth slowly curved up into a smile so naughty her nipples got hard.

By the time Jules had remembered anyone else existed, Mary was staring at her with one brow raised and a smile. Oh man, she'd never hear the end of it now.

"Gideon moved back to help Patrick run the farm."

Mary turned that pretty smile back to Gideon. "Really? That's great news. We were just talking last week about how we were worried about him out there on his own. I'm glad you're back."

He grinned. "Me too. He'd be tickled to know the ladies in town were talking about him."

Jules laughed then. "He's a big flirt."

They stood speaking for a few minutes more until Mary started to bustle around. "Don't mind me. I'm just going to get started. My staff are going to meet me at the party so that's one less thing to worry over." Mary got her things put away and an apron on after washing her hands.

Gideon took a step back from the counter and raised his hand in farewell. "It was really good to see you again, Mary. Please tell Cal I said hey. I need to head out to grab some lunch or a drink with him. I've got his number."

"He'll be happy to hear that." Mary made sure Gideon didn't catch the arch look she sent Jules's way.

Gideon put a hand at the small of Jules's back and guided her back out to the dining room. "I should get going. I promised Granddad I'd grab some groceries before I head back. He said he'd cook if I did. That's not a bad deal."

"Not at all. Grocery shopping is far more worth it when someone else does the cooking." She walked him to the door but when she moved to flip the latch to unlock it he took her hand and kissed her knuckles.

Again she noted the sheer size of his hand as he held hers. And then the warmth of his lips against her skin. It was impossible not to shiver with delight.

He straightened but kept her hand a moment longer. "I'm going to be back here to have some coffee and maybe something sweet. That all right with you?"

She felt the heat of her blush but tried not to think about it. Instead she let herself enjoy the butterflies in her belly at his sweet kiss.

"Yes. I'd like that."

He stepped back and she opened the door. "Good afternoon, Juliet. I'll see you soon."

"Say hi to Patrick for me."

She watched him lope down the sidewalk to a truck a few blocks down. *Damn*, he looked good going as well as coming.

Mary gave her a look when she came back into the kitchen before she went back to whatever it was she was preparing. "Well now."

"Well now, what?" Jules knew what Mary had meant, but that didn't mean she couldn't tease her friend into revealing it.

Mary snorted and looked up again briefly to raise her brow. "I think we've known each other far too long for that nonsense. Pretend like you don't know what I'm talking about. Pfft, I think not."

Jules laughed. "You need any help?"

"It's nearly done. Daisy hired me some new staff. The old staff will train them tonight so we'll be ready for the next set of parties. Enough of your games, missy. Tell me about Gideon holy-shit-did-he-grow-up-hot Carter."

Jules leaned against the counter and watched her friend dice something or other. "He *totally* grew up hot. And there's not much to tell really. It's at the flirting stage. He came in for coffee and a scone. We didn't have wild monkey sex on the counter or anything."

Mary's mouth lifted as she snorted a laugh. "That's really too bad. He looks like the type who just might toss you on a counter and bang you until you forget how to speak."

Jules shook her head. "To look at you, no one would guess what a filthy hoor you are." *Hoor* was the Delicious twist on *whore*, only without all the shame and yuckiness.

Mary laughed then, a full-on laugh. "Why be a hoor if you're not a filthy one? What's the point of being one if not that?"

Jules put an apron on and began to clean the espresso machine. "You want a latte before I finish cleaning this out?"

"Hell yes. Thank you. Back to Gideon, he's hot, no lie. A new boy in town is fun. For *you* obviously. He was friendly to me and all, but he looked at you like he wanted to take a bite. Also, Patrick has needed someone out there so I'm really glad for that."

Jules made the latte, set it near Mary's right hand and went back to clear everything up. And they didn't talk about Cal, though he was in between them just the same.

"You mentioned the new staff Daisy hooked you up with. They're working out then? You sure you don't need any help?"

"They're good. My short staffing issue is finally getting fixed. Thank God for Daisy. Honestly, I don't know what I'd do without her."

Mary's expansion of her catering business meant she'd had to hire more staff to work the parties and other events she was hired for.

"Honestly, I'm waiting to see if there's anything she can't do." Daisy was an artist, a dancer and she had a great way with people, which made her the perfect manager of the newly expanded Tart. It wasn't forever, Daisy had other things to do with her life, and with Tart, but they were grateful for all the help she'd provided. None of this would have been possible without her energy and ideas.

"No kidding. And on top of that, she's gorgeous and has a man like Levi. I'm beginning to get annoyed." Mary grinned as she said it.

"I think getting it on the regular-like has improved some lives around here. First Gillian and now Daisy. I'm having a long dry spell so I gotta say I'm glad Gideon is around. Maybe he can help me break that fast."

"So you think? I mean, like for real?"

"Oh well, I like him. He appears to like me. I've known him most of my life so it's not like he's a stranger and I have to wait to be sure he's not a serial killer." She shrugged and Mary tossed a baby carrot at her head.

"I'm a big girl. Old enough to be able to admit my parts would like to get to know Gideon's parts better. The rest of him too. I like him." Jules shrugged.

Mary nodded. "Too bad he doesn't have a brother."

They laughed as they worked, Jules pitching in to help load things into Mary's catering truck before she headed off to her gig. When Jules locked up it was more than past time to call Gillian about the next thing on her to-do list.

3

············

Once she got home and settled in, Jules grabbed the phone and dialed Gillian's number.

"Hello there, Juliet, how may I assist you?" Jules's godson and Gillian's fourteen-year-old son Miles answered, making her laugh.

"Hey, kiddo. How's it goin'?"

"Pretty cool. Oh! Dad said I could play with his band at the wedding. How cool is that?"

Jules smiled at the idea. She knew how much Miles loved music, and that his father, a notable musician, had given him such a big thumbs-up was lovely. She liked Adrian Brown even more at that point.

"That's totally cool. I can't wait to hear you." Though Jules bet Gillian had told Miles that if any more Ds came home he wouldn't be doing any such thing.

"Thanks. He also said he'd be cool if our band played. It'd be cool if Dad came up to play a song or two with us. Mum said he would and that I should ask him. But he's all—well, you know, he's Adrian Brown."

She heard Gillian's voice in the background. "Sure he is. And you're his son and he loves your music. Silly. I'd wager the wedding will be filled with musician types so I bet you could do one of those cool jams they have at the end of the Rock and Roll Hall of Fame events. That would be epic."

He gasped, which only made Jules smile bigger. "Dude. That would be . . . oh my god. Hey, Mum, Jules is on the phone. I have to think about this more. Jules, you're brilliant."

And with that he was gone.

Gillian's voice still held a laugh when she took over. "Are you bringing me cake tonight?"

Gillian was damned good at that stuff. Must be the mother thing. "How did you know?" She'd spent some time early that afternoon putting together cake samples for Gillian and Adrian. They'd asked her to make the cake for their upcoming July wedding. Jules had been touched beyond measure that they'd trust her with something so important and she'd insisted to Gillian and Adrian both that it was far over her head and she'd never made a big wedding cake before.

Gillian had waved it away, told her no one was better suited to make the cake for their big day and to suck it up and do it.

So Jules did. She'd spent the time since they'd asked working on different recipes. Perfecting until she'd decided on several she felt fit them both well and tasted really awesome. Gillian was her best friend and if she did say so herself, her cake repertoire had really come a long way.

"I didn't know! That was all hope and bluster. But yay, cake! Come over now. Adrian is on his way back from Seattle and he says he's bringing takeout. I'll call him to say you're coming for dinner. He'll hurry if he knows cake is involved."

"You only want me for my cake, Gillian. This makes me sad."

"It's really good cake. Come over."

"All right, I'll be there in a few minutes. Need anything else?"

"Just your pretty face. And the cake."

Gillian's house, well, the one she lived in temporarily until the renovations were finished on the new house anyway, was a place Jules always gravitated to. The front windows were ablaze with light and as she moved up the walk she caught sight of Miles, a cat in his arms, walking through the room.

Gillian would close the curtains soon, Jules knew. Now that it was common knowledge that Adrian Brown was Miles's father and that he and Gillian were getting married, photographers made their way out to Bainbridge Island from time to time to try to grab pictures. One had even set himself up in a tree across the road. Of course he fell from his perch and broke his ankle in the fall.

Gillian was a far nicer person than Jules because she called an ambulance. Jules would have turned the hose on him and made him crawl his worthless butt away.

Still smiling and feeling a little vicious, she knocked on the door. The year before she'd have sailed right in. But those days were long past, also the product of the higher profile she had now that Gillian was going to marry someone famous. The doors were always locked up tight now.

Gillian opened the door and pulled her into a hug. "Come in. Adrian just got home."

Jules put her bags down in the kitchen, out of the way of traffic and above normal cat inspection.

Still, Claypool came out and meowed at her in his scratchy old-guy voice so she knelt and gave him a scritch under the chin where he liked it best. "Hey, old man, looking good today."

The cat purred at her, turned, rubbed his side along her knees and sauntered away.

"Story of my life. Get some lovin' and you all leave afterward." Jules stood and washed her hands.

Adrian Brown, ridiculously gorgeous and equally ridiculously in love with Gillian, strolled into the kitchen, pausing to plant a kiss on Jules's cheek. "I got extra pad thai for you."

"You come in handy. Thanks."

"Do we have to wait until after dinner to eat the cake?" Miles poured juice into the glasses before he sat.

"Yes." Gillian sent her son a look and he blushed.

Jules winked at him. "I brought extra just for you."

He grinned, looking very much like his father.

They talked about the renovations. Adrian's recording studio was finished, which was a lucky thing as he'd started working on his next record with some hot-stuff producer. The rest of the house was continuing apace and should be done by the beginning of June.

The food was good, the company even better. She was so glad Gillian and Adrian were settling out on Bainbridge instead of in Seattle. Jules never would have said it out loud, but it would have been really hard to not see Gillian as often as she did. And Miles, who she loved as fiercely as she did his mother.

Jules hated the ferry. Hated all boats for that matter, big or small. Which was sort of a problem when you lived on an island and all. Thankfully the trip was just over half an hour and there was a bridge too if she had to go that way. Bainbridge had just about everything and everyone she needed anyway.

Finally, after they'd finished dinner, Adrian and Miles cleared away the dishes and brought new ones out along with some freshly brewed tea.

"All right." Jules placed five boxes on the table.

"Wow! That's all cake? Score." Miles sent a look to his dad, who also grinned.

"I told you I brought extra for you."

"Which is your favorite?" Gillian sipped her tea as Jules placed the slices out on little plates on the table so everyone could see and take a taste.

"I'm not telling. Given what I know about you and what you like and the things Adrian told me, I've come up with several different ideas. But I don't want to influence you in any way."

She pointed. "This is spice cake with cream cheese frosting. That piece there has pumpkin cream between the layers. That one has dark chocolate and that last one is cinnamon cream."

Adrian hummed his satisfaction as he tried the different pieces. "This is insane. I think I like the cinnamon one, but the pumpkin is also delicious."

"The pumpkin is my favorite. What are those?" Gillian looked to the next plate.

Jules noted the pumpkin vote and then placed the next set of plates in front of them.

"Next up are lemon, lime and tangerine. The frostings and fillings are easily substituted if you like one more than the other."

"The lemon is fantastic." Gillian looked to Adrian. "I think it could be good for the reception the label is throwing. Don't you think?"

"Is this lemon curd?" Adrian forked another bite up.

"Yes. It's a new recipe. That's only my second batch, but I think it's really good. If I do say so myself."

Gillian moaned her delight. "You'd better say so yourself! I never tire of bragging on your skills, but you have to help me, Juliet Lamprey. Also, would you happen to have any extra?"

"There's a jar of it in the bag on the counter."

Gillian laughed. "You know me so well."

Adrian gave Miles a look for sneaking some cake from Adrian's plate. His son seemed to think that was hilarious. "I think your mother would call that being cheeky, Miles, my son."

"You're the parent, you're supposed to sacrifice for your children."

"Ha. You need a kidney, you can have one. But stay away from my cake, boy." Adrian winked at Jules. "I think Gillian is right. The lemon for the label reception would be perfect."

Adrian had come to her a month before and asked if she'd be willing to also do the cake for some local event his record label wanted to give them. Mary was doing the appetizers as well.

"That's doable. I can make one with the raspberry too if you like. For some variety."

"Whatever you say. I'm all for it."

She noted that before sliding the next round of plates to them. "And this is chocolate. Seven-layer chocolate with sea salt and caramel." She pointed to her favorite but then moved on. She didn't want them to know and make a choice based on that. She wanted them to have the cake *they* wanted most.

"This one is dark chocolate and orange with chocolate buttercream and orange cream filling. Last is death by chocolate. Chocolate cake with chocolate shavings in the batter, ganache between the layers, chocolate buttercream frosting with chocolate curls. It'd be served with a drizzle of warm chocolate."

Gillian finished every last bit of the seven layer. "I love that you didn't even bother with fondant or any of that fake whipped frosting stuff."

"I know you, Gillian. You're a buttercream girl."

Gillian laughed. "Fondant is pretty but it tastes like glue. If I'm having cake, I want it to be delicious."

Adrian held his hands up in surrender. "I vote the seven-layer chocolate with salted caramel. I want to be buried in that cake when I die."

"He's right. Jules, this is all great, but this cake right here is perfect. Please make it for our wedding." Gillian put her head on Adrian's shoulder.

"Are you sure? You haven't sampled the others."

"I'm sure. Though I will sample the others as well." Gillian winked and they all dug into the yellow cake slices on the next plate.

"I guess that is that." Jules sat back with a smile.

"It was your favorite all along, wasn't it?"

"Yes, but I didn't want to unfairly influence you. It sounds heavy, but it's really good. The flavors work well together. The cake will go with just about any type of food Mary creates."

Gillian nodded. "We've gone with an all-finger-foods deal. And I made her promise to hire all the staff she'll need so she can enjoy the wedding like every other member of the wedding party. You will too of course. You're the maid of honor; can't have you working when you need to help keep me sane."

"Well, my job is simpler than Mary's. The work will be done before the wedding. You're doing it in the late afternoon so the delivery will be easy enough. I just have to swan around and accept all the love for it. Easy peasy."

"Let's go into the living room. I need to lean back a little as I'm stuffed full of cake." Gillian led the way into the other room where they settled on the couch while Adrian pulled the curtains closed.

"What's new? Other than cake and stuff, that is," Gillian asked.

"I hit some local businesses this week and spoke to a few in Seattle and outward. This 'locally produced goods' thing is working well. Mary and I are both already using some of the stuff in our products. We got Brindle Printery to do these little signs for the case that indicate what local products are used in which of our goods. We traded! That's been fun and it's enabled me to meet more people around the island. Oh, and an old friend is back in town. Patrick Carter's grandson Gideon has moved in to help his grandfather run the farm. He's also ridiculously tasty."

Gillian's laugh was easy and affectionate. "Really? Do tell."

She did, including his visit to Tart that afternoon.

"I like to hear this." Gillian smiled. "You're so pretty and fun and smart and special. I want you to have someone who sees that too."

"Whoa there, missy. I'm crushing on someone who flirted with me. That's all. We're not even dating. Don't go getting ahead of yourself."

Adrian snorted as he brought them some tea. "If she can plan your life, she won't be so stressed about the wedding. You really should let her do it. Don't make the baby Jesus cry, Jules."

Jules laughed, loving how well Adrian had Gillian pegged.

"Oy, you two." Gillian attempted a prim look but neither Jules nor Adrian were fooled. "Easy to laugh. Don't you think Jules is pretty, Adrian?"

"Don't answer that." Jules rolled her eyes and turned to Gillian. "You can't ask a man that. He's going to explode trying to figure out how to answer without offending anyone. So anyway, it's a fun thing, but it's just that. I'll let you know if we elope."

"He'd better be good to you or he'll have a bucketload of ladies raining punches down upon his head."

"He's like eighty billion feet tall. I kept looking up and then up some more." Jules knew she was blushing but if you couldn't be giddy about a new boy in town with your best friend, who could you do it with?

"Thank heavens you're not prone to overstatement." Gillian said this soberly until they both laughed.

"We chose a cake, Mister Brown." Gillian turned to Adrian, who paused, his amusement softening into something else. Something so intimate and raw between the two of them Jules was nearly embarrassed to see it.

He took her hands and kissed her fingertips. "Can't turn back now, English. There's cake to be paid for. Also my reputation is at stake. Imagine what people might do if they thought you had taken advantage of me."

Gillian blushed and Jules loved her friend very much right then. Her happiness was so well deserved. She and Adrian really were perfect for one another. And then there was a small twist of envy. Just a little.

Jules wanted that too.

She sat forward. "I should go before you two embarrass me with all your fast and modern ways."

Gillian's eyes widened and then she laughed. "You're having a go."

"Totally. But still, I'm trying a new cinnamon roll tomorrow. In case you wanted to stop in. I'm making extra for Mary and some deal she's doing in the afternoon."

She stood and walked to the door. Her bags were waiting there for her neatly. Adrian and Gillian trailed behind. Miles had disappeared into the garage out back to practice with his friends.

Gillian reached out to squeeze Jules's hand. "You guys are really doing well. So fast out of the gate too."

"It's only been two weeks but yes, it's smooth so far, which is nice. It's not hard to work with Mary or Daisy. My business is up. Mary's business is up and Daisy sold two pieces last week."

"I like that Delicious is kicking butt."

Delicious was the name of Jules's group of friends. Four women who were very different on the outside but who were close as sisters. Each artistic and vibrant in her own way. Loyal to the bone.

Adrian hugged Gillian to his side. "I love that you guys call yourselves that. Also, Levi is an art hog. I'm going on record with that. I wanted one of her large pieces for the new house and he used his relationship with the artist to get around me."

Levi was Daisy's boyfriend. He also happened to be an art collector, an ardent admirer of Daisy's art and the most breathtakingly alpha male Jules had ever met. Daisy was a lucky woman, but it must have been tiring to manage a man like that.

"Commission something. That way she's making it for you from the start. That's what Cal does."

"You're brilliant, that's what you are, Jules." Adrian grinned and hugged her before Gillian did the same.

"Love you." Jules squeezed Gillian's hand.

"Love you right back. I'll see you soon. Thanks for making my cake for my wedding. I like that. Makes me feel like I'm totally surrounded by love."

"Stop that or you'll make me sniffly."

But, as she drove home, she realized Gillian had been right. Getting married at her new home with her soon-to-be husband, surrounded by people she loved and who loved her, the food by Mary, the cake by Jules, the rings designed by Daisy. Hell, the music would be all Adrian's friends and apparently Miles too. A family affair. Like it should be.

Every night before she went to sleep, Jules meditated. She knew some of her friends thought it was loopy, but it worked for her.

Jules was not a naturally patient person. She could run toward bitchy sometimes. Meditating helped her manage her life, gave her time to reflect each day and think about the next. That appealed to the planner living inside her.

Her life was busy. Full of friends and work. It was a good thing to make herself slow down. Even if it was just a few minutes at the end of each day.

She took a shower and changed into her pajamas before

settling in with her pillows. Her house was a rental, but it was perfect for her. Her brother had offered to sell their childhood home to her at a really great price. But she'd turned it down. She'd been given Tart and that was enough. And she didn't want to live in the place where her mother's heart had been so well and truly broken.

She could have lived in the apartment upstairs from Tart, but it was important to leave every day. To walk away and have her work life over. She liked that division. Of course she baked at home, but that was different. That was for pleasure.

She'd kept that apartment open just in case her mother wanted to come back and visit. She wanted her mom to always know she was welcome and had a place to hang her coat. Her mother had used it less and less as the years went by and lately Jules had been thinking of using it as an office space for Tart. Now that Mary and Daisy were there too, it would be good to have some desks with computers and phones.

But doing that would be an affirmative step. She'd be admitting her mother probably wasn't coming back for more than a brief visit once every year or two. And Jules wasn't sure she was ready to do that yet.

Growing up, Jules and her mother had been close, but something had shifted in their relationship when her father had made his declaration. When he'd stood up at the dinner table and announced he'd filed for divorce and would be marrying the girlfriend no one had known he'd had. Oh and that he'd knocked her up.

Her mother, who had always deferred to her father, who had taken her commitment to be his partner and helpmate seriously, had been filled with so much anger it had been astonishing.

It wasn't that Jules didn't understand why her mother would be so angry. She did. She'd been totally and utterly betrayed by her husband.

But it was impossible not to feel like she'd lost her mother in a lot of ways. Her mother had divested herself of so much of her old life, sometimes even her children, who, as Jules reminded her brother, were adults anyway. She was proud that her mother had reinvented herself after a terrible thing. But Jules missed her.

And in reaching out to try to bring her back into Jules's life, their roles sometimes flipped and she found herself mothering her mother. Making sure she had enough money and was all right.

She didn't tell anyone that part. Jules knew Gillian would frown. Gillian, the fiercest mother Jules knew, would be angry that Jules's mother had—what Gillian would perceive as—walked away from her responsibilities as a mother.

Her brother had a relationship with their father that was even more strained than Jules's own. Ethan had done the right thing, had given their mother half the money from the house sale and had used the rest for his own house in Oregon with his wife and their children. He'd retreated into his own family life. It wasn't that he'd walled her out, but the distance did that anyway.

He was angry. Angry at their father, even seven years later. Angry at their mother, who'd extended a few weeks' trip to a lifestyle of sorts. And he had children, children their mother rarely saw, though she did send them presents. It wasn't the same, and Jules understood his anger. Felt it on his behalf.

So she'd taken that on too. Made sure *she* was part of her nephew's lives. She called and Skyped, and at least every month or so headed down to Portland to spend time with them. In fact she'd be going down soon to celebrate her oldest nephew Connor's birthday. Her mother was flying in to Sea-Tac and would be driving down with Jules.

Jules was looking forward to that time with her mom and also to spending the weekend with those two boys she loved so much.

It was good for her and her nephews, but she and Ethan had miles to go to get back to where they had been. And Jules wasn't sure it was possible. He hurt and she couldn't fix it.

Ethan couldn't let go of what their father had done. Jules got it. He was a father now and she knew that every time their dad pulled crap, Ethan knew he'd *never* do anything of the sort to his own kids.

So she tried to be the buffer. Their mother wasn't capable, their father wasn't . . . well, she'd always sort of thought he wasn't all the way formed as a person. Jules didn't know if it made any difference other than giving her a headache and making her stomach hurt.

She shook her head to get past it all. Going over this again and again wasn't relaxing, and relaxing was what she needed right then.

She blew out a breath and lit a few candles. There was no music but the sound of the rain on the roof.

She couldn't own anyone else's choices.

She had to accept her own path and walk it as honestly as she could.

She had to be open to all the joy her life could offer and try to get past hurts and resentments because they were not useful.

She had the family she'd made with Gillian and her other friends. She was loved and cared about. This was important to remember. Important to embrace and cherish because in the end, love was the perfect ingredient. Love was necessary, like oxygen.

She thought of Gideon and smiled. She had to be open to new people and things.

Cal's face flashed through her mind. And she had to accept what people were willing to give if she was to keep them in her life.

She kept her focus and her breathing calmed and slowed and by the time she was finished, she was feeling far better than she had before. She grabbed her journal to write in it and headed to her bed.

4

....

Gideon woke up early. Early even for his granddad, who was an up-at-four-forty-five-every-day sort of guy.

He had too much energy. His dreams had been filled with her. With Jules Lamprey looking blonde and pretty. Of Jules Lamprey naked and sweaty as she rose above him, his cock deep inside her.

Before he'd seen her approach the porch just a few days before he'd been fine. Relaxed. Happy and busy with his choice to move back.

But now that he'd seen her, now that he'd spoken to her at Tart and flirted? Now he was restless. He wanted her. Wanted to put his hands all over her body, wanted to kiss her. Christ, he wanted to fuck her and wake up next to her.

Need for Jules was hot like a fever and the novelty of how much she'd remained on his mind surprised him.

He wasn't a virgin. He'd had crushes and hot sexual flings here and there. But this thing he felt with Jules was . . . unusual. He'd known her for most of his life, though certainly he'd not been close to her as he had been with Cal. But he wanted to know her. There wasn't the same sort of urge to court, but a hot, physical punch every time he thought of her.

And her familiarity? It made this need he had greater. This wasn't someone he'd bumped into at a party or met on an airplane. She'd been there all this time and for whatever reason, it made her appeal to him all the more.

He headed out to milk the goats, grateful for the physical exertion. The opportunity to do some planning helped keep his focus. The year before he'd taken some cheese-making classes and it was something he was considering trying at Carter Farms.

It would take some doing, some equipment updating and new construction so it was a long-term idea. Until then, they sold the milk to a nearby dairy and the goats kept the hillside to the north of the farm clear of the berry vines that were the bane of many in the area. He'd even been asked just the week before to rent the goats out to help clear some public land that had been overrun with blackberry bushes.

They weren't a big, giant agribusiness. They had to make their way in a world far different than the one his granddad had grown up in. He needed to be more than a farmer, he needed to be a businessman to take the farm into the next generation. Things like a farm stand and seasonal cheese making could very well make a difference.

It excited him even as he hoped like hell he could make it work and not let his granddad down. The farm stretched out ahead of him. Neat rows of trees in the orchard to the north. Seasonal crops to the west. He loved working the land. And this land was his. Carter land where Carters had worked for three generations now.

He could see the difference in the landscape each day. If they planted, there'd be a growing cycle. If they harvested, the farm changed then too. There was something intensely satisfying about it. About seeing the results of your work every single day.

He'd taken a break from life after he'd sold the Bar M. Traveled. Done whatever he wanted whenever he'd wanted to. But now he was back, fully in his life, and he felt better than he had in a very, very long time.

Gideon worked all day, showered, masturbated, showered again and by the time he got free of the place, Tart would be near closing and he had to hope she'd still be around.

As he came up the block, he saw her inside, that pale fall of hair around her gorgeous face. He raised his hand in greeting and caught her eye as she stood at the door.

The smile she gave him as he caught her eye while she locked the door and then unlocked it to admit him was enough to soothe nerves frayed from rushing.

"Why hello. What brings you here?"

He drew his knuckles over her cheek. "Don't you know by now?"

She blushed and he wanted her so much it was like white noise in his head.

"I . . . yes, I guess I do." She'd never been one for playing at being coy. She went after things she wanted. And as it happened, she wanted Gideon. But this sort of attention, this courtly, mannered wooing was dizzying. She really liked it.

"Have you got plans for dinner?"

"Why, Gideon Carter. Are you asking me on a date?"

That sexy smile curved his mouth. "I am."

She licked her lips and his pupils seemed to swallow all the color in his eyes. Her heart pounded as her skin warmed. Oh, good gracious, he did all the right stuff to all her best parts.

This . . . this moment when things were about to happen but hadn't yet was one of her favorite things in the world. All that possibility laid out before her.

"Good. I've been waiting. I'd decided earlier that if you didn't call me by the end of the week I was calling you."

"I do like a woman who knows what she wants. I'll pick you up at six. I know you have to be up as early as I do."

"Yes." She licked her suddenly dry lips again. "Though some things are worth losing sleep over."

The way he paused, sharpened his focus, sent a shiver through her.

"Yes, they are, Juliet. Are you going to make me lose more sleep than I have already?"

He stood so very close that each time he took a breath he very nearly touched her, the heat of his skin brushed against hers.

It was broad daylight in the middle of town and yet it felt intimate between them just then.

"I make you lose sleep?" It had been a long time since she'd flirted with so much intent.

He nodded. "And even when I finally get to sleep I dream of you."

She smiled, flattered and breathless. And then she wondered if there were other things he did thinking of her. Hot, masturbatory things. A flush went through her, leaving her sweaty at the thought of him, fist around his cock, her name on his lips as he jerked off.

"I'll see you tonight." He bent and slid his lips over hers. Just a breath of a touch and she arched to keep contact as he began to straighten.

Then his arm was around her waist, pulling her close to him and his mouth owned hers.

Her heart pounded as he flicked his tongue against her bottom lip, she gasped when he nipped it, pulling it slowly and then releasing it only to lave the sting.

"You're a temptation, Juliet Lamprey." He stood back, sliding his tongue along his lips as if to taste her one last time. She nearly leapt at him.

Instead she took a deep breath and got herself back under control.

She pulled a pad from the pocket of her apron and wrote her address down. "See you at six."

"I think you should wear the navy-blue dress. It's such a pretty color on you." Gillian sat on Jules's bed as Jules tried to figure out what to wear on her date. It wasn't like she'd never dated, for goodness sake. But after that kiss earlier that day, Gideon made her nervous. In a good way.

She held the blue dress up against herself as she looked in the mirror. "You think? I don't even know where he's taking me. I should have asked, I guess. What if this is too formal?"

Jules pulled the dress on and zipped it at the side. The blue was good. Didn't wash her out and make her look like she'd been without sun for months.

"Then he clearly has no idea where to take a beautiful woman on the first date and so we won't like him at all." Gillian said it so primly it made Jules laugh. Which was most likely Gillian's intent anyway. "It's a nice evening. Not too cold. A light cardigan should be good."

Jules knew which one she needed and pulled out a bright red sweater. Soft as a breath.

"Perfect."

"One of Daisy's presents. If she ever decided to be a personal shopper she'd make a killing." Jules secured it with a pretty white belt. "Shoes. Hm." She scanned her shoe racks and smiled when she found the perfect pair.

She turned to the mirror and stepped into the navy pumps with the little white bow tied on the front. Gillian had been right, Jules thought as she looked at her reflection in the nearby mirror. The dress was flattering. Fit her just right and accentuated all her best parts. Her boobs in particular looked freaking awesome.

"My girls look like beauty queens in this dress." She waggled her brows at Gillian's reflection.

"They really do. You look beautiful and one hundred percent Juliet Lamprey in that outfit. I really don't know how you can look as if you just walked out of a milk advertisement or a magazine ad at any and all times. In the morning you look like a cereal commercial. I'd be quite cross about that if you weren't also so wonderful at baking things and being my friend."

Gillian grinned at her.

"Thanks for the pep talk."

"You don't even need one. You know him already. That takes away a big part of the anxiety. And you're gorgeous so that will work in your favor, I hear."

Jules laughed. "I know him, yes. In a way. But that's kid stuff. He's a man now. I don't know him as a man. Not yet. But Patrick is such a wonderful person it's hard to believe he grew up badly."

Gillian's features were sad a moment. "He's a lovely gentleman. I was sorry to hear about the loss of his wife."

"Yeah, they were very good together."

"What's the story about the ex-wife? Gideon's, I mean. You said he'd been married."

"I don't know much more than that. I heard it from Mary, who'd heard it from Cal. I haven't spoken to him in several years. Well, other than at his house and at Tart. Not enough to really get any details. At the funeral and wake I never got a chance to speak with him and then he left. I guess I'll find out."

"So you were quite circumspect last night in front of Adrian. What does this Gideon really look like? Spare no lascivious detail."

Gillian could be so prim and buttoned up on the outside but just underneath she had a lovely sense of humor that could be just as bawdy as Jules's.

"He's gorgeous. He's long and lean. Blond with a beard and mustache. Not like a weirdo beard, he's not starting a doomsday cult or anything."

She decided to add a few bangle bracelets and a pair of earrings her mother had sent her from Bali, where she and Jules's aunt were spending a few months just hanging out. Some lipstick—red, she decided, to match the sweater. She smoothed her hair back to catch a few flyaways.

"Blond like honey. His hair I mean. A little too long, which looks sexy of course. Curls. I bet they're soft. I can't believe I didn't get a good feel earlier when he kissed me."

"You can be forgiven. Some men have the power to kiss the sense right out of you, and before you know it you're getting married."

Jules let herself be calmed by Gillian's way. That funny, matter-of-fact teasing she did to put people at ease was one of her finest qualities.

"Yes, I believe he's one of those. He's got slow, sexy green eyes. Oh! Really nice arms. The kind of man who works with his body. I bet the rest of him is just as hard and defined." She transferred a lipstick, her phone, some money and a credit card into her bag.

"He's . . . well, for want of a better phrase, he's a cowboy, complete with boots and worn jeans."

"Well now. I can most certainly understand the appeal of that." They headed out to the living room where Gillian leaned against the couch. "I've been arguing with myself as to whether or not I should say anything."

Jules knew. *Cal.*

"I've watched you watch Cal. And watched Cal watch you for years now. This Gideon is not the same as the others you've dated. I've never seen you like this with anyone before. Just . . . what about Cal?"

"Yeah, Gillian, what about Cal? Huh? All he's done is look.

He's never made a move. I'm thirty-three years old and he's *never made a move.* Am I supposed to wait around and pine forever? I want what you have with Adrian. I want a man in my life. Gideon is different. Or, well, he feels different anyway. Who knows? He may not be. He might be a jerk who never makes me come. But I won't know if I don't give this a try. I can't wait for Cal. I have to move on and I will. Cal has moved on, for god's sake. He's had how many girlfriends and boyfriends?"

She'd waited so long and he'd never stepped up. As much as she'd wanted Cal, it was time to let go of something that would never happen.

"You're right of course. I just love you. Him too. I want you to be happy. And you should move on."

"I bet no one ever says, *What about Jules?* to him. It's stupid. And while I know everyone is just trying to be nice, it's not going to happen. There is no Jules and Cal, no matter how much I might have wished it, or you all wanted it. I've wanted Cal for a long time. I can't lie about that. But he doesn't want me back. Not the same way. It's long past time I move on. And so I am."

Gillian sighed. "I know. I know. For what it's worth, I absolutely believe with all my heart that he does want you. But you're right to say he's never moved on it and you have to let it go. I don't even know Gideon; he could be far better for you and you should make that choice yourself. I'm sorry."

She hugged Gillian. "Don't be sorry. You all have brought him up in one way or another. I think for a long time it was expected. People just assumed it would happen. Anyway, it's not going to, and I have this other thing and it's just a date, but it feels like more. Gideon is different from those other dates I've had." She shrugged. "This is a good time in all our lives."

It was. She needed to keep that first and foremost in her mind. Gideon came with all sorts of possibilities. Which was pretty cool.

Gideon drove up the street slowly; it was dark and he hadn't been to her house before. But he knew which one was hers without having to glance at the address. Just a simple white house with dark blue shutters and window boxes. He parked and walked up to her door, pausing to smile at the wind chimes she'd hung from a nearby tree and all the birdhouses she had. Pretty and classic. A lot like the woman who lived there.

This was the first date he'd taken seriously since his divorce. Juliet Lamprey was far more than some woman he wanted to get naked with. He'd been accused of being too laid back, but it wasn't that. He fought for things he wanted. He'd failed once and it was a pretty big failure. But some things weren't meant to be. Some things can't be fixed by only one person trying.

That instant sort of zing and attraction he'd experienced with Jules on his granddad's porch had woken him up from a long nap of sorts. He was awake now and hungry. For her.

He'd been looking forward to this more than he'd wanted to admit, and when she opened her door looking absolutely gorgeous, he couldn't help but smile and take her hands. "You look beautiful."

She smiled back with shiny red lips. "Thank you. I was just about to say you clean up well, but I realized you're just as alluring in jeans as you are in dress pants."

Pausing just a moment, she tipped her chin to look up at him. He leaned in to kiss her cheek but she smelled so good he ended up with his face at her nape, breathing her in.

"Um, yeah, sorry about that." He stepped back but she didn't look upset. She looked . . . interested. A good sign. "You smell good."

Her smile tipped up a thousand watts. "You're full of compliments tonight. A girl could get used to that."

He led her down the walk to his car. "That's the point."

5

....

She sipped her wine and looked at him over the rim of the glass. "So, I know you like to skateboard and ride bikes, but since you graduated college and stopped visiting here so often, what have you been up to?"

He forked up some of the crab cake from his plate. "I've spent the last few years traveling."

"Why? I mean, as part of your job or did you have an epiphany and go off on a grand adventure?"

"A little bit of all that, I suppose."

"I'd really like to travel more. That was my New Year's resolution this year. I haven't gone on a single trip yet though. My mom is currently in Bali with my aunt and I'd love to go visit."

"Did she move there?" That surprised him. He'd never really

imagined Mrs. Lamprey to be the type to up and move across the globe.

"No." She hesitated. "She and my father divorced. God, seven years ago now. Anyway, she . . . changed a lot after that. For the better." She added before he could get worried. Even so, there was an unspoken *mostly* at the end of that sentence.

"So she travels around the world now?"

Jules nodded. "Pretty much, yes. I guess she's finding herself." Her shrug was supposed to be casual, but Gideon noted the strain around her eyes. "She comes back here once a year or so. Spends a few weeks here and some time with my brother and his family. Pretty much the rest of the year she travels. My aunt sold her house and retired from her job and joined her. They've spent time in South America and Europe and now it's Bali. I admire her—my mom, I mean. Her entire life was turned upside down. She married my dad on her eighteenth birthday. They ran the diner for my entire life and then you know, it all fell apart and she remade herself."

"And your dad?"

She sighed and he watched her body language tighten up. "He lives in San Diego with his wife and their two kids. One is a pre-schooler and the other is in kindergarten."

Once again he was reminded of why he was so relieved he'd never had kids with Alana. At least he hadn't had to deal with that kind of pain. "Ah. So you don't have any sort of relationship with him?"

She dipped her bread in the olive oil and chewed slowly. He could tell she was thinking of how to put the words. He liked that.

"He's my father. I love him if for no other reason than that. But he's not the same man who raised me. Or hell, maybe he is and I'm just old enough to see it. It's easier not to be around him.

He's got a new life anyway. A new family. So you know, I get presents that only underline just how little he knows me, but he remembers so that's a plus. He doesn't come up here. I run a business and can't just jet down there, even if I wanted to or felt welcome. We have the equivalent of a Facebook friendship. Like we went to high school together or something." She shrugged again and looked lost as she sipped her wine.

"I'm sorry."

"I'm a big girl. I don't want him to be unhappy. He seems to be in love with his wife. My brothers, and that's odd to say, but they're my brothers, just the same, are sweet. She's pretty—his wife—so they made pretty kids. I wanted to hate her. I'm not crazy about her still, but she's all right. She loves him. I hope he doesn't do to her what he did to my mother. I hope he's learned his lesson. I'm not holding my breath over it, but it's really not my problem anyway. And wow, I'm sorry I've totally turned this conversation into a downer."

He reached across the table and took her hand. "No, you didn't. I asked, you answered. So how did you end up with Tart and why did you decide to change the diner into a bakery?"

"On Ethan's birthday—you remember him right? My brother?" He nodded and she continued. "Anyway, at his birth-day dinner, right after the cake had been sliced, my dad got up and told us all he'd filed for divorce that day. He was getting married to his girlfriend, who by the way is my age. Oh and she was knocked up."

He sat back, wide-eyed.

"I know, right? It's like a plotline from a television drama. Anyway, my mom just sort of lost it. She made us go and when I turned up again the next day she'd broken every last piece of

their china. That china of hers was so special. I remember growing up how she'd buy little pieces of it here and there when they
could afford it. She asked me to take out the trash and when I
got back inside she handed me the paperwork signing the building over to me. They gave my brother the house. She told me that
at least my father had been good for something and she wanted
us to have the business and the house.

"We tried to talk her out of it, but she was adamant. So. I
wanted to make the space my own. I didn't want to run a diner.
So I talked to Gillian, that's my best friend, and she suggested a
bakery because she knew how much I loved to bake. It really just
sort of went from there."

"Looks like you've been really successful there. Granddad
told me Tart was even in the Northwest guidebooks as a place
to go when in town."

She grinned. "I know! Crazy, isn't it? It's good for business,
but it's also great for my ego." She looked him over. "So now it's
your turn."

He figured he was up next and in the face of her honesty could
he really not give her the same?

"I was in college but restless. It wasn't the right place for me.
I met this girl."

She laughed then. "Oh, how many times has that sentence
been part of a story?"

He grinned. "Yeah. Well, that girl lived in Wyoming and when
she took me home to meet her family I fell in love with the area.
I got some work on a ranch, learning the ropes so to speak, and
when I'd socked enough money away, I bought a cattle ranch
with my brother-in-law. We ran it together for over a decade. It
was good. I loved the work, loved being outside so much. Loved

the animals and the land." He'd loved the feeling of looking out their bedroom window and knowing he owned all he could see around them. It had meant something to build it with her. Then.

The server came and took the appetizers away and brought their entrees. He liked the way Jules dug into her steak and sighed happily at the first bite. Liked that she wasn't afraid to eat or enjoy the process. Made him wonder again what she'd be like in bed.

"But then we got divorced. I tried to stay on but it became pretty clear after a while that it wasn't possible. So I sold my half to my ex-brother-in-law. And like your mom, I headed out to do some traveling. I didn't go to Bali though."

"Where did you go?"

"Let's see . . . I started out by going to New York to visit some friends. Hung out for a few months." He'd had a lot of firsts in New York, including his first experience with a man. "Then I went to Spain a while. England. Italy. I was in Japan for a time. I'd been consulting with an old friend who ranches beef and he invited me to stay with him. Learned a hell of a lot. The quakes happened when I was there. I gotta tell you, I've never been quite so freaked out to be on an island. When I left I visited my parents in Oakland for a while. My sister lives in Eugene so I visited her and all my nephews. She's got five kids, all boys. I don't know how she makes it through each day." But he'd loved every minute of the total and utter chaos of his sister's home. Loved his rough-and-tumble nephews.

"Wow, I'm envious of all that great stuff."

He clinked his wineglass to hers. "It was great stuff, yes. I met so many wonderful people. Experienced things I'd never imagined before. Hell, before my divorce I'd never been out of the country. I like travel. But I like roots too. So my grandmother passed and my parents and my aunt were trying to get my grand-dad to move in with one of them and give up the farm. But that's his home, you know? I came out for the funeral and the wake and he and I had a long talk about his future and the future of the farm. He asked me if I'd be willing to come out and stay on, help him run the place, take over when the time came. I've got a lot of ideas, things I'd like to try. The land means a lot to me. Working the farm with my granddad means a lot to me. And then you." He nodded. "Yes, this is all good too." He was a blunt man. He didn't like games or pretending he wasn't interested when he was. He wanted her to know up front what his expecta-tions were.

She blushed and against the candlelight she looked even more beautiful.

Though she was dying to know more about the divorce and his ex, she restrained herself from asking. Though they'd known each other as kids, they had a lot of getting to know each other to do. He'd tell her at some point, she figured, and as long as he wasn't still into his ex, it would be fine.

"Why aren't you married, Juliet?"

She loved it that he used her full name. It sounded so sexy from his lips.

She shrugged. "No one's asked. I've been busy running a busi-ness. I haven't had a lot of time to do much more than get up early, bake all day and go to sleep. I'm in no hurry."

"Can't imagine why any man would let himself be sidetracked by your schedule if he really wanted you. And I can't imagine any man not wanting you."

She gulped and resisted the urge to fan herself.

There was an intensity about Gideon. Even with the aw-shucks manners and his laid-back demeanor, he looked at her like he meant it. He spoke to her like he listened to her, with all his attention. It rendered her slightly breathless and giddy. It felt pretty awesome.

"Does this mean *you're* not going to get sidetracked by my schedule?" Flirting with him also came very easily. Oh, he was a man, a good-looking one so he would be well versed in bullshit as they tended to be. But he wasn't phoning it in with her. He meant what he said, which made it all even more delicious.

"Oh no. I don't let myself get sidetracked by much. Most especially when I want something. I don't get spooked by getting up at four thirty. Or by successful, intelligent women who are independent. Especially when they're as beautiful as the one I'm looking at right now."

"You're really good at this stuff."

He grinned and it melted her insides. Cripes.

"I'm good at a lot of things. I can fix broken toilets. I know how to run a cattle ranch. I can ride horses and repair screen doors and bad carburetors. I'm handy. You should remember that."

"I'm not sure I could ever forget it." She laughed and he did too. And then he took her hand, turned it over and pressed a kiss to her inner wrist and then her palm and she forgot her next words.

"I guess I'll have to keep on being good at the things you like most, then."

He had such an easy way about him. Just being around him was relaxing even as she found him exciting and sexy. "First you'll need to figure out what it is I like most."

He laughed and she loved the way it made him look. "I suppose knowing you as a kid isn't the same. You've grown up pretty damned well."

After dinner he took her back to her house where she promised tart and coffee. Decaf of course.

"I like this house." He sat at her table, his long legs stretched out in front of him. "I knew it was yours before I saw the address."

She slid a plate with some tart his way and then poured him a cup of coffee. "Cream and sugar if you like." She put those nearby as well before she sat. "I like it here too. I've lived here five years. I've considered buying the place for a while, but renting suits me for now. Gillian keeps threatening to build me a little house at their new place."

"Sounds like you've got some good friends."

"I do. You know a lot of them. The Whaleys. Mary, Cal and Ryan are all close. I don't think you know Gillian, but she's my bestie."

Her smile was quick and it sent his heart racing it was so pretty. He really wanted to just lean in and lick up that neck of hers, taste the salt of her skin, feel the weight of her against him.

"Do you like really good food?"

He had to chase away a particularly dirty fantasy of taking her from behind to focus on what she said.

"Who doesn't?"

"This is true." She forked up a bite of the tart and he followed, pausing to enjoy.

"This is so good. I don't know how you get anything done. If I had this around my house all the time I'd be as big as one."

"Believe it or not, I don't always have tart here. If I have left-overs at the end of the day, I try to fob them off on friends. If I brought food home all the time I'd be in trouble. But I was hoping you'd want to come over so I made sure to bring some home."

"I like that." He liked that she'd thought about what might please him. "So you were about to invite me to dinner?"

She laughed. "Not me. I mean, I'll be there but I won't be the cook. Mary runs a supper club of sorts called Delicious. There's no menu. She makes all the choices and presents you with whatever she's decided to create, and I've never had better. This Sunday is the first time we're using Tart. She used to have it at her place but was outgrowing it. That and the kitchen at Tart is bigger than hers at home. Anyway, I've got room for one more at the table if you're up for it."

"Yes, definitely."

They ate and drank coffee and they talked a lot about music. It pleased him that she loved music as much as he did. Her tastes were eclectic and ran the genre gamut. He expected he'd find some new favorites now that they had connected again.

He wanted to take her to bed. Wanted to kiss her from head to toe. If she'd been a woman he'd just met and been attracted to, he'd have made his move right then. She was interested, that was clear. But she wasn't a woman he'd just met and wanted to nail.

This woman was different.

But he wanted to know her more before he did, so he made himself wait.

But not for a kiss.

At her door he paused. "I'm going to go, but I don't want you to think it's because I don't want to take you to bed right this very moment. Because I most assuredly do."

"So why aren't we getting naked?"

"Are you annoyed?" He paused there in her doorway, caught between amusement and agitation. "Back when I was a kid I remember thinking all your bold ways were sort of annoying."

She grinned, her hands on her hips. "And now? Because, well, of course I can't tell you how to express yourself to a lady and all, but if you just said that to pass along info and not as a segue into why you think it's awesome and how much you enjoy a gal with moxie like me, I'll be quite annoyed with you."

He laughed. Damn, he loved her sense of humor. "Yes, it was a segue into why I think it really turns me on now. You know, a gal with moxie and all. You're bold and brassy and you organize your music in a slightly scary but overall impressively catalogued fashion. It's nearly religious. And your spices are color coordinated. I bet you don't have a single junk drawer."

He took a step and pressed her against the doorway. She'd taken her heels off when she came into the house so while she was a long, tall woman, he was a lot taller. She was nearly petite as he got in close, holding her in place.

"There's something sort of dirty about a woman who organizes her kitchen in a ruthless fashion and can also create what is, most assuredly, art on a plate. You're salty and sweet. All that big, blue-eyed, blond-haired stuff, goddamn, Juliet, you get me all fussed up."

She paused and her mischievous grin slid away. But he wasn't disappointed because the smile she replaced it with was slow and sexy. Mischievous couldn't begin to describe what that smile promised.

Her breath caught. His words, the tension in that normally slow and easy voice of his, snagged her attention. Tugged low in her belly. This whole week had been utterly delightful. He was this boy she'd known but so much more. The man he'd become interested her.

The intensity of this connection knocked her for a loop. She'd never had this, not with anyone. She was bold. A take-charge woman who got what she needed and gave as good as she received.

Gideon made her feel so damned alive.

Sexual tension vibrated between them. His weight against her body. No harming. But he wanted her there and that was . . . well, it ran over her hot and fast. Sex wasn't something she was ashamed of enjoying. She sought it out when she needed it. Enjoyed the men she had it with. For a time.

But this wasn't enjoyable.

This heat between them was hot and intense and it got under her skin that he wanted her the way he seemed to.

They would end up in bed. No doubt about it. And when they got there, it would be absofuckinglutely fantastic.

For now he held her there, slowly seducing her into a wobbly-kneed mess of a woman frightfully close to begging a man to have his way with her.

"I'm glad I'm not the only one." She slid her palms up his chest and to his shoulders. "And yet you're going." She tiptoed up and nipped at his bottom lip.

It would be a whole heaping helping of just what she needed to get naked and sweaty with this man. Right then. And for a few hours more.

"I'm hungry for you, Jules." He took a deep breath and stepped back. "I'm hungry for you and it aches."

He bent and took a kiss, this one more bold than the last. His tongue slid in, against hers and then he was gone again.

"I want to enjoy that ache a while." He bent and kissed her again, but with this kiss he settled in. This wasn't quick. No, he took a long, leisurely tour. Little kisses against the edge of her mouth, nips of her bottom lip, the slide of his tongue against hers. He stole her breath as she held on. Held on as he kissed her until her spine eased and all there was was his scent on her skin, his lips on hers, hands at her hips.

He pulled back and tipped his forehead to hers. "When does Tart close tomorrow?"

"Eleven. I'm shortening my Saturday hours and Mary will take over and close up at two. She's doing these nifty little box lunches. When they're gone, they're gone. This is the first week she's doing the weekend lunch boxes so I hope they'll kick butt for her." God, she needed to stop talking. He made her blurty, which was not something she'd experienced with too many people.

"How about we go on a picnic?"

"Really?"

"Yes. Let me deal with the food. Can you meet me at the house?"

"All right."

"I'll see you tomorrow at eleven thirty." He kissed her, fast, and then stepped away; this time he stood on her porch and put his coat on.

She lifted a hand and waved, watching as he walked away.

6

Cal looked up to see his sister Mary come through his door holding one of his favorite things: a canvas tote he knew would be filled with food.

"You're an angel sent from heaven." He went to her, taking the bag and kissing her cheek. "Come in. Do you have time to eat dinner with me?"

"Calvin Whaley, it's nine at night. You haven't eaten dinner yet?" Mary looked around the room, one eyebrow raised. "You can't work every minute of the day. It's not healthy."

"I have work to do. It's do it here or in the office. I prefer here where I can drink a glass of wine and take my shoes off." He led her to the kitchen where he began to unpack the tote while she got plates.

She was petite, his baby sister. Curly hair like their grand-mother and while Cal's eyes were blue, Mary's were brown with flecks of gold. She was like a sprite on speed as she bustled around his kitchen, muttering to herself.

"You need a woman. Or a man—I don't care which—who cooks and will make sure you eat." She dished up some cucumber salad to go with the skewered chicken she plated. "Hang on, there's a sauce." She opened containers until she found what she was looking for and pushed it at him.

He hopped up onto a barstool at the island in the kitchen and began to eat. "Holy crap. The problem is, Mary Whaley, you're such an amazing cook that no matter who I was with, I'd be unhappy with their cooking. You're too good."

"Ha." She frowned.

He'd known her all her life, of course, which is why he could tell she wasn't there just to bust his chops about not eating right.

"So why don't you tell me why you're really here. Not that I don't appreciate the food, but you have that look you get right before you deliver a lecture and it's not about my work habits."

"I've been wrestling with myself for the last few days. Telling myself I shouldn't say anything. But of course that argument never wins."

She sat next to him and pushed a glass of juice his way.

"What? You're starting to scare me."

"Jules is seeing someone." She blurted it and Cal tried to keep his expression casual but this was his sister so she saw right through that.

"Not the first time. She's had dates before. Why tell me? Unless." He sat forward and held her eye contact. "Is this guy hurting her?"

Mary made a face and he felt better. "No, no. At least I don't think so. This guy is . . . you know him actually. It's Gideon Carter."

"Gideon?" He knew his old friend had recently come back to Bainbridge for good. Gideon had even called and left a message, saying he'd love to get together soon.

"Look. I've watched you watch her for years. Unless you want it that way forever, now's your time to move."

"How could it be serious? He's only been back a week, right? Maybe two?"

"Yes. But they . . . she talks about him differently. I've seen him look at her. This isn't some fast, shallow thing. This isn't *fun*. It could be more. And you know, it should be if she wants it to be. He appears to be into her and all."

"So why tell me?"

Mary just stared at him.

"She's not for me." He pushed to stand. "We've been friends a very long time. It suits us."

"Does it? Must be why you're pacing at the mention of her dating someone else."

"Well of course. I worry about her like I'd worry about you." He cringed as he said it. Despite the jokes about unethical attorneys, Cal hated to lie. He was pretty shitty at it, as it happened.

His sister snorted at him. Staring right past his excuses.

One of her brows slid up. "Really? So your feelings for Jules are *brotherly*. This is the bill of goods you're trying to sell me right now? I'm insulted that you're actually saying this to me. I've let you go on this subject for too long. You're being a dookiehead. God." She punched his arm pretty hard.

"Ouch." He rubbed the spot. For a little thing she was totally strong.

"I don't want to ruin the connection we have. I appreciate your concern and all, Mary, but things are better this way."

She blinked at him, saying nothing for a long time.

And then she sighed. "What to do with you, Calvin? What would you do without me? Don't even try to pretend you don't know I'm right. Poop! I call total poop on you for this lame-ass excuse."

He started laughing before he took a risk and leaned in to hug her, kissing her cheek. It wasn't that she was afraid to curse, she did and often quite creatively. But between the three Whaley siblings, their old childhood insults often reigned.

"I'm duly chastened. But I'm not going to ruin what I have with Jules. Sure, there's a little spark. But I'm not going to act on it. If things went bad, I wouldn't have her in my life. I like having her in my life. But not to date."

She actually stomped her foot and glared at him. He backed up a step, his hands up.

She pointed at him. "You are a serial monogamist. Oh, you like one guy or one woman at a time, you're not a cheater. But you always have an expiration date in your head. I know you, Calvin. You can be a dick sometimes. You're messier than you should be. But you're smart. And you're good and kind and you help people when you don't have to because that's who you are. You don't normally pretend away the truth." She stood and smoothed the tote, folding it carefully.

"I want you to think carefully on this. Because if you lose her because you're too . . . whatever it is that keeps you from admitting just how much you want Juliet, you'll hate yourself for it. And her eventually. Maybe even Gideon for doing what you didn't have the courage to."

She headed to the front door. "Stay for a late dinner with me." He tipped his head to the table where the food lay. "I have wine. We can hang out and not talk about Jules."

"No. I need to go home. I've got a long day tomorrow and I want to go to bed. Plus you're harshing my mood." She opened the door and turned back to face him. "I see the way he looks at her. He is not the kind of man who will miss what an extraordinary woman Jules is. He's moving in on her. They're forming a relationship right now. He's taking her on a picnic! I shouldn't even be telling you this."

His stomach twisted a moment.

"Don't be a dumbass, Cal. Don't let her go." She waved and left him there alone with the thought of losing Jules.

Jules Lamprey was a person he'd always loved having in his life. She ran with his sister and had pretty much been a fixture in his house from an early age. Over time they'd grown close and at this point in his life he counted her as one of his very best friends.

But when he'd just about finished high school there'd been *more*. He saw her as she'd grown and developed as a woman and he'd found it pretty irresistible. There'd been a kiss. But she was so young and he left for college right after. And then he'd thrown himself into his life as a student. He'd developed a taste for men as well as women. He'd learned a lot about himself and he wouldn't trade that for anything.

His family had always been accepting of who he was, but it was when *he* could be that accepting that he'd felt like he'd truly grown up. Heartache had been part of that process and he couldn't imagine making her hurt the way he knew he'd hurt other people when he'd broken things off in the past. He never wanted to see hurt that he'd caused in her gaze.

Whenever he'd been single she'd been with someone. And even when they were both single, he'd hesitated at moving their friendship into anything else. Because he counted on her. Jules would always be there when he needed her. She loved him and supported him and he didn't think he could recover if he lost that.

Even if he did want her so badly it took all his energy at times not to change the tenor of a hug and finally kiss her for real. He cherished Juliet Lamprey. This thing with Gideon probably wouldn't last. The others hadn't, after all. Some day she'd find someone to settle down with. But probably not for a while.

She'd still be his friend even if she loved another man. And he'd have to deal with that. When it happened.

She showed up at eleven thirty, as he'd asked her to. She went to the main house, not knowing if he was there or elsewhere, but Patrick would most likely know.

It was Patrick who answered, a big grin on his face. "Hey there, pretty girl. Come on in. Gideon's back in the kitchen."

She entered the house, pausing to kiss Patrick's cheek and squeeze his hands. "How are you today?"

He closed the door behind her and then smiled, taking the pastry box. "Better now that you've brought me one of these boxes. I do like something sweet in the afternoon with my coffee."

She linked her arm through his and he led her through the house. "Clearly I've been remiss in bringing things by then. I'll have to add it to my to-do list." She didn't tell him she'd made adjustments to the recipe of the turnovers she made him. Lowered the fat considerably and added some whole wheat to the pastry too. What he didn't know wouldn't hurt him.

He grinned and patted the hand on his arm. "Good. I like the idea of a beautiful woman coming over here to bring me goodies. Gives me something to look forward to."

Gideon turned at the sound of his granddad's voice. He'd known Jules had arrived, but seeing here there, her arm linked with his granddad's, made all his nervousness wash away.

"Juliet." He dried his hands off and moved to her, taking her from his granddad with a wink. "I hope you're hungry. I may have gone a little overboard with the food."

"As it happens, I'm starving so it's a good thing. Looking like rain out there though so I hope you didn't have anything super picturesque in mind."

"I remember that much about living here. I have backups in place." He grabbed the ice chest with one hand and took hers in the other.

"Have a good afternoon, boy. Don't rush back on my account. Mainly because I have a date with the game and some cherry turnovers and you're not invited."

"I put a pot of tea in the front room for you. It's still hot. Hiram should be over soon. There's plenty of snacks for him, even if you don't want to share the turnovers."

He led her out the back door and down the steps to the golf cart parked to the side. "I'm out at the creek house."

"I haven't been out there since, gosh, since I was twelve or thirteen I guess."

He put the ice chest in the back and she got in.

"I'd planned a picnic. Forgetting how silly an idea that was for May. So when it was clear it was too rainy to have one outside, I shifted and decided to have one inside."

The farm was large enough that the little golf cart was a

necessary evil. But the cart had an electric motor so it was quiet enough and it was perfect for getting his granddad around.

The creek house was a one-room A-frame five acres away on the other side of the land from the house. It had been built as a place for Gideon's father to live in while attending college. But then his dad had gotten married and moved to California. Gideon loved it out there though. Quiet solitude was often what he needed at the end of a long day, though given his granddad's age, he'd have to move into the main house at some point he knew.

"You're living out here now?"

He pulled up next to his truck and helped her out. "For the time being. It's good to have a place to get away to at the end of the day where I can turn my music up really loud and not have to worry about it. It's unlocked. Go on inside. I want to get this stuff."

She raised a brow, but grabbed a blanket and one of the bags to carry into the house. He repressed an annoyed sigh, grabbing the ice chest and the other bag.

"I can hold a blanket and a grocery bag for ten feet. Just for future reference."

She opened the door and moved inside, pausing as she took the place in.

He dropped the stuff in the small kitchen to the left and returned, taking the blanket and other bag from her hands.

"This is gorgeous." She walked over to the wall of windows, looking out at the creek running just beyond.

"It's quiet back here. I can hear the water, but that part is nice."

He unfurled the blanket in front of the fireplace.

"Sit. Let me get the picnic laid out."

"Are you sure you don't want some help?" She toed her shoes off and left them neatly by his front door.

He made a mental note to pick up some slippers or something for her so her feet wouldn't get cold when she was over.

"No. I'm good. I have a few tricks up my sleeve."

She laughed and sat on the pillows he'd set out.

"This place still had the fireplace from when they first built it when my dad was in his late teens, early twenties." He flipped a switch and the fireplace danced to life. "I had them take it out and put in this one. Energy efficient and really warm."

"I like it. It goes perfect with this view. Wow."

He joined her, looking out over the view. Trees surrounded the place on both sides of the creek, lending a lushness he loved to the whole space. "Granddad wrote this creek into a land trust so that it can't be developed. I can make some internal improvements but I can't make this place bigger." He handed her a glass. "Warm pear cider."

She took it from him, breathing in the spice on the steam. "Thank you." She sipped as she watched him taking his shoes off before heading to the kitchen to push his sleeves up and wash his hands.

"This hits the spot. It's not as cold lately, but the wet is a soaker today."

"I'm still getting used to the weather here." He brought plates over and a little basket of silverware.

She looked so perfect there, reclining near his fireplace, against his pillows. The firelight lit her just right. He brought the tray of cheese and the crackers over.

"Thank you."

"You're the kind of beautiful that lifts a man's sprits just looking at it." He brought the remaining plates and bowls over, joining her at last.

He clinked his glass to hers.

"You're pretty good at this sexy picnic thing."

It was impossible for him not to notice the easy grace with which she moved. "Now don't laugh, but I learned how to pack a good picnic from all my trips to see my sister. She's in Eugene and she's got five kids. All boys." He laughed and stole a slice of apple from her fingertips.

"Hey!"

He popped it into his mouth. "One of the things I learned is that you've got to be fast when you see what you like. Snap it up before someone else does."

He paused, momentarily transfixed by the way one side of her mouth slid up just a breath.

She sat back a little. "When you look at my mouth like that it makes me sort of light-headed."

He took a deep breath but all he got was more of her.

"Tell me about them. Your nephews, I mean."

He smiled, thinking of them. "My nephews are all nonstop tussling, wrestling, dangerous action. It's insane. I don't know how my sister does it. They're great boys. A lot of fun. Super smart. And when I visit we all hang out by the pool and have picnics and play Marco Polo until all hours. It's wild and crazy."

She laughed. "Ethan's got two boys and they're so funny. One is four and the other is eighteen months. I try to get down to Portland at least once every few months to see them and we Skype and do FaceTime. They're two of my favorite people in the world, but they're rambunctious. Ethan jokes that everything in his house is broken. He's not that wrong."

"So really, that you'd enjoy what a seven-year-old boy thinks is awesome picnic food is a pretty big compliment. To me and them."

She reclined and he did as well. A spring rain soaked the world outside as they lay quiet and warm, away from the cold.

"What did you like most about cattle ranching?"

"Hmm. I liked working with my hands. If I had to be in an office all day long I'd go crazy. The best thing about ranching and farming is that while there are lots of times I work behind a desk, I'm also outside. I'm all over my land all day long. I know what's going on where."

"You're connected to it."

"Yes, that's true, I think. It's my job to be sure I'm using the land in the best way I can. Some people describe it as a sense of freedom. But to me, it's a sense of commitment. Of putting down roots and being connected, mind and spirit with the land. At the same time, this is a business. I have to remain relevant and solvent. It's not just my life but the staff, my grandfather, the people we do business with and so on."

To Jules that seemed like an awful lot of pressure. Even as she admired his ambition and commitment to the farm.

"I admire that. So many times people just go through life without ever feeling any real passion for what they do. I'm so fortunate to have that in Tart. I'm glad you do as well here at the farm."

He waved her comment away and turned the conversation back to her. "What's your favorite part of being a baker? Pastry chef. Whatever it is you call yourself."

She finished chewing one of the little sandwiches he'd made.

She doubted those boys of his were fans of watercress, but maybe they were. Either way, the sandwiches were pretty awesome.

"My friends call me the goddess of pastry." She laughed. Gillian had been the one responsible for that one. "But you can call me Jules if you'd rather."

He leaned in and kissed her and she couldn't remember what they'd been talking about before.

She slid her fingers through his hair, pulling him closer. He smiled, his mouth against hers for a brief moment and then he was gone again. But it wasn't long before he was back. This time at the spot behind her ear. And down again to the nape of her neck, leaving her shivering with delight.

And again, he moved away and she opened her eyes to glare his way.

"If you stop again, I will hunt you down and maim you."

He paused from where he'd been putting the glasses out of reach and then he laughed. "You're vicious." Which only made her sexier.

"I am when I'm being denied something I was promised. You need to get back up here and kiss me some more."

He leaned in and kissed her chest, right over her heart. Her heart that sped when he touched her. His own kicked in response.

She sat up, pulled her sweater off before folding it and placing it a few feet away. So neat, even when she was partially naked and ordering him to sex her up.

He sucked in a breath and it didn't help. "I'm trying to take it slow and you go and take your shirt off. How can any sane man be expected to not want his hands on those?" He indicated her breasts, mounded up perfectly at the top of a pretty navy polka-dot bra. "Can I confess something?" He played with the bow just between those two, perfect B cups.

"Yes. Especially if it has anything to do with sex and having it with me."

"B is my favorite size." He squeezed her breasts for emphasis and she arched into his touch.

She'd had a hand on the middle of his chest but she reversed her hold and sent it down. Down to grab his cock through his jeans. "This is my favorite size. Whatever size it is. I mean, it's big." She started laughing. "Sorry. I'm unable to make sense apparently. Your cock is in my hand and I want to have sex with you so bad it's a little embarrassing."

"The most sensible thing I've heard all day." He got to his knees and she got to hers, her hands going to his shirt, which she unbuttoned quickly. "You sound like you want it as much as I do."

"You can take your time. The next time."

"Why do I get the feeling people rarely tell you no?" He shrugged from his shirt and then the T-shirt he wore beneath it.

"Because most don't. And wow. This is way better than I imagined. And I can admit I did imagine a time or two."

He pushed her back and she looked down her body as he slid her zipper south and pulled her jeans off, leaving her in her panties and bra.

His want for her was so powerful his hands shook just a little. He was barely holding back the impulse to jump on her, and when he took in all that bare skin it only made things worse.

He wanted to take. To gorge and take more until neither of them had breath. He gulped. "I want to kiss you some more."

"Bring it."

He did, resting his upper body against hers. Her arms encircled his upper body, her fingers digging into the muscles at his shoulders to hold him close.

Pears and cinnamon. He doubted he'd ever smell either and not think of that moment.

She tasted of pears and cinnamon. She was warm and solid and she kissed like she meant it.

The warm weight of her breasts in his hands when he popped the catch on her bra blew the last of his control. There was no turning back. Not with this woman.

He wanted Jules and all she had to give. He gave over to it and let himself want.

Jules reeled. Gideon was so . . . unexpected. He touched her so shyly at first, nearly reverently. But then he'd warmed up and those touches had grown bold and insistent.

He lavished attention on her breasts and she had no complaints. His fingers were work rough, adding to the intensity of the rolls and pinches of her nipples until she seemed to throb along with her racing heart.

She arched into his hands, wanting more and he gave it to her. Pinching harder, bringing a gasp of his name to her lips.

But that gasp turned into a snarl when he dipped his head, the cool softness of his hair brushing against the curve of her breast. His mouth, hot and wet, slid over the same nipple he'd teased. Arcs of electricity singed her nerves.

He kissed over to the other nipple, rendering that one equally tingly and hard once he'd licked and nibbled over it. While she contemplated hauling him back to her nipple when he wandered away, his lips cruised over her ribs and she sighed, melting against the pillows stacked behind her.

He continued to kiss and lick down her body. Over her hip bone and the seam where her leg met her body. He breathed warm over her pussy, through the material of her panties.

She was so wet she ached, so swollen and ready that each movement she made sent ripples of pleasure all through her system.

And it still wasn't enough. She needed more. Of him.

"You're so soft. You smell good. Damn." He kissed against the edge of her panties, catching them between his teeth and tugging down.

"Taking off my underpants with your teeth. You have so many talents. I'm in awe."

He tossed her panties back over his shoulder and loomed over her as he knelt between her thighs.

Where to look first? There was so much. He was so gorgeous her brain didn't know where to settle in. He was shirtless, but his jeans were still on. His upper body was lightly covered in chest hair. Gold, like the hair on his head and his beard. She reached up to run the pad of her middle finger over his nipple a few times. He grunted, pressing into her touch, so she figured nipples were in the plus column for them both.

This was unreal. He was so gorgeous and totally male above her. She swam through all his testosterone and held on as he took what he wanted, teasing, caressing, driving her wild with little fluttery kisses.

"I need you to understand I'm going to be masturbating to this exact moment a whole lot in the coming years." Her tongue was thick, but she managed to get it out, wanting him to know what he did to her.

His intensity faded a little as a grin lit over his features. "I like you a whole hell of a lot, Jules." He picked up one of her legs, kissing her ankle. Her breath stuttered from her lips.

"Thank God." She arched up as heat rushed through her. Each kiss seared her in a totally different way. The barest touch of his lips at her ankle, but behind her knee he flicked his tongue at the end of the kiss and it shot straight to her clit.

"You seem to have responded to that quite positively. You should put your arms up over your head. Look at you all long and golden. Like a sunflower. Strong and vibrant. Large and bright. Lovely."

She got to her elbows, moving to get close enough to steal a kiss. "The things you say." She closed her eyes a moment. "They make me dizzy."

"Wait'll you see what I have up next."

She giggled as he brushed his beard against her belly. Lower and then the giggle died on a moan as he dragged his beard against her pussy and then spread her open with his fingers, taking several long, quick licks until he drove her right up to the brink of orgasm before backing off again.

Her eyes snapped open as he backed away. "Hey!" She reached for him and he caught her hands in his, kissing them.

"Back up above your head."

Hoo boy. She did and he lunged up to kiss her mouth quick and hard and was back at her pussy while her head reeled.

He caressed her belly and her sides and then back down her inner thighs, pushing them up and then out. She was wide open to him then, utterly bared to his gaze.

The rawness of the moment stretched between them, taut. Heat. So much heat between them.

He bent his head to her and kissed her long and slow, his lips and tongue exploring every single part of her pussy. He flattened his tongue against her, teasing her clit, building her higher and higher.

And then he sucked her clit between his lips. Three times until she gasped in a breath and orgasm crashed into her hot and sharp until she was sure she'd burst with it.

When she opened her eyes, he was looking at her, his head on her thigh. "That was spectacular."

He smiled and she rolled on top, grabbing his belt and unbuckling it before attacking his button and zipper.

"I want you in me." That she managed to say it without sounding desperate was a miracle.

She scooted down his legs, pulling his jeans and shorts along with them, down and off.

He'd never actually been with another person who was so unafraid to ask for what they wanted. She was bold and unapologetic. It was incredibly hot.

And then she turned back to face him and crawled up his body. "I must have been a saint in some former life to have merited this moment." He meant every word.

She laughed, bending to kiss his knee and then the other. Her hair trailed up his thigh as she kissed her way up, past his cock, up over his belly and over his chest.

He hissed his pleasure when she licked over his left nipple, dragging her teeth against it until he made a sound awfully close to a plea.

Her ass was perfect. He noticed this as she bent over his body, kissing down his belly again.

Better than any porn he'd ever seen, she grabbed his cock and licked around the head, all while keeping her gaze locked on his face.

He nearly swallowed his tongue when she sucked him in deep and then backed off, keeping his cock wet and slick.

Her fist slid up behind her mouth and then she moved back to palm his balls. He couldn't look away from that beauty there spread out before him. That mouth on his cock. Her eyes, so brilliantly blue, locked on to him. He was exposed and raw.

She drew him achingly close to climax. So close he pushed against her shoulder. "I want to fuck you."

She pulled up with a soft pop of sound.

He held up a foil packet and she grabbed it, ripping it open.

Transfixed, he watched her roll it on his cock. Her eyes went half-mast as she caught her bottom lip between her teeth. Need beat at him but he continued to watch as she moved up and then sat, pressing herself onto him. She was so fucking tight. Sweat sprang to his temples.

"I should confess to you that having you on top is my favorite thing." He loved having a woman above him where he could touch her nipples and get at her clit.

"I'm amenable to that," she said on a gasp.

Orgasm had lent a pretty flush to her cheeks. Her hair was tousled around her face and she looked like a thoroughly debauched girl next door.

She leaned down to kiss him, slow and long before backing slowly onto him again, taking him deep.

She pushed herself upright, her head tipped back, arched, sliding her cunt over his cock again and again until he was nearly blind with it.

She rose above him, all that glorious hair sliding over her skin, over those pale pink nipples.

"You're so hot. Christ."

He'd known, somewhere in the back of his mind that it might be like this between them. But it was more, more than he could have imagined.

She circled her hips slowly. She'd braced her hands on his thighs behind her body so she was arched toward him, her head back. He slid his hands over every part of her he could touch.

Her upper body was toned. He figured it was most likely due to all the kneading and mixing she did. Whatever the cause, she was beautiful there above him as she undulated. He tiptoed his fingers down her belly, heading to her clit.

"Again for me."

He squeezed it gently and her cunt rippled around him, tightening and fluttering. She groaned low and deep and he continued a slow squeeze and release of her clit.

And then she sat straight up with a gasp and began to come, her pussy clamping tight around him as she increased her pace, pressing herself around him harder and harder, faster and faster until he grabbed her hips and held her in place as he came so hard he saw stars against his closed eyelids.

It went on and on until he wasn't sure he could take it. But she lay against him, his cock still inside her, as he caught his breath.

"Be right back." He rolled from the blanket and headed into the bathroom to rid himself of the condom.

When he got back to her side, he pulled her close, taking a deep breath and letting it all out. Just being. He buried his face in her hair, his arms around her from behind. The world was all around them, just outside the little A-frame surrounded by trees.

Just Gideon and Jules. For the moment he could forget everything else. The complications of dating and relationships. His granddad's needs, her business, their friends. None of it was necessary to think about right then. He knew what he wanted and it was her.

7

....

She painted her nails as she waited for Erin to answer the phone. They'd see each other later that day at Delicious, but she wanted to get this out of the way and out of Gillian's earshot.

"Hello, Jules!"

Erin Brown was a person like no other Jules had ever met. Adrian's big sister, she was larger than life with Technicolor hair and an infectiously jovial manner that was impossible not to respond to. She was a musician just like Adrian; in fact they still recorded together, though Erin didn't go out for full tours.

She was talented and lovely and really fun to be around. And she saw Gillian for the treasure she was, which went a hell of a long way in Jules's book.

"Hey, Erin. How's it going?"

"Not bad. Todd took Alexander out to the park and Ben is working. I am blessedly alone. I can't tell you what a rarity that is."

Jules knew there were people out in the world who had more than one partner, but Erin was the only person she knew who lived within a committed threesome. She and her husband also had a partner, Ben. And the three of them had a sweet little boy named Alexander. For all the piercings and wild hair and rock-star life, Erin was also refreshingly old-fashioned and family centered. They made a beautiful family and it was clear they all loved each other very much.

Erin and Adrian were very close. As Adrian also was with his older brother, Brody. He had a strong commitment to family and Jules admired that. He and Gillian were perfect for each other in that way.

Very few people would have been good enough for Gillian and Miles. Lucky for Adrian he was one of them. Most of the time anyway.

Jules looked down at her calendar for a moment before speaking again. "I was wondering if you'd like to plan an engagement party with me for Gillian and Adrian. Now that they've chosen a date and things are moving forward I thought it could be a good idea."

"Yes! I was just thinking about this a few days ago. Ella brought it up. Let's do it."

They talked places and dates and decided on mid-June, which gave them about a month to get everything in place.

"Get me a list of people you think Adrian would like to have invited and I'll get them on the list."

Erin assented. "Gotcha. Also, I know a really good printer. How about I take on that part?"

"All right, that works. I'll work on food with Mary."

"I'm sure she has connections for good bar staff, so can you get me a few names? I'll volunteer to get that hooked up. Nothing wild." Erin laughed. "We're all too old for wild these days. But a nice open bar. I know Brody wants to help with some of this too. How about he pays for food?"

Jules tapped her pen a moment. "We've got the food. If you want to get the booze, that's fine. But we've got the food and the desserts. Mary and I already talked about it." They weren't rock stars, but they wanted to do their part for their friend.

"You're going to tell Brody no?" Erin laughed. "Oh, never mind, I bet you would. It would be worth it to see his face. How about he gets the printing then? For the invitations."

"Do you always get your way?"

"Not always, but most of the time I do."

Jules could imagine the grin on Erin's face as she said it. She was too lovely to be annoyed with. Erin only wanted to do for the people she loved and Jules couldn't fault her for that.

"I'll get you the contact information later today for the invitations, then. And I'll get you the info on the menu and all that stuff too."

"Perfect. Brody and I are so thrilled for Adrian and Gillian. I'm so glad you called. We'll see you in a few hours at Delicious. I'm super excited. We've got a babysitter and everything. A real adult meal in a place without paper tablecloths? I'm in heaven."

"It's Mary's first Delicious at Tart. She's nervous and pretends to be worried she'll pull it off. But she knows, like we all do, that she'll kick ass. I'll see you and your dudes later tonight."

She hung up. As the maid of honor and Gillian's best friend, it was Jules's job to be sure everything went smoothly. Gillian tended to be a worrywart, wanting everything to be perfect for everyone else. But this was her day and Delicious had banded together, united to be sure Gillian's wedding was the best day ever.

For now though she had to finish getting ready for dinner. Jules wanted to head over to Tart a little early to check Mary's progress. She'd been forbidden from helping, but not from coming in to her own shop.

Mary insisted on people staying out of her kitchen when she did dinners unless she'd chosen them for helper status.

Jules wasn't a helper this time, but if Mary needed the extra hands, she'd pitch in.

But first her nails needed to dry and she planned to think over which pretty underpants she was going to wear. As she had a man and all.

Grinning, she managed to get the drawer open to look, all without messing up her nails.

It was good, this thing with Gideon. The sex had been . . . well, stunningly good. But more than that, he made her laugh. He was the kind of man who cared about important things, who took care of those who needed it.

They shared history. Which was . . . well, she knew plenty of people she'd gone to school with and had been lifelong residents of Bainbridge along with her. But this was unique. Even back then he'd been exotic. He'd come for a month or a week or two and was gone.

That shared history meant something to her. And to him too, she believed. They shared a comfort level she rarely had with others.

Gillian would want details, Jules knew. Jules had tried to talk with her last night, but Miles had been home and they had a movie marathon going. She'd stayed for something suitably horrifying and had slept with her damned lights on, which was often part and parcel of family movie night with Gillian and her men.

She had some juicy post-date gossip and it was about time. She hummed as she got dressed. Things were really looking up.

Jules let herself in the back door of Tart and her phone started buzzing in her bag so she fished it out. "Hello?"

"Do you still have my copy of *Tigana*?"

She smiled at the sound of Cal's voice. "I don't think so. I gave it back. I'm not home right now, but if you can't find it, let yourself in and check my shelves."

"It can wait. I'm sure it's around here somewhere."

She rolled her eyes. He had a beautiful home with a beautiful view and he was the messiest person she knew. Clothes everywhere, books all over the place. Thank goodness he'd gotten a housekeeper the year before.

"Did you get a sudden yearning to read fantasy? Do you want me to come over and look for it?"

"You would totally do that for me."

She cocked her head, though he couldn't see it. "Of course I would. Just like you'd come over to my house to fix my leaky faucet." Which he had done only the month before.

"I take it you're going to Delicious tonight? Save me a seat. I have to run over to Seattle to grab some paperwork so I might be late."

She frowned. "Will do. Gideon will be here tonight. I know he wants to see you."

"What about you?"

"What about me what? Will I be there?"

Mary poked her head out into the hall and narrowed her gaze when she caught sight of Jules. "Uh-oh, your sister discovered me. Protect me."

He laughed. "You're on your own for that. I have to run; I'll see you later."

It wasn't until he hung up that she remembered he never answered her question.

He hung up and paced a little.

She'd brought up Gideon.

Brought him up in a friendly way, but it was unmistakable that she'd been in contact with him and that they'd discussed Cal.

He really did have to run over to Seattle to pick up some papers. He may as well get it done. He had to push it to make the ferry in time, but he'd done it enough that he had the pattern down.

Regardless of any business between him and Jules, his sister was having her first night at the new space and he needed to be there to support her.

He pulled his shoes on and grabbed his work bag. The rest of his house was a mess, but his office was always spotless, so at the very least he always knew where his car keys, work bag and anything else work related and important was.

He got in his car and the first thing he noted was Jules's hair thingy on his stick shift. It made him smile to see it. They'd taken a drive up to Vancouver together in the fall. Mary had come as well. They'd all stayed in a fabulous little boutique hotel and had shopped and eaten too much and had a great time.

Her smile. It hardened his entire body just thinking about it. Juliet had the most beautiful smile. Open. Big, perfect white teeth. There was nothing wishy-washy about a true Jules smile. Her joy was apparent on every part of her face.

They'd been close for decades now. Each boyfriend or girlfriend Cal had had was jealous of her. And he understood why in retrospect. While he'd never cheated on anyone he was with— it wasn't part of his makeup to do so—he'd been closer to Jules than any of them. Had sought her out to relate a funny story with or to share a secret.

He liked to tell people she was his best friend. But that wasn't entirely fair, he knew. He wanted Juliet. Had wanted her since he'd been eighteen and she'd been fifteen. He'd been her first kiss. She'd made him do it, convincing him someone else would do it if it wasn't him and she could trust him so why not just show her what she'd been missing.

It had been an exciting moment. One he still recalled from time to time. One moment she'd been his little sister's annoying friend and the next she'd been, well, a girl worth kissing.

But he'd shoved that part away. She was too young. He had older girls to sniff around, and, as he'd come to discover, some boys too. That part of him and Jules had gone dormant, but it was still there, sleeping, not always so quietly, beneath the surface.

She'd been a fixture in his life. Always there for him when he needed her. If he lost that he'd never forgive himself. As long as she stayed in the friend camp that had been possible. To always have her in his life.

He'd been repeating this to himself over and over since Mary had come to his house to tell him about Jules dating Gideon. It was true. Mostly.

If she was with Gideon, he could have them both around. It would be good. Wouldn't it?

8

....

By the time Cal arrived, Delicious was in full swing. But true to her word, Jules had saved him a seat. On the other side of Gideon.

He frowned but covered it quickly as he entered the doors and everyone looked up. Jules smiled and moved to him to grab a hug. He kissed her, like he normally would, on the lips. But it felt different because she smelled like another man.

"Saved you a seat. Gideon is going to hog you, he said." She indicated the chair. Seemed to Cal like Gideon was hogging *her*, not Cal. But he kept that in his head where it belonged. He smiled at Gideon, who looked good, even while his hand slid over Jules's shoulder before he reached Cal, who he pulled into a hug.

"Good to see you."

"You too. Welcome back to Bainbridge. Mary says you're back for good. I'm glad." Cal said it and realized it was true, even if the guy was poaching Jules.

He hugged Gillian and Daisy, nodded to the others and sat. Jules wasn't even in his line of sight, which sucked. Though Daisy and Levi were, and they were both beautiful and funny to be around so that would be fine. Ryan was at the other end of the table and his brother sent a quick look to Gideon and Jules before moving his attention back to Cal as if to say *See*.

And he did see.

Erin, Todd and Ben were at the other end of the long table. He waved to them. He was glad to see them there supporting Mary.

Speaking of his sister, Mary came out of the kitchen and headed to them with a dish of something beautiful. "You missed the first plate." She kissed his forehead as she slid it in front of him.

"Sorry. Ferry traffic. But I knew you'd save me something. It's perfect in here." He looked around the room. They'd transformed the dining room into something more intimate.

"It's all Daisy and Jules. I was having a little crisis earlier about it. I wanted it to be as intimate as the house, you know? So Daisy shows up with these heavy red drapes and Jules wound the white lights along the edges of the ceiling. The linens are perfect too."

Daisy waved a hand. "I can't take credit for any of it. It was all Jules. The curtains are her mother's. They were upstairs. As were the linens."

Jules shrugged and Cal wished he were close enough to reach

out and give her hand a squeeze. "It's nice they get used. They close out the outside world just perfectly and should be easy enough to take down and put back up at will. Same with the tablecloths and linens. I'm leaving the lights for a while. I think they add something."

She'd done it because it had made his sister feel better. He knew her so well. She'd come over there early, when he'd spoken to her before. Just exactly to be there for Mary when she got freaked.

He hoped Gideon realized how amazing Jules was. Sort of.

It was crowded, but not overly so. He was so proud of Mary, who'd taken her love of cooking and had made it into this. Into this little supper club idea everyone had laughed at until she had a nearly two-year wait list for people who wanted to join just to see what the fuss was about. She was a genius in the kitchen, his sister.

"This is amazing. I haven't eaten this well in forever. Jules has been talking you up, and she wasn't exaggerating." Gideon winked at Mary, who blushed as she oversaw the delivery of the next course.

Jules put her head on Gideon's shoulder with a smile. "I'm telling you, she's magic."

"Did Jules tell you guys we finally chose a cake flavor for the wedding?" Adrian sipped his wine and then his sister made an oooh sound from the end of the table.

Erin leaned over to look down to their end of the table. "You did? You didn't say. You bogarted cake details from me? Where's the love, Blue?" Blue was Erin's nickname for Miles, and the boy blushed in response.

"Mum swore me to secrecy."

Erin looked to Gillian as both women laughed.

"Shall we tell, Jules?" Gillian looked across the table to her friend.

Jules lit, all for Gillian. "Oh, all right. Go on. It's your cake. And your day."

Gideon put an arm around her shoulder and she leaned in to him. They were, Cal had to admit, beautiful together. Jules had an easy way with people she trusted. An open, bold personality, and she was that way with Gideon. It made sense; he was part of their extended group of friends from childhood. Gideon used to spend hours at Cal's house in his room listening to music and talking about cars and girls.

He'd make her happy.

But would he make her as happy as Cal could? And did Cal want to know? Did he want this to be the new reality of Cal and Jules? This third person he had to mediate past?

Gillian nodded thoughtfully. "I think I'm going to keep it a surprise then. Just trust me that it's going to be the best cake you ever had."

"You're a tease." Erin laughed. "Once someone gets to know you, they get past that careful reserve and underneath you're a vicious tease."

Gillian laughed. "I have to be to keep up with you all."

The food was delicious. His sister had outdone herself and he got up to tell her so. And also to leave behind the image of Gideon kissing Jules's temple.

"I told you." Mary said this as he snuck back into her kitchen.

"You didn't bark at me to get out."

"That's because I wanted to say I told you so. Hello, that

trumps everything else. Now that we know I was right, what are you going to do about it?"

"I can't talk to you about this right now. I wanted to say you did an amazing job tonight." He hugged his sister and she hugged him back.

"Fine, fine. Thank you. It's going quite well. I tried some of these new local-sourced ingredients and that worked well, I thought. The space is really perfect. It's so much easier for me to work in this kitchen than at home."

"Relieved not to work the truck anymore?"

"I miss the truck and this summer I have a few jobs I think I can cater from it. It'll be fun. But I don't miss trying to find a place to park or dealing with all the city regulations and rules. The catering business is more stable for me. And more lucrative. That part is really nice."

"I'm glad to hear it. Do you need help?"

"My staff is just fine, thank you. Now go on. It's dessert time and Jules has outdone herself."

He tried to peek but she pushed him from the kitchen without another word.

"You knew she was going to kick you out." Jules grinned as he returned to the table.

"I did, but I had to push my limits. Plus I like to poke at her. It amuses me and keeps her from obsessing about how everything needs to be perfect."

"You're a good big brother."

"I am. So tell me what dessert you made for tonight."

Jules laughed and sat back in her chair to take a sip of wine. "Incorrigible. You'll find out yourself in a few minutes. Be patient."

"I'm not very patient; you know that about me."

Gideon snorted. "Remember how you almost lost your thumb because you kept cutting the fuses on all those M-80s shorter because you hated to wait for them to blow?"

He and Gideon laughed at that one. His mother had nearly lost her shit when she came outside to discover Cal covered in black powder, Ryan and Gideon patting him with a broom to put out all the little smolders on his clothing.

Ryan apparently still found it hilarious. "You two got into a lot of trouble every damned summer. It was a boon to me, as Mom watched you two so carefully I got away with a lot more stuff."

Cal looked down the table to his brother, still laughing. "You're an asshole. You still do that."

Ryan shrugged, unrepentant. "Hell yes. You're still a trouble-maker so as long as you continue, I keep flying under the radar."

"It occurs to me that the two of you have a great capacity for troublemaking." Jules leaned across Gideon, who kept his arm around her. It was an open, easy affection between them and it twisted through Cal's gut.

"I don't cut the fuses on my cherry bombs anymore."

She laughed, reaching out to pat his arm. "That's a start, baby."

And then the dessert came out and he nearly fell to his knees with gratitude because it was his fucking favorite, a rustic apple cranberry tart. Complete with vanilla bean ice cream.

"You rock," he said to her as he dug in and moaned.

"It's his favorite," Jules explained to Gideon.

"I can see why." Gideon forked up a bite and sighed happily.

"I can also see being involved with you is filled with plenty of awesome perks." He kissed her quickly and she leaned into him.

Cal put his gaze back on his plate, but not before Adrian caught his attention and raised a brow.

Nothing like a secret crush everyone knew about.

He'd get used to it. Right?

9

....

Two weeks after that dinner at Delicious, Jules took the back door out after work. The street out front was still busy and she was *so* done with the day. Mary didn't have any jobs that night and so she'd locked up, cleaned up and headed toward home.

Jules wanted a hot bath, a good book and maybe even a movie. She'd been up late several nights in the last two weeks and it was really beginning to catch up to her.

Smiling, she thought about the reasons why she'd been up late. She had a boyfriend. Like a real one. A man who brought her flowers and knew how she took her coffee. He was in her life but didn't dominate it. He loved her friends and respected her business.

Gideon had shown up at her house with dinner and a bottle

of wine and they'd eaten, played cards and fucked so loud if she had close neighbors they would have called the cops.

Things were very good.

"Hey, I'm glad I didn't miss you."

She turned to catch sight of Cal headed down the alley toward her.

"Hi, you. If you want a cup of coffee you'll have to get it at my house. I'm closed for the day."

She stepped close, knowing he'd hug her. But what happened was far more than a hug.

She saw the look on his face and worry sliced through her for just a brief moment as he pulled her to him and then he kissed her and she forgot everything.

He kissed her, pouring all his energy into it. The heat of his mouth against hers, the taste of him was shocking as he slid his tongue into her mouth.

Years. Years and years she'd wanted exactly this and it was better than she'd imagined. All her words skittered away. The scent of him filled her senses, his taste overwhelmed. He'd backed her against her doorway and kissed her like there was no tomorrow.

He nipped her bottom lip and she held on, her fingers in his hair. Somewhere she knew she needed to tell him to stop. This wasn't okay. But it was . . . goddamn, it was everything she'd imagined and more.

He set her on fire and all the want she'd carried for him spilled between them and he feasted on it, feeding it back to her.

And when he stepped back, she gasped for breath and held a hand out, warding him because she was weak and nothing had prepared her for the reality of what he kissed like as a man.

"What. Was. That?"

He licked his lips and began to pace the alley. "That was a kiss, Juliet."

"No duh. I've seen you kiss lots of *other* people enough to know. But why me? Why now? What's wrong?"

He threw his hands up in the air. "What's wrong? What's wrong is that you taste so fucking good I'll never forget it." He continued to pace, shoving his fingers through his hair, disheveling it.

"What?" She gave in and licked her lips, tasting him again. Damn it.

"I'm tired, Jules. Tired of telling myself I don't want you when everyone on the planet knows it's a lie. I *do* want you. I'm tired of seeing you with another man when I wanted you first."

She blinked, trying to clear her head. Luckily he was being a guy, which made it easier to put the kiss to the side to get to the real issue.

"You've had a long time to make a move. Through, hmm, let's see." She paused to count them all. "Candace, Elvin, Shaun, Carrie, and what was the last one? Oh yes, Diego. Funny how your move only comes when I'm seeing someone, instead of the other way around."

He gusted a sigh. "Yes, I can see how it looks that way. But it's more than that. Don't tell me you can't feel it."

"You know, Calvin, I used to tell myself it was that you were really gay. I said to myself, *He can't admit it all the way yet, but if I push him and then we get together, one day he'll be unhappy that I can't be what he wants.* I'd have been that woman, you know the one. The one who gets dumped when her husband finally comes out. More than how *I'd* have felt, I never wanted you to have to fake who you were. Because I love you."

He started to speak and she held her hand out to shut him up.

"No. I'm talking now. And then, well, then you dated women too and I realized something else. You truly do like men and women both. So what that meant was that you were choosing *other* women. Other than me I mean. You made your choice, Cal. You made it and you can't just come down the alley and kiss me like that. You're screwing with my emotions and that's shitty."

He shook his head, miserable that he'd fucked it all up so much. "No, I'm not. I wouldn't do that to you. I know what it looks like. But you know me. Better than anyone else in the world, you know me."

"I'm with someone. I'm with Gideon and now I have to confess this . . . this kiss to him." More than that, she had to process how it had lit her up from the inside out. How he'd brought her to the brink of an orgasm just from a damned kiss.

"I want you, Jules. This kiss wasn't just a drive-by moment. It was my declaration. You and I are meant for each other. Do you have any idea how many people came by work or my house since Gideon has moved back to town? Everyone knows we should be together and I've known it too and I kept telling myself that I couldn't risk our connection." He swallowed hard. "We are meant to be. You know it."

"What I know is that *I'm with Gideon*. He's a good man. He takes care of me. He's good to his granddad. He makes me happy. He respects me. And he makes me feel wanted and beautiful."

"He's a great guy. I can't argue. But you and he have been together just shy of a month. I've loved you for years. I can't let you go without a fight. You kissed me back, Jules. You were just as into that kiss as I was. And if you were so totally committed to Gideon, you would have socked me."

"I should sock you right now."

But she didn't argue.

"You don't get to judge how long I've been with him. You're not the boss of my fucking emotions! He and I, well, he's special. What we have is special. I'm falling *in love* with Gideon. You're too late."

Which was worse than arguing.

"I know what you need. I know what you are, who you are." He stepped close enough to brush the hair back from her face and then he kissed her again. This time she pushed him back after a few beats.

"Stop that."

"Are you denying your attraction to me?"

"I'm attracted to lots of people. I don't fuck them all. I have self-control. Attraction doesn't mean anything."

"You said you've wanted me for years. As long as I've wanted you. I know the timing sucks, but you can't expect me to let you lie to yourself. If it was anyone but you, I might just step back and let Gideon have you. I know you two have something, I can see it. But I loved you first."

She swallowed hard and he knew he'd landed a few direct hits. But this thing between her and Gideon was far more serious than he'd thought. He tried to wall back the panic. He could do this. This was his job after all. He made arguments for a living.

"I have to go. I have to talk to Gideon." She tried to move around him but he took up next to her and walked along with her instead.

"Fine. Let me come along."

She stopped. "Are you high? No. Go home, Cal. Jerk off a

few times. Call one of your many, *many* admirers and fuck one of them. You only want me because someone else does."

He grabbed her upper arms, bringing her close. "That's a lie and you know it. Don't demean it that way."

Her hurt had washed away, replaced by anger. "Fuck you, Cal! Demean it? You've fucked your way through dozens of men and women when *I wanted you* but now you've decided you want me? Isn't that convenient? Now that someone else does?"

"Convenient? Is that what you think? You think it's convenient to watch another man touch you the way I want to? When I know it's my own fault for waiting too long? You mean too much to me and I won't accept that I've lost you until we have this out with Gideon."

"How dare you give me ultimatums. This one-sided bullshit pisses me off. You have had *years* to make a move and you didn't. Now that I'm happy with someone you decide you want me and that if I don't break up with Gideon to be with you, we're not friends anymore?" Her voice broke and he felt like a shithead.

He shook his head; the hurt on her features tore at him. He never wanted to cause her all this upset. "No, that's not what I mean. I'm *always* your friend. Always. That won't change. I mean lose my chance to be with you. It's not an ultimatum, it could never be. I'd sooner cut off a limb than lose you in my life."

He leaned in and kissed her again. Softly this time. "I don't want to imagine a world without you in it. I know this is unfair. I know I should have done this years ago. But I can't go back and change my mistakes. I'm trying to learn from them."

"I have to go. I was going to have an early night. A bath. Some reading or a movie and now I have to go to Gideon's and tell him another dude kissed me and that you're the other dude. Oh my god."

There was no way she could skirt who it was who'd kissed her. Cal knew that. She was an honest person. She'd never let this go without telling Gideon because it was the right thing to do. But man, Gideon would be pissed off. Cal didn't want to lose his friendship with Gideon either.

Since Gideon had come back they'd had dinner one night and talked a lot of cattle ranching, some gaming and books and then family law as they'd discussed his grandfather and the divorce too.

Gideon and Jules together would have been a hell of a fantasy to fuck his fist to. The both of them so beautiful and perfect. He liked to watch them together, liked the way Gideon had spoken about her.

Except for that part about how Gideon had the woman Cal wanted. That part wasn't so sexy.

"I'm sorry that this will be uncomfortable."

She rolled her eyes and shoved past him, muttering. She was well and truly angry by that point and he wanted to smack himself because it always got him off when she was like this.

All that pretty blonde-haired, blue-eyed sweetness turned topsy-turvy into righteous anger. She was truly the hottest pissed-off person he'd ever seen. He'd made enough people pissed off to have a sizable comparison to make as well.

She spun when she noted he'd blocked her car in. "Really, Calvin?"

He grinned. "I had to be sure you couldn't get away before I spoke with you."

She shook her head. "Move your car."

"Not until you agree to let me come out to Gideon's with you."

"I will knock the shit out of your pretty little car, Cal. Don't test me."

Goddamn, he wanted to fuck her right then. Oh, she meant it. She was dangerous, pissed off and frustrated. But she'd never have gotten this far along if she hadn't cared about him.

He knew she wanted him. That kiss had been all the proof he'd needed. And then her confession about how she'd watched him with men and then other women had shredded him.

He'd spend every moment until forever proving to her that choosing him was the best choice. He just had to get her to that point.

Gideon had received a short and somewhat terse call from Jules, asking him if she could come over. Silly, that, considering her open invitation and the way she'd been with him most nights since that evening at Delicious just two weeks before.

He could hear the upset in her voice though and when she said Cal was coming along, Gideon began to wonder if his suspicions were correct.

It wasn't very long until she showed up and he met her at the door, hugging her tight. Their connection clicked into place and he felt a little less worried.

"Are you all right? What's wrong?" He lifted his chin in Cal's direction as he moved to the couch and settled in, Jules snuggled next to him.

"There's no other way to say it." She licked her lips. "Cal kissed me."

"You mean back when you were fifteen? I know about that." He kissed her forehead.

"No, back just about half an hour ago. Outside Tart's back door."

He froze and narrowed his gaze at Cal, who shrugged as if it wasn't a big deal to have laid a kiss on Gideon's woman.

"Without your permission? Do I need to punch someone's face?"

She laughed and he felt better. And then worse.

"Not against my will. He's got issues, but he's no rapist."

"She'd cut my balls off if I tried."

Gideon interrupted this little exchange, brushing his fingertips over her cheek. "Why are you upset?"

"I'm not prone to kissing other people when I'm in a relationship. It was icky of me. He caught me off guard. I did kiss him back for a few moments. I'm sorry."

Cal cleared his throat. "Yes, we're both sorry. But I want Jules, Gideon. I want her. I loved her first and I wish it didn't have to be this way."

"Oh my god, Calvin, shut up!" Jules's spark came back and it made Gideon feel better.

"If she was breaking up with me, why is she snuggled into my side?"

Momentarily off balance, Cal tossed back, "You're awfully calm for a man whose girlfriend just confessed to kissing someone else."

"She kissed you back for a few moments in an alley. And then came over here to confess to me. I'm old enough to cut her a break. You on the other hand, I don't know about. I'm on the fence between punching you and being magnanimous because I happen to see Jules's appeal just as you do. I can afford to be the bigger man here because Jules is worth it."

And as he'd thought, she snuggled into his side more. Oh, he'd known about the attraction between Cal and Jules. He'd seen it, heard others refer to it. He'd seen the way Cal watched her at dinner. But Jules was *his*.

None of this bullshit shenanigans in the alley was going to stop that from being true.

Cal sighed. "Jules knows I want to be with her. I believe Jules wants me too. I'm sorry it had to happen this way."

"But she's *not* with you, Cal, she's with me. *She came to me.* Because I'm here. And I have been since day one."

He caught Cal's flinch and knew that arrow struck true.

"Hello?" She snapped her fingers. "If you two would like to continue this manly conversation without me, great. Otherwise, as I'm *right here* and all, let's move on. Okay, Cal, you made your confession, now go."

As Gideon had expected, Cal rolled his eyes and tossed himself into the chair across from the couch.

"I'm not going anywhere."

"Why? Do you want to watch as I kiss her? Touch her?" Gideon slid a hand up her thigh and she slapped it.

"Don't be an asshole."

"I'm not." He tipped his chin to Cal. "I'm trying to figure out what Cal's bottom line is. What mine is for that matter. Or yours."

She put her face in her hands. "Good lordamighty."

"My bottom line is clear. I want Jules. I want to be with her. I'm sorry to do this because I know this is not what a friend does and it'll undoubtedly impact or even ruin our friendship. But it's Jules. Anyone else and I could be honorable. But . . ." Cal shrugged.

She looked at him and Gideon saw it there, the spark between them. But her hand remained in his.

He knew she'd choose him. They'd begun to put down roots and grow closer. He was in love with her. He knew this as well as he knew his own name. He knew her feelings for him were deepening.

But there was something between her and Cal. It would probably die as his relationship with Jules went along. But he saw on Cal's features that it wouldn't be over. That the kiss in the alley was his way of staking a claim. He'd never give up until he had her.

"I'm not a pork chop. You can't walk in circles around me, growling." Her voice held frustration, yes, but also amusement and maybe a little bit of curiosity. He could work with that.

Gideon laughed, surprised. He kissed her. At first it was meant to be reassuring. But it deepened and she opened against him. He tasted her and the rightness of it sang through his system. But there was Cal too, that subtle taste and he sucked her tongue into his mouth and she groaned, clutching his biceps.

Cal's attention on her, on *them*, was so sharp Gideon felt it.

"As it happens, I also want Jules. I've said this already." He licked his lips and she pushed to stand.

"What it is you want, Jules? Hm?" Gideon watched her carefully. He knew from experience what a terrible poker player she'd be. Everything she felt broadcast all over her face and in her body language.

Right then she was annoyed, which amused him though he took care not to let that show. "Do you think I'd have come over here this way if I wasn't with you? If I didn't want to be with you?"

Gideon shook his head. "No, which is why I'm not feeling entirely angry or jealous right now. Because I can see it, Jules. I can see the spark, that connection you and Cal share. I've known you both a long time, but I've been friends with Cal just as long as you have. He's not going to let go or give up. And I can't say I'm interested in even the idea of letting you go. I'm in love with you, Jules, and that's that."

Her lips curved up as her emotions softened. "You are?"

"Hell yes. But the thing is the problem is still there. He's still going to want you. You're still going to want him. And you're friends. Close friends so you'll see each other and it'll be there. Between us all."

He sat back and put his ankle on his opposite knee and tapped a forefinger on his leg, thinking.

"What are you up to?" Jules, being her usual self. It made him laugh.

"You're a very suspicious woman."

Cal snorted.

"You like cock, don't you, Cal?"

She froze in place, her eyes widening at his question.

"I do. But that doesn't mean I don't want Jules, or that I can't give her my whole self. I like cock, but I like cunt just as well. And that one"—Cal tipped his chin toward Jules—"well, I don't need anything else if that's what's waiting for me every day when I get home from work."

Her brows flew up and Gideon knew they needed to tread carefully. "Shall I box it up for you? Gideon can have my tits. Cal can have my pussy and you can take them out and pet them every night and everyone can be happy to have a piece of Jules. Don't bother, you know, consulting me about it or anything."

Cal got up and moved to her, his gaze darting back to Gideon, who allowed it for the time being. Hell, Jules might kick or punch Cal, which would be interesting too.

Cal addressed her. "I know you're worried about that. It's best to just get it out in the open. It's not about a preference for cock or pussy. It's about the person. It's about *you*. You're all I want or need."

"What I propose," Gideon interrupted, "is that you come into our relationship."

"What?" They both asked this, in unison.

"Rather than fear it being torn apart, which is what I think will happen. Things can't be the same now. Why not invite him in? To share. Unless you're opposed." He spoke directly to Jules because this whole thing was up to her.

"I . . . I don't know what to say." She hadn't rejected it out of hand though, Gideon could tell that much.

Cal raised a brow in her direction and then over her shoulder at Gideon, who stood just beyond.

"As it happens, I like cock too."

Cal threw his hands up in the air and Jules grabbed her bag. "Nice one," Cal hissed as he followed her out the door.

Confused, Gideon got up and went after both of them. He didn't have to go far; she'd walked down from the main house so she hadn't made much progress.

"Wait, why are you leaving?"

She spun. "I can't do this. I . . . I can't always wonder if he's in it for me, or for you. Or if you are. I just . . ." She tried to keep walking but Gideon moved in front of her, taking her arms.

Cal moved him over. "Baby, it's you. Always and only you. He's trying to make you happy. In all the years I've known him *nothing* sexual or romantic has ever happened. Nor have I wanted it to."

Fuck. Now Gideon got it. "He's right. Stop thinking, even for a moment, that if it was a choice I'd do anything but choose you. What I'm proposing is that we share you. I look at Erin, Todd and Ben and I think I'd prefer that to anything else. I want to be with you and if that means sharing you with Cal, I'm willing to try it. And yes, in the interests of full disclosure, I enjoy men."

"I have to think." She stepped back.

He was fucking things up, damn it. "Don't go. Forget I said anything."

She tiptoed up to kiss him. "It's more than that. It's this whole night. It's the way I felt when you kissed me in front of him. It's the way I felt when you made the offer and said you liked men. It's all a jumble and I need some space to think. Please, just back off, both of you, and give me some space."

Gideon reached for her but she stepped back. "Let me drive you home."

She heaved a sigh. "So glad you both listen so well." She pushed past Cal and kept walking as they both watched her walk away.

"Jules, it's your choice. I'm here either way," Gideon called out.

She kept walking.

"Nice going, dickhead." Cal stomped past him as he continued to watch her walk away.

10

·······················

Cal couldn't believe the way his life had turned in the course of just a few weeks. He riffled through Gideon's kitchen until he found a bottle of good scotch. If he smoked, he'd probably have lit one up too.

When he'd gotten up that morning it had been after a night of going back and forth about what to do. He'd gone to Tart full of resolve to win her but he hadn't expected anything that had happened after the kiss.

Gideon came back inside fifteen minutes later. "I watched her until she got to her car."

"What the fuck did you do?" Cal turned slowly, holding the tumbler of scotch so his hands wouldn't shake.

"Me? What the fuck did *you* do? You kissed my girlfriend, asshole."

Well, put that way . . . "Yes, but she's not yours. She was mine long before you blew back into town and stole her."

Gideon's brows flew up. "I stole her? Really now? From who? You? A guy who could have had her for years but couldn't be bothered to make a move until someone else treasured what you took for granted? I didn't need to steal her. You neglected her. I saw what a wonderful woman she is. Don't cry about it now."

"You pushed her button, dumbass."

"What? You should be grateful I'm not punching your teeth down your throat. She and I have been dating for nearly a month. What the hell possessed you to pull this shit now?"

Cal sighed. "Okay, so yes, I probably should be grateful you didn't punch me. But that whole bit about liking cock pushed her away."

"I had no idea it was an issue. It's an issue *you* gave her, Cal. So you laid a kiss on my woman, came into my house and when I saw what was up I tossed out a solution. Again I'm asking you, why now?"

"I've loved Jules a long time. So long I guess I just took it for granted that when I was finally ready to stop lying to myself she'd be there. But I was too slow. I tried to let it go. I know you make her happy. But I couldn't. I couldn't just let her go without trying. I sure as hell wasn't expecting you to propose a three-way."

Gideon pushed past Cal and poured himself some scotch. "Yeah, well, look. I'm not an idiot. I know she'd have chosen me over you. She did that by coming over here and that makes it easier for me. I can't lie to myself or to her. I see how you look at her. I see how she looks at you. You two have something deep and I know you well enough to understand you're not going to just walk away. I don't want to put her in a position of always having to make choices."

Cal scrubbed his hand over his face. He'd made a choice, one he didn't regret in the big picture, but he'd done it without really thinking about Gideon and how much he loved Jules too. Oh, he got it on one level. How could you not love Jules?

He sighed. "I'm sorry for springing it on you. I can't regret kissing her and making it clear I'm going to fight for her. But this outcome has hurt her and you. I do regret that part."

"I need to go after her."

Cal leaned back against the counter, watching Gideon pace. Goddamn, the man was beautiful.

"Let her be for a while. She has to process."

"I don't want her thinking I proposed the idea of a threesome as a way to get at your cock. Why don't you tell me why she'd think that, Cal?"

"I didn't realize the extent of it until earlier today. I own it. I think part of her believes I'd only truly be happy with a man. I tried to explain to her it wasn't like that. And it isn't. Cock, cunt, whatever. It's about the person I'm with. For me, it's been Juliet and because I waited so long she has doubts. And then you went and phrased it that way and it pushed her buttons."

Cal levered away from the counter and began to pace. "I didn't mean for any of this to spin so totally out of control. I don't want to hurt her. Or you for that matter." He paused, turning to face Gideon. "Did you mean it? About the threesome, I mean."

Gideon looked Cal up and down, torn between wanting to punch him and wanting to comfort him. The need to run after Jules drove him, but he also knew Cal was right about giving her some space.

"Yes. She wants you. You want her. I'm not letting go of her, but I don't relish her being in between us when you won't stop fighting for her. It's not what I'd imagined with her. But . . . it's not something I hate either. In fact, well, she's not the only one sexually attracted to you. You and I have been friends as long as she and I have been. It could work. I'm not an expert, but I know it'll take a lot of work to get it right. We'd have to go step by step. I just think it's a way forward. I look at Ben, Todd and Erin and I know they have something special. What about you?"

Cal sucked in a breath. "I don't want her to doubt me. Do you understand that? I made a mess of this whole thing, I know. But it would break my heart to think she didn't believe my commitment to her. You're hot as fuck, I'm not denying that."

Gideon's heart sped a moment.

"If we do this, we need to let her make the choices and take the steps."

Gideon nodded. "I agree. I'll hold off on the punching for the time being. For now, let's focus on how to get her back."

"What's going on?" Gillian walked in to Tart four days later with a look on her face that made Jules suck in a breath and steel herself.

"Um. A clue perhaps? What do you mean?"

Gillian put a hand on her hip and glared. "You won't return my calls. Your texts are boring and lack even a basic amount of snark. Cal is moping around. Mary says you're not here when she arrives in the afternoon and Gideon called my house looking for you. What in God's name is going on?"

Jules sat in a nearby chair and told Gillian everything.

"Well, I can see why you needed the space to think. But why you wouldn't come to me to let me help, I can't imagine."

"You have enough going on in your life. This is just . . . it's . . . I don't even know."

"Don't be daft. *Enough going on.* Sure, a wedding and a bossy fiancé and a teenaged son who is at turns sweet as pudding and then surly. But you're my best friend, it's my job to listen to you. Also, really to deny me the story of how two ridiculously gorgeous men offered to share you? Mean." She fanned herself. "Well, are you interested? You know, in both?"

"The thing is—and I've been thinking on this nonstop since that damned kiss—I'm with Gideon. I chose him when I went to his place to tell him about the kiss. But then he was all, hey, take us both and now I'm torn."

"Torn because you'd rather have just one than both? And if that's true, that's okay too, you know. I'm not sure I could manage two men at once. Adrian gives me more than enough to do."

Jules wiped a counter down to keep moving. "Do I want them? Individually? Sure. Look at them! It's more than their looks, of course. I'm falling in love with Gideon in a big way and I'd be a liar, liar, pants on fire if I denied how long I've loved Cal. But together? At the same time? I don't know."

"Is it the overabundance of penis? Or worry that they're not interested in your parts best?"

Jules laughed and then hugged Gillian tight. "Thank God for you."

"I say this about you all the time."

Jules was so glad Gillian had come in. She needed this so badly. Needed the support and honesty she got from her best friend.

"Gideon loves you. I admit that I've got a natural bias toward Cal. I've known him longest. He's like family. But since I've met Gideon he's been nothing but good to you. And you do deserve to be happy. If you can't imagine being with them both, then don't do it. Cal will get over it. He'll have to."

"What kind of flesh-and-blood woman with a pulse *wouldn't* imagine being with them both? I'm only human, Gillian. I've imagined it all right." So much her wrists hurt from masturbating so often.

Gillian grinned and cocked her head. "Have you thought about talking to Erin? I know she can be sort of bold and wild, but she's a wonderful listener. She puts a lot of work into her relationship with Todd and Ben. It can work if you do it right and you have the right combo of people."

"Honestly if you were telling me this story, I'd yell at you to get out of here and jump both men. You're very patient."

"You love them both. I know this about you. You're thinking this over because it would change everything. No matter what decision you make, everything will be different. There's no way around it, I'm sorry to say. Once Cal kissed you, things were thrown onto a wholly different path."

"I know." She paused and then blurted it out because she needed to say it. "It was a really, really good kiss. If he'd kissed me like that six months ago, we'd be happily together right now. He's quite a dumbass for a man who looks as good as he does." Jules chewed her lip a moment and then just said it. "I'm afraid Gideon will think the same thing about his kisses and they'll get sick of me. It's stupid and petty and I can't stop thinking about it."

Gillian made one of her polite little growls of annoyance.

"He's a fool for waiting so long. As for the kiss? I'm glad. I mean, I figured it was. You two, well, there's years and years of built-up stuff between you. But back to the threesome thing. I don't think this is about them both secretly being totally gay and then they'll find out and dump you. I can understand why you'd worry. But they both want *you*. I'm telling you the total truth when I say I've watched Cal watch you for years. He's in love with you, Jules. Not with anyone else. Same with Gideon."

"So you think I should give it a try? The, um, threesome thing? I mean, we didn't make rules. It's not like it has to be all double penetration all the time or anything. Or any." She shuddered. "That just seems sticky and messy and not entirely pleasant for the person who is being stuffed full of cock."

Gillian blushed and then laughed so hard she started to choke.

"I'm with you on that. So why not, you know, have a conversation with Gideon and Cal about this? You can't avoid them forever. They're pretty alpha dudes. They're only going to be patient so long before they come to track you down."

"I asked them for some space and some time. They left me alone for a day." She laughed. "In the four days since there've been several phone messages. The last one was Cal telling me he was going to hunt me down if I didn't stop ignoring him."

"He's adorable for a boy with so much cheek." Gillian winked.

Yes. He was. And yes, she needed to confront this whole thing like a big girl.

Cal showed up at the farmhouse on Friday. Patrick led him though the house to the kitchen where Gideon had been making a pot of tea.

"I'll bring this through in a bit. I'm just letting it steep." Gideon spoke to Patrick, who snorted.

"I have plans, boy. I'll see you later on."

"You're driving?" Gideon had been trying to wean his grandfather away from driving, at least on the city streets instead of on their land.

"No. I'm off to Ernesto's place. His daughter should be here any moment to pick me up. She's a pretty one. Don't wait up."

Gideon watched out the window until a car pulled up and then his father got in and left. Then he turned back to Cal.

"Have you heard from her?" Meaning Jules. He'd called and left voice mails but she hadn't responded.

"No." Cal's expression was as frustrated as Gideon felt.

"Have some tea. There's a fresh pot."

But then his phone rang. Her number. Gideon picked it up quickly and hoped he didn't sound as forlorn as he felt. The time away from Jules had only convinced him of how right they were for each other. He'd missed her like crazy.

"Will you be around later? I wanted to talk to you."

"Can I come to you? Or do you want to come out here? Granddad's gone and I'm in the big house with a pot of tea. And Cal, he just showed up here, but I can make him leave if that's what you want."

Cal flipped him off, but Gideon knew he'd leave if that's what he thought was best for Jules. Despite the idiocy of that kiss in the alley, it was totally clear to him that Cal adored Jules.

"No, that's fine. I have to lock up and then I'll be over." She hung up.

"She's coming over. She didn't say you had to go so I guess you can stay."

Lauren Dane

Gideon put one of his grandmother's cozies on the pot to keep it warm. It would only take Jules about five minutes to get there if she avoided the after-high-school traffic.

"Before she arrives, one last time. Do you really want to share her with me?"

"I want her in my life. You're not going anywhere and I'd rather have you in my relationship than outside it, working to break it apart. It's not optimal, but I can live with it. You're all right to look at."

"So you're really into men too?" Cal looked dubious and it pissed Gideon off. He'd said so already.

"When I was in New York—this was about a year after my divorce—I was with a man. It was unexpected. But not regrettable. I find the older I get, the better able I am to accept that my sexual identity isn't so easy to put into labeled slots. I like who I like." He shrugged.

"Hm. Have you had a cock in your ass? How bi are you then?"

He spun and got in Cal's face. "I've had my cock in an ass. I've had a cock in my mouth. I've enjoyed the person the cock was attached to. Is that bi enough for you? Do you have a checklist? Do I only pass if I get a certain number of gay points?"

Cal grimaced. "Okay, I admit it, I was being an asshole."

"And still I didn't punch you."

"You do love her."

"I do. And if having you in our life instead of just outside it makes her happy, I'll do it." He shrugged. "We should wait to hear what she thinks."

Cal sighed. "What if I don't want to share?"

"Then I'll fight you for her. Not with my fists, but with everything I am. I don't lose." Gideon wanted to be sure Cal realized that while he was totally amenable to sharing his bed with the other man, he wasn't going to let Jules go. It was share or back off.

"Neither do I."

"So you can see how difficult things would be. She'd be the loser in the end because no matter which one she chooses, she'd miss the other. I don't want that. I don't want to come into her life and force her to cut off people she cares about. No one wins in that scenario, even if she's with me. I don't want her to be unhappy."

Cal ran his hands through his hair, sending it into a disarray that still managed to look gorgeous.

"I guess we wait to hear what she has to say then." Cal sipped his tea and slumped into a nearby chair.

11

....

She arrived and went straight up the steps. Not bothering to knock, she went in, making enough noise to let them know she'd arrived. She found them sitting in the front room sipping tea and pretending to be casual. She dropped her bag on the bench near the door and moved to the fireplace.

Gideon stood and moved to her, pulling her into a hug. She went willingly, pressing her ear against his chest, listening to the heartbeat she'd missed so much over the last days.

He dipped his head down for a brush of his lips against hers. "I'm glad to see you."

She nodded. "Me too." Jules sucked in a deep breath and stood taller. Time to be a big girl. "Let's just say I was on board with this sharing thing. How do you envision this working?"

"I'm going to return the question. How do *you* envision it

working?" Gideon paused a moment. "I want you to set the boundaries here. If that's what you want. Only if that's what you want. Cal and I don't want you to make choices you aren't totally behind."

"Well, do you want—what—separate date nights?"

"I want you however you want to give yourself to me."

"This isn't helping." She turned to Cal. "And you?"

"I want to fuck you, Jules. I want to see you naked as the sun rises. I want to lick you in all the parts I've dreamed about for years. I want to wake up next to you and I don't care that it's only Wednesday and Friday, or that on your other side there'll be Gideon. I want *you*. I'm sorry this was sprung on you the way it was. I'm not sorry I kissed you and I'm not sorry I finally worked up the nerve to make my move. But I put you in a bad place and that I do regret."

She rolled her eyes. If she did this, she needed to do so knowing what a handful these two were going to be. Cal as her lover would not be as easy to blow off and be amused by when he got entitled.

"So if I said I want you both to fuck me, you'd be on board?"

Gideon laughed then. "Honey, you know I'm on board for fucking you any time."

"That's not what I asked."

He nodded. "You're right. I want you. I'm on board. We can make it work no matter what you choose. Unless it's not me and then I'm going to be really bratty about that. I can't lie."

Jules repressed her smile. Incorrigible, the two of them.

"Cal, you're not the one who proposed this whole sharing thing. What do you think?"

"I think I'd rather be doing it than talking about it. We've talked about it. We're all adults. Gideon and I want you, you clearly want us both. So let's do it. I'm going insane not touching you. After finally making that move I'm impatient."

She narrowed her gaze on him and then to Gideon. "If we do this, it's got to be exclusive to the three of us. No fucking anyone else. No kisses in alleys. None of that. No other men, no other women."

Cal got up and approached them and her heart skipped a beat. "That's entirely fair. As if I'd be interested in anyone else." He snorted. "I want you, Jules."

Gideon was on her other side, touching her. She turned and he smiled. Every part of her saluted with joy.

"And you?"

"I'm with Cal. Totally reasonable." He nuzzled her neck and she moaned.

"Not here. If Patrick came back . . ."

Cal kissed her temple and spoke into her ear. "My house then. I have a king bed, a full fridge and a great security system." Cal held a hand out. Gideon took her other hand and she took Cal's and they headed out.

Her hands shook she was so damned nervous. She, Juliet Lamprey, the person people thought was bold and decisive, was having a nervous fit over a threesome with two of the hottest men she'd ever seen. Two men she loved. Two men who had declared their love for her.

She was glad she drove over alone. Both men had invited her to ride along with them, but she needed the time to get herself together. So she turned her music up loud and drove, pretending she wasn't looking at Gideon in her rearview, or that Cal wasn't looking at her through his.

This was fantasyland. Now, she wasn't opposed to handsome princes, especially when they wanted to have sex with her. But her favorite place had always been Adventureland. Which, she supposed, was also where she was headed.

This made her laugh. And then she realized Cal would see it and it made her laugh harder.

She just needed to deal with it. She'd tried, at first, to pretend it away. To go to sleep and wake up and go to work and not remember she had this thing to deal with. But when she went to sleep it was alone. And she woke up alone and instead of talking to Gideon daily she didn't talk to him at all and Cal didn't come over either and she was miserable.

Thank goodness Gillian had shown up and made her confront it all.

Cal's house was just ahead and she followed him up the hill to his garage. He opened the door and she saw the imperious flick of his hand where he indicated she take the second, empty spot so she could park out of the elements. He always did that. She knew to keep her warm and dry. He was bossy though. Which probably meant he'd rock her world in bed.

The giggles surfaced again and she managed to wrestle them back under control by the time Gideon opened her door and she got out.

"I missed you." He said this softly, right before he kissed her and she melted into his touch as she always did. He tasted so right, so perfect.

Cal closed the garage door and approached, his hand out. She took it and he stayed in place, pulling her to him. His kiss wasn't slow and lazy like Gideon's had been. He was so intense; his mouth on hers demanded a response, which she was happy to provide. His tongue slid in like it was meant to be there and she sucked it, delighting in the way he straightened with a growl, hauling her even closer.

His cock pressed into her belly. And then she realized it was real. She was actually and truly going to have sex with Gideon *and* Cal. At the same time. Good lord.

Cal spoke, his lips still against hers. "Come on inside or I'm going to eat your pussy right here in the garage and it's too cold for that."

She swallowed hard. Gideon leaned in and licked over her mouth, stealing what little breath she'd managed to get back.

She followed them both, each man holding one of her hands, and she wasn't sure if she was comforted or constrained and then she thought, well, sometimes it's both and that was okay too. Why not? Since she was going insane and all and about to embark on a three-way with her boyfriend and best friend who she'd fantasized about for a good seventeen years.

"Are you cold?" Cal entered the house and tossed his coat on a chair. She snorted and picked it up, hanging it on a nearby peg. Gideon put his next to it and took her coat and bag, hanging them as well.

"I'm . . . um. Not cold. Thank you."

Cal stalked to her, backing her into Gideon. "Are you nervous? After all these years, baby? I finally get to touch you the ways I've dreamed of and you're nervous?"

She nodded.

"All you need to do is tell me to stop and I will."

He was so close. Gideon's chest rose and fell at her back, his strength holding her up.

She managed another shaky nod. And watched as Cal slowly unbuttoned her cardigan, spreading it and exposing the soft camisole just beneath. Her belly button peeked out at the waist and he slid a fingertip around and then inside. Just a ghost of a touch but her knees nearly buckled at how good it felt.

"Come on." He stepped back and indicated they go upstairs where his bedroom was.

She wondered if it was too early for a drink.

And then forgot about it as Gideon paused just inside Cal's door and pulled his sweatshirt off. She moved to him, needing to touch all that skin. She kissed over his chest, pausing to lick each nipple.

She turned to catch Cal watching, his hand unzipping his jeans. "I knew it would be hot."

"What?" He made it hard to think clearly. Jules could only think in giant capital letters about how hot this whole thing was.

"The two of you together. All that golden hair and skin." Cal shoved his jeans down and stepped from them.

She licked her lips and thought about licking his abs instead.

"Why did you leave your underwear on?" Though he looked like a super hot, real-life underwear ad. But instead of Times Square, he was right there and she was about to touch all of him.

He laughed then and Gideon pulled her cardigan off and came around behind her, reaching to unzip her jeans, exposing bright red panties.

"I was just trying to take it slow but . . ." He tipped his head toward her.

Gideon pulled the camisole up and off, leaving her in a bra.

Cal pulled his underwear off and fell to his knees before her, pulling her jeans and panties down.

He leaned in and breathed deep before pressing a kiss to her pussy, leaving her shivering.

"Well now." He got to his feet and she watched, unable not to. Cal Whaley was absolutely gorgeous. His hair was dark, but long on top so it always made him look as if he were up to something. Normally at work he had product in it, she knew. But he'd had his fingers in it, most likely as they were talking. One rakish lock had fallen over his forehead. His eyes were blue, fringed by dark lashes.

Acres of taut, olive-toned skin. She'd seen him in shorts and swim trunks. So she knew what he had lurking beneath his clothes. But this . . . Well, fantasy had nothing on reality. His cock was fat and meaty and it set her heart pounding.

His legs were long and powerful, particularly his very muscled thighs. A high, tight and toned ass. He had great arms and hands.

"You're giving me a complex just staring at me without a comment."

She smiled, her fingers still tangled with Gideon's. "I'm glad I had never seen you naked until now. I don't think I could have taken it."

He smiled, the worry gone. "I can say the same thing. Though I have seen you in a bikini and from that I have a general idea of how amazing you look naked. But there you stand all stingy with your bra still on. Gideon, have a heart and set those tits free."

She looked down as Gideon's palms slid around her waist from behind, and then up to cup her breasts before popping the catch. The bra slid open, her breasts free until he caught them in his palms again.

Cal sighed. "You're so much more than I imagined." He approached slowly, his gaze darting to Gideon's every once in a while to be sure everyone was on the same page. She liked that even as it sort of drove her nuts because she wanted to just jump in and have sex with them right then.

He touched her nipple and it stood for him. "Once you wore this dress. Flowers all over it, one of those numbers you wear all summer long. But it was slightly sheer and you had this other thing on underneath. But the shadow of your nipples, Christ. All day long I kept seeing them and thinking about you. Wondering." He bent his head and flicked his tongue against the nipple where his fingers had been and she gasped.

"You taste good." He grinned up at her and then straightened.

"Gideon isn't naked." She turned and looked up into his face and felt better when she didn't see any shadows in his gaze. Just Gideon looking at her as if she were the finest thing ever.

"I am so lucky," she said, meaning it totally.

He gave her a smile as he came around her body to face her. "That I'm not naked?"

She tugged on his beard and then while she kissed her way over his chest, got his jeans opened up and off, along with his shorts and socks, until they all stood there totally naked.

She looked back and forth between them. "Wow."

Cal grinned. "Yeah."

"I want you on the bed." Gideon nodded toward the very large bed she'd only fantasized about fucking Cal in a few million times.

"Where will you be?" She fluttered her lashes up at him.

"In you."

"Oh." She moved quickly to the bed and Gideon followed. Once there, though, he turned and held a hand out to Cal. She got to her knees and did the same thing.

When he took her hand first and then Gideon's it was suddenly so much more real. She took a deep breath and looked back and forth between these two men and then she laughed, falling back to the bed.

Gideon followed on one side and Cal the other. "What's that for?" Gideon smiled at her.

She took Gideon's cheeks in her hands. "You." She kissed him. "You're amazing."

"I am? I haven't even done any fancy sex-type stuff yet."

She laughed more and Cal dipped to kiss her shoulder and she turned, her mouth meeting his. She tangled her fingers up into his hair, her other hand in Gideon's. And he bent, joining them in the kiss.

That giggly sort of need she'd been sitting on exploded into something else. Something far hotter and less controlled. There may not be rules to contain what she felt with them right then.

She wanted everything all at once as her tongue slid along Cal's as Gideon's taste spiced them both.

Gideon broke away and he kissed down her neck. His cock was hot and hard, insistent at her thigh as he moved. Her fingers left his hair and dug into the muscle at his shoulder. She cried out when he bit her nipple just this shy of pain. He nibbled around her breast, licking and biting over the skin until she writhed against them.

Then Cal's mouth left hers and followed along. His mouth on

her other nipple was different. Both men had scruff, both looked amazing with it. Both men's beards scratched the tender skin of her breast. But Cal knew how to use his tongue, no lie. He fluttered it against her nipple until she gasped out a cry so ragged she didn't know where it had come from.

"I want to lick your pussy until you scream." He flicked his gaze to hers, holding it as she swallowed hard, nodding.

"She doesn't scream. She makes this *mmm*, a whimper of sorts."

Cal looked to Gideon and then he leaned over her body to kiss him. She watched, thrilled, breathless, as both men opened up. The flashes of tongue while they kissed drove her to distraction. So bold. This felt way less horrifying than when Cal kissed anyone else.

"I think we should get her to make that sound together."

They turned to her as one and she knew her eyes widened like a cartoon character at the sensual impact of that look.

"I want to hear *all* your noises. God knows I've fantasized about them enough." Cal licked over her hip bone and then slid a fingertip over the tattoo there. "I've wanted to kiss this since you got it. I used to get so jealous imagining Brody getting to touch you as he inked you."

She'd gotten a dandelion just a few months before. Adrian Brown's older brother was an artist and he'd done an amazing job with the floating seeds over her side and belly.

Cal kissed over them and Gideon pushed her thighs wide open.

She lay there, breath held, as both men spread her labia apart and bent, in unison, dark hair and blond, two tongues slid through her cunt and she probably did make a whimpering sort of sob.

• • •

Gideon had lost any and all worry about sharing her when she'd gone into his arms back at his granddad's place. Her kisses were just as ardent; she was still lodged inside him where she was supposed to be.

Her nervousness had been touching. And he supposed it made him feel a little better that she hadn't immediately jumped on Cal when it was so clear the two had chemistry.

But with her lying there on the bed like the most luscious slice of cake he'd ever had, with Cal next to him, their hands and mouths on her, it was all right. Hot. Sexy. It totally worked.

"What do you like?" Cal spoke to her. "Tell me."

"You're doing just fine." She said it in a rush and then she squeaked when Gideon sucked her clit just a little.

"Ah." Cal turned to Gideon and watched for a few moments. "You have the prettiest pussy. All pink and glistening." He took a long lick of her clit, tickling it when Gideon backed off a little.

She pounded the mattress with a fist and her head whipped from side to side.

"Yes, yes, yes!"

Cal chuckled and fisted his cock a few times, his gaze sliding to Gideon's.

Chemistry there as well. A different sort of electricity. That would work too.

"I want you on my face." Cal sat up and she made the sweetest little frustrated growl.

"She comes often," he said to Cal.

"Does she? Good." He lay back. "Come on, Juliet, make my day and sit on my face."

Gideon helped her up, her hair sweeping forward. Her nipples stood hard and dark, her skin was flushed. "He's going to make you come, baby. And then I'm going to fuck you."

Her gaze on him was clear until she settled and Cal grabbed her hips and held her as he began to lick and nibble her pussy. Then she went blurry, her fingers in Cal's hair as she rocked her hips.

She made it then, the sound Gideon had jerked off to more than a few times. A ragged whimper. So much desire there. Her spine arched as her head went back, her eyes closed, and Gideon was pretty sure he'd never seen anything hotter than Jules perched on Cal's face as he made her come.

If that made him wrong, or bad, or odd, he didn't care. He'd spent enough time caring what other people who didn't matter felt. Jules mattered.

He helped her off, watching as Cal kissed up her thigh and to her belly. "Hurry, Gideon. I've dreamed of that cunt for a very long time."

She opened her eyes; her smile was lazy. "Oh, you two."

"Hands and knees." Gideon saw the mirrors just across the room and settled her where he could watch.

Cal pressed a condom into his hand and Gideon nodded his thanks as he rolled it on quickly. Sweat broke out over his brow as he slid the head of his cock through her, easing in slow. She fluttered all around him as he forced himself to be patient and wait as her body adjusted. And then she pushed herself back onto him, taking him in all the way.

He grunted and met her gaze in the mirror. She caught her lip between her teeth and he grabbed her hips and thrust hard. Once. Twice. Three times. She grinned at him then.

A thrill raced through Gideon at the look on her face. "Is that a challenge in your eyes?"

She tightened around him in answer.

"Yes, more, more, more," she whispered.

Cal had been watching them in the mirror and then he looked back. "Christ."

Gideon knew exactly what he meant. "I know."

Jules tipped her chin in Cal's direction. "Cal, move over here. I want you in my mouth."

He blinked at her a moment and then adjusted himself to fit so she was over his waist.

Dipping her head down, she slid her tongue up the line of Cal's cock, keeping him nice and wet. Gideon licked his lips as he watched and then went back to the sight of his cock disappearing into her pussy and then coming out, dark and slick with her honey.

And then to the mirror again.

He'd fucked around, had a variety of sex with a variety of people in a variety of ways. But this was hands down the most exciting and compelling fuck he'd ever had. She was beautiful there between them. Long and lean, her hair sliding around and paying peek-a-boo with her mouth on Cal. The three of them moving on and with each other as he watched in the mirrors across the room.

Now that he'd had a taste, he craved more. He understood the allure of what Todd, Ben and Erin had on a whole new level.

Wanted more.

"That's so fucking good. I've imagined your mouth on me so many times. This is better than I ever dreamed." Cal had eyes for no one but her, for her mouth on his cock as she swallowed him over and over. Her taste was still on his lips, her scent on his fingertips.

He'd not expected it to be so damned good. He knew it would be enjoyable, but she was addictive. The feel of her skin, the way her weight rested against him, the feel of her hot, wet mouth sucking his cock. Christ.

He'd worried—and still did—that this would be a strain on her. Both men were dominant. Cal wasn't really that surprised she'd be attracted to them. Jules would be the kind of woman who'd run right over some men. It wasn't shocking that she'd seek out aggressive men like Cal and Gideon. She seemed to handle them both just fine though.

Her body made him want to weep. Just perfection. Her tits . . . he looked up at them as they moved with each thrust Gideon made into her body. Perfectly sized, lovely pink nipples, very sensitive. He liked that.

As he shifted his attention to the mirror, he noted Gideon was watching them with greedy, half-lidded eyes.

It didn't surprise him that Gideon liked to watch, though it did make him hot. Given the way they all were together, it was a good thing. Ridiculous how something that'd only lived in his fantasies could be even better in reality.

The mirror held his attention. Her back was arched, her shoulders and arms, toned, held her upper body in place as Gideon fucked her harder and harder. Held her in place as she rose up and fell again, taking his cock into her mouth, so deep it touched the back of her throat and he groaned.

His gaze met Gideon's and a full-body shiver ran through him. Goddamn, the man was hot. What made him so was the way he was so into Jules. But Cal did fine on his own too. For that moment, his hands were all over Jules, where he'd wanted them for so very long, as she arched back into Gideon. As her moans echoed and vibrated around Cal's cock.

"Yes, yes, yes," Gideon snarled and grabbed her hips, holding her still. Her eyes snapped open and locked with Cal, blurring slightly as he realized she was coming again.

Gideon bent and kissed the small of her back as he pulled out. "Be right back."

"Bathroom is through there," Cal said and then turned his attention back to her. "Enough. I've waited for you so long. I want you on me. I want to be in you."

She pulled up and off and she was so lovely and perfect that he drew her down with him, down to lay next to him so he could kiss her again. And before he realized it, he'd rolled on top and her legs were wrapped around his waist and she rocked her hips. His cock was naked and sensitized from her mouth. The feel of her slick pussy against the head sent a little shock of intense pleasure through him.

"Stop that or it'll be over before we begin."

"Here." Gideon put a condom in his hand this time.

She rolled him again, scrambling atop and putting the condom on.

Gideon sat on the edge of the bed, a smile on his mouth. Watching as she sat up enough to get Cal's cock just where she wanted and then pressed down, taking him deep. They both had to pause a moment when she'd taken him all. She was unbelievably tight and hot, so hot even through the condom.

He looked up at her, into all that pretty pale hair and her blue, blue eyes. And he was home. The certainty that of all the people he'd been with, it was this woman who held the key to his heart settled in.

"Fuck me."

She smiled and then she did. Undulating slowly, keeping him deep, sliding herself around him, back and forth or in circles. Her nails dug into his biceps but it just added to the pleasure. This time it would be slow and sweet. But the next time? He had plans for her. Hard and fast plans. He supposed it would have been nice to have let her know up front that when it came to sex he liked it in heaping amounts.

The way she was on him just then underlined that preference. It'd be a challenge to get through his workday without running to her house to fuck her.

But right then she was his. He was where he'd wanted to be for years and years.

"You're beautiful." She caught her lip between her teeth after she said it.

Surprised, he focused his attention on her face. "That's my line."

She laughed and Gideon joined in, crawling over to rest just behind her, straddling Cal's calves. His balls brushed the hair there and their gazes met briefly before Gideon slid his mouth over Jules's bare shoulder and she turned to receive Gideon's kiss.

Cal pinched and rolled her nipples, taking pleasure in the way her pussy gripped him and then he wet his fingers in her mouth, nearly losing his shit when she sucked them. He was so close to coming he had to take a few deep breaths and get his focus back.

He took those wet fingertips to her clit and began to tease it gently.

Her moan was guttural as she pressed harder down on him.

"Hmm, do you like to come with a cock in your pussy?"

She swallowed hard and found her words. "Yes."

"Good." He increased his pressure and it was only moments until she began to unravel all around him, her body hugging his so tight there was nothing else to do but come and come hard, along with her.

12

·····················

She couldn't quite believe what had just happened. So she lay there, her head on Cal's biceps. Gideon moved to the other side and she turned to face him, smiling as he took her hands and kissed them.

"This wasn't exactly how I'd planned to spend my afternoon. But as afternoons go, this one wins." Gideon grinned and she felt the weight of worry over his potential reaction to what had just happened lift.

She was still reeling from it though. It had been so much more complicated than she'd imagined. Who to touch? Was she paying more attention to one of them? Were they all right with everything? Was she necessary? And yet, there was a rightness there too, which scared her even as she embraced it.

"You all right?" Cal asked, his voice lazy and relaxed. He brushed a fingertip up her spine and she shivered.

"Probably going to be sore tomorrow."

He laughed. "Well, you're a lot more flexible than I'd originally imagined. We'll have to keep you nice and limber."

Gideon grinned over her to Cal. "Good idea."

She looked over her shoulder to Cal and then back to Gideon. "So, um, not that I want to ruin this lovely moment or anything, but what's next?"

"Give me a few minutes. I have great recovery time and all, but you wiped me out."

"Ha! Insatiable. I meant with us, the three of us. Tomorrow, the day after. Not just in bed."

"I imagine this will take some measure of coordination and patience from all of us as we figure things out. We could probably take it day by day. Step by step." Gideon brushed a thumb over her bottom lip and she kissed it.

"But we're together. Period." Cal spoke from behind her.

"So just the three of us?" She sat, bracketed by them.

"No one but you for me and Gideon."

"What about, you know, you two?"

Cal raised a brow and then looked to Gideon a moment before answering. "He's beautiful. You have good taste. It'd be a shame not to enjoy him when we're all in bed together. Is that all right with you?"

Jules frowned a moment. "Why would you ask if it was all right with me? You want him or you don't."

Gideon adjusted his body to look her in the face. "Baby, what's this all about? Are you bothered by me and Cal together?"

It was stupid hot to see them kissing. She found them both attractive so why shouldn't they too? Why shouldn't it be a true threesome? Wouldn't it make everyone happier that way? To share each other?

"Hot and bothered," she said. How could she say to them that she worried they'd chose something she couldn't provide? Especially when they were both loving and good to her, when she knew they both wanted her as much as she wanted them?

It wasn't the time for silly, petty fears. It was time to be a big girl and make this work. She hoped.

"The two of you are hot together. And I know you like men, the both of you. It'd be silly to say no when you're so pretty touching each other. If this is going to work, it's better to have this be a relationship between all of us."

Cal looked her over carefully and she knew he was wary of her answer. He'd known her a long time, knew when she was evading. He was sneaky that way. But she hadn't lied. She did find them sexy together and the fact was, there'd be enough challenges and to add some sort of silly you-can-only-want-me thing would only make it worse.

"Good." Gideon pulled her back to the mattress.

"You two should spend the night." Cal moved closer, kissing her chin and up her jaw.

"Calvin, gorgeous, I get up at four thirty. You like your sleep." She lazily leaned against him.

"I'm up that early too."

She leaned to kiss Gideon. "And you have Patrick to worry about."

"He's an independent guy. He gets annoyed if I bug him too much. But he likes to go on a ride in the early mornings so we get the horses and he can oversee most of the farm that way."

"Really? Can girls come too? I haven't been horse riding in eight or nine years. I'd love that."

Gideon's smile was slow and sweet. "Hell yes. I had no idea you'd be up for it. I know mornings are crazy for you so you can come by when you close up and we'll go then."

"Yay."

"Jules has a tiny bed." Cal looked her over. "And I can wake up early you know, if there's a promise of warm, naked Jules waiting for me if I do so."

She'd slept over at Gideon's several times and the total truth of it was she loved waking up with him. She liked being with someone.

And now she had two someones.

"My bed is bigger than Jules's but my place is smaller and doesn't have this view." Gideon slid a hand up her leg.

"Problem solved then. Stay over here. I won't complain about getting up early. Hell, I'll get a lot more done at work if I did."

"I'm hungry." Her stomach growled.

"Want pizza?" Cal kissed her neck.

"Only if beer is included."

His smile sent a wholly new kind of thrill through her. "How about champagne? I have some chilling now."

"Works for me."

Cal got up and she hummed at the sight of all that bare skin. He looked back over his shoulder, caught her stare and smiled all sexy-like. "Call the pizza in; you know the number. I'll get the champagne."

Gideon held her to him once Cal left. "Are you all right?" He kissed her softly.

"Yes, I am. I'm still processing, but you . . . this was . . . yes, I'm good. Are you? Was it . . . okay to see me with Cal?"

He took a deep breath. "I admit I wasn't sure how it would feel, but"—his mouth curved up at the corner—"I like to be watched and I like to watch. You're gorgeous and sexy and having sex with someone else who is gorgeous and sexy and I'm here, enjoying it too. It was more than okay. It was mind-numbingly hot. I want more. But not at the expense of your feelings or of Cal's."

She touched her forehead to his.

He continued. "This isn't just sex. It's feelings. We have to take it step by step because I know we've made things way more complicated and if it fucks up, I could lose you and I don't want that."

She sighed, hugging him tight. "That was exactly what I needed to hear."

"Good. Now, order that pizza. I need to call in and check with Granddad to let him know I'll be out late but up early."

She got up, Gideon noted, pretty comfortable with the space. It had been sort of odd at first to see how close she and Cal were. They had memories Gideon wasn't part of.

But he had her first. He'd had the luxury of those quiet first days when they'd gotten together and he'd slowly but surely fallen for her.

She'd put on a shirt and some socks—Cal's, he supposed—by the time he'd finished the call with his granddad. Patrick had urged him to stay out as long as he wanted and enjoy his little missy. He'd gruffly added that he was eighty years old and totally capable of managing his life.

She smiled from where she'd propped herself up against the headboard. "Pizza is ordered."

He got in bed with her and Cal showed up with champagne. "Let's toast to beginnings."

He filled their glasses and they did just that.

Cal looked up at the knock to find Jules in his office doorway with a cup of coffee and a box containing what he knew would be delicious. It had only been a few days since that first, amazing time they'd all been together and he loved the sight of her, loved knowing she was his at last.

"Hey." He got up and went to her, kissing her quickly and motioning her inside. "Sit. What brings you here?"

"You do. I had a break. My new staff are so awesome I actually have breaks. I wanted to go for a walk and so I decided to bring you a treat. I know you're working. I just wanted to pop in. Your secretary said it was all right."

He put a staying hand on her thigh and realized it meant more than it had before. He slid it up just a smidge and her mouth quivered before a slow smile marked her lips.

"I like that you came by." He sipped the coffee and poked open the box. "You're awesome."

She grinned. "I was up early and made extra. I set aside two just for you. The blueberries are fresh. Patrick brought them over himself this morning. I think it makes Gideon crazy that he drives. I can't blame him." She raised a brow and he tried not to inhale the little lemon blueberry tarts he loved almost as much as her apple cranberry tarts.

"Go on, you can eat them both. I took some home too."

He laughed and kissed her quickly.

"I'm still not used to that."

He sat back and watched her, content that she was his to do so. "To what?"

"To being kissed by you."

"I kissed you all the time before."

"Not the same as you do now."

He made himself save the other tart for later, putting the box on the corner of his desk.

"I'm getting used to it too, I guess. It just seems natural to touch you. It always has been."

She blushed, so fucking pretty.

"Are we on tonight?"

"I'm going over to Seattle for a fitting in an hour or so. Then dinner with Erin. We're planning an engagement party for Adrian and Gillian."

"You're taking the ferry? Oh, the things you do for your friends."

"I'm going to take a Xanax first." She blushed. "A small enough dose that I can drive afterward. Don't worry."

He tipped her chin up. "Baby, why are you so embarrassed about it? Everyone's got a few phobias." And hers came from a very real place. She'd nearly drowned when she was seven years old. Her father had subscribed to the old and incorrect adage that all you needed to do to teach a child to swim was throw them in the water. Only he threw her into Puget Sound in twenty-five feet of water.

Worse, he'd missed the deepest part and she'd hit her head on a submerged log, knocking her unconscious.

She'd been in the hospital for four days. Cal could still remember his mother going on about what an ass her father had been to do it.

And she'd been terrified of the water ever since.

"Why don't I drive you? Then you don't have to worry about driving at all. I have work to do in town anyway. You can call me when you're finished and I'll pick you up."

She smiled at him. "That's very sweet. But I'm thirty-three years old and I live on an island. Having to take a ferry comes with the territory. I can handle it." She jutted her chin out and a wave of tenderness hit him square in the chest at the sight.

"You're being stubborn for no reason."

One of her brows rose slowly and it got him hot, though he didn't share that part.

"Do you think that because we're together now you get to boss me around?"

He laughed. "I wish."

She rolled her eyes. "No, you don't. You'd get bored with me if I let you boss me around. Remember Candace?"

He cringed.

Jules straightened and stood with a smile. "Careful what you wish for, Calvin Whaley. You wanted me and now you get me. Me and my memory of every woman and man you had when you should have been with me."

He stood and hugged her. "It's worth it. Please let me go with you tonight." He hated the thought of her sitting in her car, gripping her steering wheel until the ferry docked in Seattle. "I can call Gideon; he and I can go to a movie or something while you're with Erin. Does Erin know how much you hate the ferry?" He looked at her suspiciously and her eyes widened and then narrowed.

"No and if she finds out I'll know from who. Let me handle this myself. I'm not incapable of doing things like taking the damned ferry. Don't make me sorry I shared."

She was wily, this one. He was damned if he did, damned if he didn't. So he sighed and nodded. "Will you call me when you get back? Or while you're on the ferry if you want to talk?"

Jules smiled, fixing his tie and then tiptoeing up for a kiss. "Yes. I'll see you later. I need to get back."

He watched her go, smiling and still wanting to fix things for her. Knowing she'd kill him if he even tried.

She preferred not to think about the ferry. She often put her sunglasses on and closed her eyes on the trip over. It helped. Today she listened to an audiobook, Lara Adrian, one of her very favorite authors. It helped take her mind off the deep water beneath the boat. By the time she was able to drive off, never a moment too soon really, she'd swallowed back her fear enough to be proud that she'd overcome her stupid damned fears once again.

As promised, Erin had arranged for her to park in the building's garage and she was buzzed up immediately. The building they lived in was amazing. Breathtaking views from pretty much all sides. The hallways were quiet, but once she got off on Erin's floor, it was easy to tell which door was theirs.

Erin Brown loved color. It was apparent in everything she did. It was something Jules found totally wonderful as she also loved color. But Erin took it to another level. She was bold and vibrant and just being around her was exhilarating.

Todd, one of Erin's men, answered the bell, grinning down at her, Alexander, their son, on his hip wearing a matching grin.

"Well, hello there, you two." She grinned right back, charmed.

"Come on in." Todd stood back and motioned her inside.

She walked past them and Alexander reached out to pat her shoulder. "Hi!"

"Hello there, young man!" Some babies were all joy. This one had been and as a toddler he was just as happy. He made her want to smile.

He began to tell her about the big yellow truck he saw earlier, a mass of dark hair in curls about his face swaying as he excitedly explained the entire setup from the moment they decided to go out for a walk to Pike Place right up to the truck sighting. He spoke quickly, and in toddler speak, so she had to go with the energy and feel of the story rather than the narrative. The boy was ever so much like his mother it touched that need she'd begun to feel.

Jules had been an active part of Miles's life. She knew she could deal with croup and diapers. Though the part about raising a good person seemed a great deal harder and she admired Gillian more than her friend would ever know.

And Alexander was a pretty freaking delightful kid too. Made sense as Erin was a delightful woman and her men were the type anyone would want their sons to be. Big and strong. Protective of their loved ones. Thoughtful. Alexander came from some pretty awesome genes.

Ben had paused in the kitchen to listen to the story about the truck, looking at his son with so much love something tightened in her chest.

Todd swung the boy down and he took off quickly, heading toward his mother as she entered the room.

Erin's face lit when she saw Jules. "Jules! You're here. The invitations went out today. I've got some in my office if you want to check them out. Then we can talk about the rest." She bent to kiss Ben, who'd knelt to speak to his son.

"Are you sure I'm not interrupting?"

Erin laughed. "We don't have a quiet, peaceful life. It's always sort of loud and busy. Wouldn't have it any other way."

Ben smiled up at Jules. "Hey, Jules, good to see you."

Goddamn, Erin was fortunate. Then again . . .

Alexander plopped down and Ben did the same. Todd, laughing, joined them. "What should we do, monkey?"

Beautiful, this family. Unique and vivid and solid. It gave her some hope that maybe she could make it work too. They were such a great example and suddenly she felt better because she wasn't alone and it wasn't impossible so maybe they could really do it.

The look on Erin's face as she took in her men made Jules want to sigh. "Let me know when the oven dings. We'll be in my office."

Alexander looked up at his mother. "Okay."

Todd laughed and assured her they'd keep an eye on dinner.

Erin turned with one last look at her boys and led the way through the apartment and then down the hall to her office.

"Dang, you even have snacks in here already? That's pretty host-tastic."

Erin's smile lit her entire face. "I love that word! Truth is, I cheated and picked these up at Pike Place earlier today. Alexander and I went on a walk. He loves to see the pig."

"I love that pig too," Jules said of the brass pig at the mouth of Pike Place Market. "I heard about the yellow truck." Jules paused. "You have a really fabulous kid."

Erin reached out and squeezed Jules's hands briefly. "Thank

you. I'm obviously biased but I think so too. Adele was like that too. Totally fearless. Never stopped talking. Was everyone's friend right away."

Erin's daughter Adele had been killed during a standoff between the police and Erin's stalker. Jules couldn't begin to imagine the pain of that.

"Anyway." Erin sat up straight and her smile was genuine. "Thank you." She pointed. "Those are the invitations that went out today. There are some extras in case we think of someone else to invite. I even sent you one."

"Cool! Thanks." She sat, looking at the invitation as she nibbled on the cheese Erin had laid out. "These turned out so well. I love them."

"They really did. It's the same people who did Brody and Elise's wedding invitations. Gillian and Adrian used them for that too so they had all the info already."

Erin liked Jules. She was the kind of friend Gillian could count on. She knew Jules had helped Gillian past some trust issues with Adrian as well. That made her even more likeable in Erin's book as she loved her brother very much and he'd found something so special with Gillian.

"Mary has the food planned out already. She also has the chairs we'll need. Smart to know a caterer." Jules pulled out a folder.

"Color-coded charts. Wow."

Jules blushed. "I know. I'm pretty . . . um, organized."

"Don't be embarrassed at all! I love color-coded charts. I'm not even lying. Plus, it's a great habit. You don't seem to have been hindered by it and your business is successful so you clearly find it useful there."

Blushing, Jules slid the charts out on the table between them. "All right. So the front lawn of Carter Farm is really perfect for this. It's level and the tenting—also something Mary has access too—is easy to install. Gideon has already volunteered to get that taken care of. I don't think we need to worry about assigned seating. We've planned for enough tables so people can mix and match if they like. Everyone knows everyone else, after all. Oh and there'll be security. Gillian was not happy about it, but Adrian talked her past it."

"I bet you did too. And thanks. I know she has a hard time with all the attention and fame stuff."

"It's a shitty thing that my best friend can't have an engagement party without security and strategically placed curtain panels and floral arrangements to block paparazzi pictures. But that's what it is and she has to deal with it." Jules shrugged. "She wants a normal life. But Adrian's job isn't normal. She knows that."

Erin smiled. "Well yes, we know lots of things. But you help her past stuff." She wasn't a fan of having to deal with security either, but Jules had the right of it. Erin knew just exactly what *worst-case scenario* meant.

"That's what friends do." Gracious and humble, two very good qualities as far as Erin was concerned, and Jules had them in spades.

"Not always. But you do and I like that. Oh music! We've got that part handled. Now that Gillian and Adrian know about the party, I ran some music choices past him. I think instead of live music, we'll do a DJ for dinner. We'll handle some live stuff for later in the night. It's a secret, but Adrian has some new material on this record he's making and he wants to give a song to Gillian as a present. He'll do it live for her that night."

Jules's eyes widened. "That's so cool. She'll love it. He's perfect for her."

Erin nodded. "They're pretty perfect for each other. And for my nephew. Great kid, our Blue." Blue was Erin's nickname for Miles and only she and Alexander used it. Erin loved that boy to distraction. Gillian had done a fine job with him and her brother had stepped up and been a great dad as well.

Jules made a note. "I'll tell him to coordinate with Gideon then so they get the right kind of flooring and staging up."

"I'm giving them a present at the party. In public so they can't refuse it." Erin giggled.

"You're such a schemer! What are you giving them?"

"A honeymoon trip. Ben just gave me a trip to Fiji. We leave next week, as it happens! Anyway, I'm going to check it out for sure, but if it's as fabulous as the paperwork and website make it look, I'm sending them there for two weeks. I'm laying claim to Blue though."

Jules frowned. "You're a Miles hog."

Erin laughed. "I am! You had him all to yourself for thirteen years. And you're his godmother. He talks about you all the time. I suppose I should add that you're always free to come see him here. Stay over if you like. We've got the room."

"When he's with me, he talks about you. He has good taste, I'll give him that much. And exciting on the trip to Fiji. I've never been but it looks so beautiful."

"It was a very pleasant surprise. We don't get much time, just the three of us. We do date nights. We're fortunate to have so many capable babysitters so close by and all. But ten days with no toddler up at the crack of dawn? I really can't wait for that. Though I'm going to miss that little monkey."

"You need that though. The time with Todd and Ben. Alexander will do just fine. As you pointed out he's surrounded by people who love him. I'm sure there'll be a tussle over who gets to keep him while you're gone."

Erin nodded. "Ha! That's true. Brody and Adrian will probably get into it. Todd's mom has surgery on her ankle the week before we leave so at least that's one less person they'll have to fight with." They were lucky indeed to have so many people in their lives to love.

"Having a baby with them has been incredible, but the alone time is necessary for sanity and to keep our relationship nurtured too. I love our family. It's a challenge of course, but it's been wonderful."

"Watching all these children makes my ovaries hurt." Jules winked.

"We'll get to that in a moment. Did you go to the fitting?"

"I did. I was a little worried the dress would be a wee bit tight. I've been sort of busy of late and I haven't exercised as much."

Erin looked her over and laughed. "Please. You're ridiculously pretty."

Jules laughed. "Well, thank you, but I still love to eat a lot of pizza."

"And beer." Erin snorted a laugh. "So before we go out there you need to give me the scoop on what's happening with Gideon."

Jules took a deep breath.

Erin continued. "I know you're close with Gillian, but we're friends too. I hope you'll feel comfortable talking with me about stuff. If not, that's okay too."

Jules laughed. "You have *no* idea. As it happens you're sort of perfect for this discussion because it's . . . I'm not just with Gideon. I mean it started out that way but then . . . Cal."

Erin's brows flew up. "I have to tell you Calvin Whaley is one gorgeous specimen. Gideon works that long, tall cowboy thing to distraction too. And . . . so is it both at the same time or a triangle situation?"

Jules blushed and then Erin laughed, reaching out to pat Jules's knee. "Really it's pretty hard to embarrass me. Just say it and I'll try not to ooh and aah about it."

That's when Jules eased up a little and embraced the relief of being able to talk to Erin. A woman who managed to do what it was she was on the verge of trying.

"I started with Gideon. We've been dating a month or so, but I've known him pretty much my whole life. He used to come to Bainbridge every summer and also at the holidays a lot. So he came back and we had this amazing chemistry and things were very intense very fast. He's impossible to resist and why should I? You know? So I didn't, and we got serious and things were pretty amazing until Cal walked up to me in the alley behind Tart and kissed me. Like whoa. The kiss was . . ." She fanned herself. "It was everything I'd ever wanted from Cal."

Erin grinned but one of her brows slid up. "But the timing, not so much? I mean, I guessed you and Cal had something maybe a while ago. There's smolder there. Smolder is good."

"Oh, I know people talk about it. About me and Cal I mean. Yes, I've wanted Cal for a long time. I had a crush on him as a teenager. He was my first kiss actually. And then never again and he started dating boys and then I thought he was gay and couldn't give him what he needed and then he started to date women too and then it was like, why not me! And then I just figured he wasn't ever going to move and I committed to Gideon and then he kissed me and told me he wanted me. That he couldn't bear the idea of letting me go without telling me his feelings."

"Wow."

"Yes, *wow* is a good word for it. But you know, I'm with Gideon. More than that, I *like* being with Gideon. So I went over to his place and Cal followed. I needed to tell him obviously. I can't go kissing other people in alleys when I'm someone's girl-friend. That's not done." She snorted.

Erin nodded and pushed the snack plate closer, so Jules took a few bites.

"And then Gideon, well, he shocked the hell out of me and Cal both by suggesting Cal come into our relationship rather than try to tear it apart from the outside."

"And how did you feel about that?"

"I left. I needed to think about it. And then it happened. I took the time to think and realized how much I missed Gideon and how things with Cal couldn't be the same again either way. And if I had him in my life in the way I've wanted for so long and Gideon is okay with it, why not try it? So we did and, wow. I . . . I don't know. It's a lot to process."

"But things worked?"

Jules laughed so hard she nearly choked. "Yes."

Erin slapped her knee. "You know what I mean!"

"It was . . . *complicated* and took some coordination, but it worked. We seemed to click. They're good to me and no one punched anyone else. And for me, sometimes that's really a good day."

Erin laughed. "I hear that. So it worked chemistry-wise and no one is outwardly hostile. They can share you? Without issue? There'll be enough of you for both?"

"I have no idea. I don't know anything other than I suddenly have two boyfriends. They're both bi. Cal pretty much his entire adult life. Gideon later on. But they don't seem threatened by the other."

"But they're attracted to each other? I mean, that's a good thing. I say that because I think if you mean to make a triad work, you can't get around the jealousy and attention issue. If you have two people who are totally into each other but not that third, or someone ends up feeling left out, it eats away at the foundations."

"What if they, you know, decide I'm not what they need?" She *knew* it was silly, but it was hard to get around how it felt sometimes.

"Ah." Erin sat back. "You're not going to be immune to jealousy either, you know. I don't know Gideon that well, but it seems to me that if he wanted to fuck Cal, he would have. He doesn't seem to have trouble speaking his mind. And Cal didn't lay that kiss on Gideon in the alley, he kissed you. Trust is hard. Probably the hardest part of any relationship, but especially the one I have and you're thinking about. Each person has to trust the other two. You have to find a way to trust that they both are what they say they are. You can know it here." Erin pointed to her temple. "But here is sometimes harder." She rubbed her gut. "However, I don't know about you, but watching my boys kiss and get down together? The hottest thing in the world."

Jules blushed and nodded. "They kissed each other and it was, wow. I appreciate it, the advice, I mean. I'm a planner." Jules held up her color-coded sheets of paper. "I can't schedule this. I can't organize and plan it. I'm trying to let go and remind myself this will be something we have to blunder through sometimes. But it's hard."

Erin leaned forward again and took her hands. "I imagine so. I'm not going to lie, it's not easy. And not just between the three of you. People on the outside judge. You'll lose people. I wish that part wasn't true. Some people you think you can count on will let you down because they can't handle it. Others will come around after a time."

Jules knew it, but it scared her nonetheless.

"I want you to feel free to come over or call any time, okay? I mean even for just everyday friend-type things, but if you want to talk about the triad stuff. I'm not an expert, but as there aren't any anyway, I guess I can stand in as one. Sometimes it just helps to say it out loud to someone who'll understand."

"You can't know how much this means to me. I'm so *relieved* to know I'm not alone. Thank you so much for listening and for all the great advice."

Erin sat back with a smile. "That's what friends do, remember?"

13

....

Gideon stood under the hot water for a long time. He'd
dug fence-post holes for hours that day. Not his favorite
thing, but totally necessary as the old ones were a mess
and the goats kept getting out.

It was late. Later than he'd planned to finish up. What he'd
really wanted, all day long, was to sink into Jules's arms and hold
her. Damn, he missed her smile. The rest of her too.

It'd only been a few days since he'd seen her last, but it felt
like a year. He wasn't a teenager anymore, but she made him feel
that way.

Six weeks he'd had with her. Seemed a silly, short period of
time to feel so deeply for someone, but he did. And he'd been
with enough people to know the difference between infatuation
and love.

And Cal? Well, Cal was his buddy growing up and as it turned out, they still managed to keep that relationship. In the two weeks or so since the first time they'd all been together, he and Cal had managed to continue their friendship with this new facet. They were outwardly different. Cal with his buttoned-up, designer-suit-wearing ways, complete with swanky house and car, was still the same kid who cut the fuses short on his fireworks because he'd been impatient for the boom.

Gideon liked that. Liked having someone he could talk to, though as it happened, sometimes he wanted to talk about Jules, which made it a little complicated, as she turned out to be what Cal wanted to talk about most often too.

But it was working. Slowly but surely the three of them were finding their way to make this threesome thing work.

He walked out into the main room in his shorts, needing some dinner, but started when there was a knock at his door.

He opened up to find Jules there with a smile and a bag. Instantly his exhaustion faded and he found himself smiling because she was so beautiful and he'd been wishing for her and there she was.

"Hi. I know you're tired. I just wanted to bring you something to eat." She cocked her head. "Nothing fancy like Mary makes. Soup and some bread."

"Come on in here and give me some sugar."

Once she'd put her things aside, she moved into his arms, lifting her face for a kiss.

He took his time. Needing to soak her in. She tiptoed up, wrapping her arms around his neck, smelling of spring and rain.

"I need to bring you food more often." She stepped back, licking her lips.

"It's been a long day. You're just what I needed."

"I'll dish the soup up since you brought it and all." He motioned to the table. "Sit and tell me about your day."

Before she got a word out, her phone rang and she answered.

"It's Cal. He's sad without us." She looked up to catch Gideon's eye. He really liked that she checked in with him and also that Cal wanted to be with them.

"Tell him to come over."

She did and hung up shortly after. "He's on his way." She put her phone in her pocket and stood, moving to him again. "Why was your day long?" She kissed his neck. "Would some hot tea help?"

He leaned back into her "God, it's so much better now. It was fence-post-digging day. We're done now, but I'm not as young as I used to be."

"When you finish your meal, I'll give you a massage. I'm a pretty good hand at them." She kissed him again and wandered over to the stove to get the kettle on for the tea she'd offered to make.

"I'll take you up on the tea and the massage. If you're naked it will work better. Just sayin'." He winked at her and she snorted.

"I'll take that under advisement." She sniffed.

She moved around his space and filled it up just right. He ate, content just to watch her.

"What did you do today? I missed you."

Her smile was all he needed really. The sight of it filled him with warmth. "I was a baking machine. A machine, I tell you." She grinned and put a cup of tea on the table for him. "You know I had that job for Mary's catering gig tonight so I baked an ungodly number of sweet little baby tarts."

He found her dedication to her career admirable. She loved

what she did and spent a lot of time making herself better. But it was her sense of whimsy that always pleased him so much. Baking was more to her than a job.

"And yes, there are some for you and Cal both in the bag I brought. Cal's sort of addicted to them, so you have to be quick if you want any. He's an unrepentant lemon tart hog, though for heaven's sake I have no idea where he puts it."

He stood, swept her up into his arms and carried her off to his bed where he kept her close as they got situated.

"All this for lemon tarts? I had no idea you were so easy for them or I'd have made them for you far sooner."

"While your goodies—the baked ones, I mean—are tempting, it's the way you always think about me and Cal that pleases me so much."

She blushed a little. "We all do for each other."

"We're lucky that way." He rolled on top and ground himself into her. She made a lovely little gasp that caught his attention.

"I can't very well massage you with you on top of me." She kissed him quickly.

"I'm sure we could figure out a fair exchange for the loss of massage."

"I'm guessing that's also to be done while I'm naked."

He laughed. "You catch on quick."

He kissed down her neck as he unbuttoned her sweater.

"I bet you were a menace back in high school with those magic unbuttoning fingers."

He popped the catch on her bra and sent her a raised brow. "It's a skill, what can I say?"

"You're doing all the work." But it didn't sound like a complaint at all.

He bent to lick over a nipple. "It's work I love doing."

She laughed and hugged him tight and he realized this is what he never had. Not with anyone. This sort of funny, intimate, easy relationship. Oh, they were going to fuck, hell yes. But she lightened his heart. Made him laugh even as she sometimes got stubborn and made him mad too. She was his partner, not his dependent or someone he had to manage.

It was sexy. And exciting.

She wasn't like anyone he'd ever known and though he had grown up around her a few times a year, the woman she'd grown into . . . and the man he'd become . . . seemed to be right together.

There was a knock on the door that reminded him there was an added facet to their relationship.

Gideon rolled off her and made his way to the door he'd locked to be sure his granddad didn't go stumbling into something that would send him into therapy.

A shiver went through Gideon as Cal came through the door and closed it, locking it behind himself.

"Hey."

Gideon leaned in and brushed a kiss over Cal's mouth. Cal hummed his satisfaction and opened his lips, breathing Gideon in. Something so arrestingly delicious that Gideon groaned.

Jules lay on the bed and watched the two of them together. Cal was so confident and self-assured, freely giving in to the kiss. Gideon had his own sort of surety. He eased his way in, but he kissed Cal differently than he kissed her. Held Cal differently as well.

Her breath came out sort of shaky. Just watching them made her hot and not a little achy. It was sexy and gorgeous and totally uniquely male. A little fear twisted through the shiver.

She shoved it away as far as she could.

When Gideon straightened, he turned and looked at her. "Cal's here."

She laughed, unable to help herself. "I can see that."

"There she is." Cal tossed his stuff to the side, toeing off his shoes, and moved right to her. She'd wanted him for so long, had watched him be with other people. Most of the time she hadn't been bothered by it; she'd dated too after all.

He'd looked at her like she mattered. Even when he'd been with other people he'd looked at her like she mattered. He'd been her friend and someone she loved like she loved his sister and Gillian.

But *this* Cal? The one who moved to her like there was nothing else he wanted to do in the world but touch her? Yeah, his attention was like a hundred billion times better this way.

This was laced with their friendship and the trust they'd formed after knowing each other so long. They confided in each other, cheered each other on. But his gaze burned with something a lot more than friendship.

It was as if he'd suddenly turned the dial up. That intensity he always carried had deepened. Aimed it at her. She'd seen him with enough people over the years to know he never looked at any of them the way he did her.

That thrilled her to her toes.

And scared the hell out of her.

He got on the bed and didn't stop until he'd laid on top of her and touched his nose to hers. "Hey. This is good. Goddamn, I've needed this all day long." He kissed her, slowly at first, nearly sweetly. And then once she'd wrapped her arms around him, it deepened. He slid his tongue into her mouth, his taste filling her up. His taste mixed with Gideon's.

He didn't stop that kiss until she was thoroughly boneless and her fingers dug into his upper arms as she held on.

"Now I'm feeling a lot better." He smiled at her and she smiled back.

She rolled her hips, grinding herself against his cock. "I can feel."

"What did you do today?"

Gideon joined them on the bed. "She baked."

Cal laughed. "She bakes every day. Even when she's not working. Not that I'm complaining."

She told him about the tarts and he kissed her quick before jumping up to go procure one. That was nearly as flattering as the way he looked at her.

"Did it bother you that I kissed Cal?" Gideon brushed his lips over hers and she sighed happily.

She thought a moment before answering. "No. It's sexy. Hot. I don't know if this thing we're doing would work if you two didn't also dig each other."

"You hesitated. What's the unspoken *but* in that sentence?"

"I wanted to be honest. I had to think it over."

"Which means you had something to think past. Look"—Gideon licked his lips—"I want this to work. I don't think it can if we all aren't honest."

"What happened with her? With your ex-wife?" she returned.

He laughed. "Nice try. I'll tell you mine if you tell me yours."

Cal returned, brushing crumbs from his shirt. "What's going on?"

"I was asking Jules if she was all right with me kissing you."

Cal's gaze went straight to her then.

"I said I was."

"And there's that unspoken *but* again."

Cal got on the bed on her other side. "I'm with Gideon here. I know I messed up in waiting so long. Tell me. You've shared so much over the years; this is the most important part."

"I just . . . I don't want to . . ." How could she put it into words without sounding stupid and petty? "I don't know how to say it without sounding stupid and petty." She sat up, pillows at her back.

"You're not stupid. Nor are you petty." Cal tangled his fingers with hers as he settled in, sitting at her left. Gideon mirrored that on her right.

"I just don't want to wake up one day and discover I'm not enough."

Neither man spoke for long moments. She wasn't quite panicked by that; she knew both of them were that way. Cal was so good with words, given the job he had. But he rarely spoke rashly, especially when it was important. And Gideon, well, he liked to work things over in his head a while before he spoke.

"What do you mean by *not enough*? Like we have two partners because we can't get by with one?"

"I don't have a penis."

Gideon seemed to find this hilarious. "I've noticed that. It's a fine quality in a woman."

But Cal watched her carefully.

"I can't do for you what Cal can."

"Ah." Cal sighed and moved into her line of sight. "I'm a little old to pretend I don't like men. I'm a little insulted that you think I'd use you to get at Gideon."

"That's not what I think. I told you it was stupid and I told you I was okay with it and I am. It's sexy and beautiful and I believe it's a good factor in making this threesome thing work. If not, one of us would feel left out all the time. I *like* that you two are turned on by each other."

"Do you really doubt what I feel for you is real?" Gideon asked.

"No. Which is why when you asked I gave you my honest answer, which is that I am *not* bothered by the kiss. *You're* the one who wanted to hear the *but*. I told you it sounded stupid and petty and you made me say it and now you're going to make me feel bad for sharing."

She tried to get up but they both kept hold of her hands.

Cal wouldn't let it go. "I'm not trying to make you feel bad. I'm trying to figure out what I've ever done to make you think I'd do something like that to you."

She would not cry.

"I would like you to let my hands go."

They both did but eyed her carefully.

"I never said any of that." And now she regretted saying anything at all.

"You think I'd leave you because Gideon has a cock."

She pushed up from the bed, needing some distance. "Don't cross-examine me or put words in my mouth, Calvin. That's not what I said."

Cal started to speak again but Gideon shook his head. "She's right. She never said that. It's clear she hit a sore spot with you, but that's not what she said."

"I don't want to be here right now." She eyed the door.

Cal wasn't going to let it go though. She saw it on his face. "Bullshit. You don't want to face what you said."

She sighed, blinking back tears.

"That's not true. I just don't want to have this argument. I don't want to debate things I never said. I'm tired. I came over here to relax and have a nice, quiet night. That's not happening."

Gideon got up and moved toward her. She held a hand out. "Please don't. I want to go."

"Too fucking bad. I don't want you to go. I want you back here in my bed. This is spinning out of control and it's silly." Gideon glared at Cal, who, she noted, did appear to feel bad.

But it didn't stop him from saying, "You can't just toss that out there and leave."

She narrowed her eyes and spun to face Cal. "Toss it out there? Fuck off. You both asked. You told me to share. I said I didn't have the right words but I was *honest* like you both urged me to be. And then you turned it all around and attacked me with it. You came over here, Cal. You told me to share. I did. I'll think twice the next time."

Cal still managed to look beautiful when he glowered. "And now you threaten me?"

"If this is how you react to my expressing my fears? Yes. And it's not a threat. It just means I don't know if I can trust you like that. Not when you're this way about it."

"So if I don't like what you say I have to shut up about it?"

"Cal, try shutting up for a damned minute, please." Gideon took her hands and she allowed it for the moment. "I did ask you to share and I'm thankful you did. What I need doesn't come with a gender. It's about the person. I chose you, Jules. I chose to be with you. I don't need a cock, or a cunt for that matter. I need *you*."

He looked into her face, his love for her written all over his features. She *knew* it was silly to worry over it. She'd said she knew it.

"I know."

He smiled. "Yeah?"

"Yeah. I told you I did. If I was really worried about it, I wouldn't have said yes to this thing to begin with. But I can't lie and say it's not a fear. I can't. Not when you asked me for it. It's an irrational fear; I said I knew that. But it's there. I can't always control what's in my gut."

He pulled her to him, hugging her tight. "Juliet Lamprey, you are something else."

She kept her eyes closed. Face pressed to his chest, inhaling his scent, letting the strong, steady beat of his heart make things better.

"I'd never do that to you." Cal's voice was small in the background.

Jules kept her face buried, not wanting to face him. "I never said you would. I said it was a fear."

"You won't even look at me now?"

The thing about knowing someone and being friends with them for decades was that she and Cal had been through a lot together. They'd had spats over the years. Jules knew she could be bitchy, easily annoyed. But with her friends she was far more easygoing. Chipper most of the time. Unless she got pushed. Cal was far more intense with everyone. If he got lit up about something, they'd go a few rounds because he knew her buttons and she his. This wasn't the first time she'd told him to fuck off and she doubted it would be the last.

"Cal, I swear I'm gonna kick your ass."

She squeezed Gideon before stepping back and looking the pretty handful in Gideon's bed straight in the eyes. "You know,

Calvin, if you wanted me to look at you, you should try being nicer. I brought you tarts. You brought me an argument."

He grimaced. "You make me crazy."

"Why? Because I have feelings?" She winced. "I'm sorry, that was a cheap shot."

"You always have to do that."

Her ire was rising again. "Take cheap shots?"

Cal's mouth twisted into a smile. "No, do the right thing. Apologize when you're supposed to. Be reasonable. I have wanted you, *you*, Jules, for a very long time. Gideon is hot, no lie. He's sexy and smart and he makes me laugh. But what is most exciting is that he looks at you the way I probably do."

Jules took a breath, looking for the right words. "For years I watched you with men. And then there was Candace. God. Anyway, I remember thinking." She had to stop because the tears crept into her voice and she wanted to get it back under control. Unfortunately Cal heard them and she saw the change roll over his features. "So you found a woman and maybe you weren't totally gay but she was . . . horrible. My god, she was horrible and you two were so horrible together and you were just a total asshole."

Cal nodded. "I was. It was a bad relationship for us both. Please don't cry. I don't want to make you cry."

When they were younger, Cal would be so fierce with his siblings. Competitive. They'd all get into epic fights. But if Mary cried, he'd lose his hardness. Get all soft for his sister. Jules could see it broke his heart to see her cry. It's why she tried so hard not to cry right then.

She didn't want to be the woman who cried to get her way, damn it. "I'm trying not to!"

He came to her then and hugged her. "Baby, I'm sorry I made you upset."

"Let me finish." She swallowed it back. "So then you broke up with her and there was another man. He was nice. You have great taste in men, not so much with women, and so yes, in the corner of my mind I wonder if you really want me, like forever. Or if I can't be what you need. I can know things and still have those fears."

"I've thought about that. Why my relationships with men were better than with women. Mainly? I think it's that I wanted one woman only. You, Jules. I looked around for women you weren't, because I didn't think I could have you. I was scared to lose our friendship. It's not because I like women less, it's because there was one woman for me. I'm not going anywhere. If it bothers you, Gideon and I can just not."

She sighed. "I said it before and I'll say it again. I like that. It's sexy and I think if we are all together it'll work better." She looked back to Gideon.

"I don't want to hurt you." Gideon was so lovely she reached out to squeeze his hand.

"Oh, you will. Cal will. I'll hurt you guys. It's inevitable with people you love."

"With my ex," Gideon began the story she'd asked for earlier, "we had a really intense beginning. So intense I probably ignored things I should have focused on. She was spoiled. Her family had given her everything and she was sort of . . . helpless, I guess. But at first it was good to give to her. I liked taking care of her. And when we bought the ranch, her brother and I ran it together. I had a great bond with her family. Hell, I miss them more than I ever missed her once things went bad. Anyway, if you run a ranch, you can't be helpless. Things need doing all the time. I started to resent her. She didn't really care to learn anything. So she started to travel. At first with her brother's wife and that was fine. Then my sister-in-law got pregnant and traveled less. Also she worked the ranch too. So she, Alana, started traveling alone. That's probably where the first lover came along. There were so many."

Jules found it hard to understand this woman who'd ignore what a fabulous man she had.

"Anyway, after a few years of it, she finally fell for one of her boyfriends and filed for divorce. I stayed on; it was my ranch after all. I'd built it with her brother, who was a close friend. But things changed and after a while it was just too awful to see my ex. My brother-in-law felt put in the middle and was arguing with his parents, who always took her side. So I sold him my share and got out."

"She never knew what she had." Jules wanted to punch this Alana bitch in the face. But she owed her too. Without the way she'd acted, Jules wouldn't have Gideon now.

Gideon's smile wasn't laced with pain at all. "She didn't really care one way or the other. It's just . . . it's not nice to feel like you don't matter."

Jules hugged him, as did Cal. "She was a total idiot. But it brought you to me. I can't regret that part."

"I don't want you to. I don't regret any of it. I learned a lot from it. Skills I use every day here with Granddad. Skills I hope I use with you. Because let me underline something. I know what it feels like to get a shadow of someone's love and attention. It sucks. I never, ever want to be that with you. When you look at me, I can see it in your gaze. I can see that I matter to you. That's what you give to me. A place of belonging."

Her tears had broken free by that point and Gideon thumbed them away.

"I'm sorry I got pissy," Cal said.

She turned to him. "You're a pissy guy sometimes. The pretty ones often are."

He snorted. "I can't hide behind the stuff I do with other people. You're the one person who knows me flaws and all. It's scary."

"It was scary before you began to put your penis in my hoo-ha."

Cal burst into laughter. "Goddamn, let's all fuck, please."

She held her hand out to him, keeping her other in Gideon's hand. "Let's."

Need nearly blinded Cal. Need for her. Need to connect with her after their silly fight.

He let go of her hand long enough to push off her already unbuttoned sweater and unhooked bra from her shoulders, baring her to his gaze. "So pretty, God. Juliet, you're perfect." He kissed her shoulder.

Gideon took care of her skirt and she stepped from it, pausing to pick it up, along with her shirt and bra, to place them on Gideon's dresser. Their woman was tidy. A direct opposite of his more sloppy ways. But instead of annoyance, Cal had always been charmed by the way she had to put things in order. Plus she was naked because Gideon had rid her of her panties as well.

She waved a hand at Cal. "You both aren't naked and I am."

"I've always had a weakness for that." Gideon had only been in his shorts and shoved them off.

"What?" Her gaze moved to Gideon's cock.

Cal liked the way Gideon got addled around her. He knew the feeling. "Being clothed while my partner was naked."

She grinned. "Yeah? I like it too." She turned to Cal. "Sometimes. But right now I'd like you naked too."

She shoved his shirt up and over his head as he got his pants and shorts off, returning to her as naked as she, and as ready too.

"Now then, I feel as if we can get on with our business. I want to fuck you from behind. Hands on the bed, feet on the floor. I think it'd be even better if you were sucking Gideon's cock while I fucked you."

Gideon laughed and moved to the bed. "I like that idea. But don't make me come yet, Jules; I want inside you."

Cal turned her, walking her to the bed, all the while his hands roamed over her skin. Her nipples were hard and dark, drawn up tight. Gideon got to his knees and kissed her, through and around Cal's fingers, which was hotter than the sun. She liked it too, making one of her sexy-sweet sounds.

"Now." He pushed her upper body, having her bend at the waist. "Your bed is the perfect height for this, Gideon."

"Good to know." Gideon handed him a condom, which he donned quickly as he found her pussy swollen and ready for him as he slid his fingers through her. "So hot. I think about this all day long."

She tightened around the finger he'd slid into her pussy, thrusting back at him. Impatient. When it came to sex, he'd discovered Jules was demanding and greedy. It drove him insane, it was so hot.

Impatient himself, he pressed the head of his cock to her gate and slid in, bit by bit.

This was something he'd dreamed of for so long. The ability to put his hands on her this way.

Jules being his.

He pressed in totally and paused to catch his breath. And to watch as Gideon slid closer and took her mouth in a kiss.

The kiss Gideon had laid on Cal when he arrived had been a surprise. Oh, they'd kissed before, while the three of them were together in bed. But this was more natural and easy. It had felt like another step in their relationship.

And of course he'd ruined it by being testy when Jules had confessed her fears.

Cal had wanted to scream that he'd wanted nothing and no one more than her. That he'd seen her face so many times while he'd been with other people, wanting her yet being convinced he'd never have her. Instead he'd barked at her for giving the difficult truth.

She hadn't broken, though he'd made her cry and he hated that. Gideon had gotten between them and calmed her down and when she'd calmed, it allowed Cal to realize what he was doing and to step back and approach it differently.

This thing between them wouldn't be easy. But if they didn't stick together it'd be even harder.

"I want your cock," she whispered against Gideon's mouth and Cal thought he'd come right then.

Gideon slid back, angling himself so she could grab him at the root and as they both watched her, she sucked him in slow and deep.

Cal began to fuck her equally slow and deep and for a long while the pleasure built bit by bit. Her mouth on Gideon. Cal's cock buried deep inside her cunt. Gideon's eyes were for her, but occasionally he'd look up and meet Cal's gaze, or turn his head to watch them all in the mirror above the nearby bureau.

Gideon loved to be watched, loved to watch. Cal found that very hot. Found it hot that Jules got off on it too.

"Stop, stop, stop," Gideon murmured to her, brushing a hand over her hair. "I'm too close and I want to fuck you. Watching you and Cal is already enough, but your mouth on me? I'll never make it another two minutes."

Jules frowned prettily and Gideon moved to watch them better. Jules met Cal's gaze in the mirror, pushing back against him.

"You telling me the slow and deep is over, baby?"

She nodded and tightened all around him.

"Can you reach her clit, Gideon?"

Gideon moved, stretching out an arm. He must have been close enough because she gasped and her inner walls tightened. Then Gideon's fingers quested back to Cal's cock, back to his balls, which he cupped and then dragged his short, blunt nails over until Cal stuttered out a curse.

Then Gideon went back to her clit, bringing a soft moan of pleasure to her lips.

It wasn't too much longer until she began to come. Cal loved being in her when she did. Her body superheated, got so wet and tight. It was so good he wanted to be in that moment forever, suspended right before orgasm when everything was becoming, filling him up with so much pleasure he was about to burst from it.

And when he did, it was all her. Jules. His at last. Yes, he shared her with Gideon, but that was good too. So much better than he imagined it would have been. Not perfect, but so good it nearly was.

The tenderness mixed with his arousal and satisfaction as Cal picked her up and helped her to the bed. Gideon put his arms around her and held her tight as Cal came back and did the same from the other side.

"I'm sorry I made you cry."

His whispered confession made her tear up again, but she pushed it back.

"It's over. It's all right. We worked it through." For the time being anyway. All she could hope for was that time would weaken that bit of fear she carried.

He kissed her shoulder and she turned to him, needing him to know she meant that it was over. Wanting him to understand it was good between them, and that she chose him.

Cal frowned. "I hate it when you cry. You never cry."

She laughed and then laughed some more. "Sure I do."

He made a sweet sort of growl and only looked prettier so she leaned closer and kissed him, sliding her fingers through his hair, holding him in place until he'd lost the tension in his muscles.

She arched back against Gideon, needing him too. He shifted, and his cock rubbed against her ass, sending a shiver through her. She reached around, turning her head to kiss him. He put one of her legs up on his thigh and slid in, sending her breath and all her words very far away.

Gideon took it slow, drew her pleasure out so long she was sure she'd die if she couldn't come. And when it happened, it shocked through her system.

All the while, Cal's gaze roamed all over her body. He pulled the blankets back so he could see everything. She knew Gideon got off on it, which worked for her really well.

She watched, a little breathless as Cal crawled up the bed, bending to kiss her calf, pausing to kiss the hand Gideon used to hold her in place as he fucked her, over her belly and to her breasts.

"I think I need to return the favor you did me earlier, Gideon."

Gideon rumbled his approval.

"I'm going to make you come while Gideon fucks you." Cal's mouth, so beautiful, curved up into a naughty smile.

She nodded and barely resisted yelling out *"Yay!"*

And when he touched her clit she jumped a little.

"Sensitive?" He nuzzled her neck and gentled his touch.

She swallowed and let it wash over her. The inexorable thrust and retreat from behind and the featherlight touch on her clit. She closed her eyes and just felt, let them take her where they knew she needed to be.

And she splintered. Flying apart as Gideon held her, as Cal stroked her and soothed, kissing her mouth, swallowing her cries.

14

....

Gideon stirred as the light was a faint hope on the horizon. Jules stretched and opened her eyes when he started to get up. "Where you goin'?"

Damn, she was beautiful. He had no idea how he ended up so lucky.

Gideon bent to kiss her and she pulled him back into bed. "I need to go home for a bit. I'll see you later this afternoon. Go back to sleep."

Cal laughed sleepily. "Baby, she's not going back to sleep. Our girl has been waking up at four for so long I'm not sure she knows what it means to sleep in."

"Sorry to wake you." Gideon leaned over to kiss Cal as well.

Jules liked that Cal used pet names with not only her but Gideon too. She'd been concerned that the week before when she'd brought up that small fear it would ruin things between the two men, which really wasn't what she wanted in any way.

Fortunately, Gideon understood her well and hadn't changed his demeanor with Cal. There was an easy affection between them, they'd been friends a long time anyway. Only now there was a sexual and romantic side.

Each time they were all three together it got easier to see and the fear got smaller and smaller.

"Unlike Jules, I'm just fine napping later. In fact, come back to us, Gideon, and we'll fuck and then sleep."

She propped herself on Gideon's chest as he sifted his fingers through her hair. He was warm and smelled all yummy and male. "Or we can fuck now and then you can go and come back and we'll do it again."

Gideon's mouth canted up slightly. "I mightily enjoy the way you're always ready for sex."

Cal did as well. There had always been a sense of needing more before he'd ended up with them. Of not quite being sated when he'd been with other people. Oh, the sex had been great and all, but he'd never been truly satisfied. Until Jules and Gideon.

Now his muscles weren't tight. His appetites were quenched. If he wanted to come, he did. And she wanted it as much as he did. Add Gideon to the mix and the sexual energy between them was electric.

Gideon kissed the tip of her nose. "I've got to run just now so all I'd have time for is a quickie. And I like my sex in the long, slow ride category."

She laughed and moved back, allowing him to get out of bed.

Cal held her as they watched Gideon at the bathroom sink,

brushing his teeth before he came back into the bedroom to get dressed.

"I'll be back in a few hours. Cal, keep her out of trouble."

Jules got up, naked and gorgeous, and hugged Gideon. "Let me walk you out." She grabbed her robe and the scent of her skin, the almond lotion she used, teased Cal's senses.

"Deal."

Cal got up too, he was awake after all, and once Gideon left he had plans for all that naked Jules had on under the robe.

"We'll both walk you out."

Gideon grinned as Cal joined them.

After a kiss for the two of them, Gideon jogged to his truck and was gone.

"Now, we're awake. Whatever shall we do to spend our time?" Cal spoke as he stalked her back up to his bedroom.

Her answer was to drop the robe and head into his bathroom. "I'm dirty. Want to help me get clean?"

Shower sex with Jules? Yes, that would do just fine.

"I love your shower. Really, it's like a fantasy come to life."

He struggled to follow what she was saying, which was difficult given how she looked bent over to turn the taps on.

She stepped in and groaned as the water hit her from all sides. "Damn, this is almost as good as whatever you're going to do to me when you stop staring and get in here."

He snapped out of it and moved quickly, grabbing some towels and then joining her. "It's like I knew I'd be nailing you in here."

She laughed. "You're so fancy and genteel with your love talk."

He needed her to understand. "What you make me feel, each time I look at you, isn't genteel. It's feral. I want to eat you up in one bite. I want to touch every single inch of you, lick and kiss, nip and lap away the sting."

"Wow, that was . . ." She shivered. "I'm all yours to eat up. Any way you like."

He slid his body against hers a moment because he wanted to and as she'd said, she was his. "I plan to, gorgeous."

"Me first though." And then she sat on the bench just behind where she'd been standing and took his cock into her mouth, sucking the air from his lungs.

He watched, rapt, as she licked his cock, straight down the line of him where she kissed his balls. Christ, that was good. She sat back a moment, squeezing some soap into her palms and making a lather. She took him in again as she caressed his balls with soapy hands, dancing her fingers back to his asshole and pressing just right, setting all sorts of nerves alight.

"Yes," he rasped, spreading his feet a little to give her more access.

As she gave the crown and that spot just beneath kisses and licks, one of her fingers pressed in to that first ring of muscle. She took her time, stretching him slowly until she got in deeper and added another finger.

His muscles burned as he locked his thighs and fisted his hands to keep from yanking on her hair and fucking her face. She filled him with so much raw need it was a challenge to his control not to ravish her at all turns.

And then her fingertips found his sweet spot and stroked, fucking him that way as she sucked his cock.

She broke down his control. Tore his intention to take things slow to shreds and he went with it. Let her suck him deep, fuck his ass, whatever it was, he'd give it to her because it was so good.

Each draw of her mouth, each stroke of her fingertip against his sweet spot drew him closer and closer to the edge. A sound, deep and raw, broke from his lips and he wasn't sure where it came from.

He wanted to draw it out, but she was too much. It felt too good with her and he couldn't resist her long. When he came and she pulled back, she licked her lips and his cock began thinking about fucking her. So damned soon. Every time.

She stood and began to soap him up as he recovered, pausing to tiptoe up to kiss him here and there. She took care of him in ways no one else ever had. He hadn't needed it, he'd thought. He was capable of course. But she ministered to him and it soothed him.

"I love how you touch me." He kissed her again and held her tight. Her nipples brushed against his chest and reminded him he had some tasting to do.

"Now, it's my turn."

He dropped to his knees and spread her open. She gasped and the sound echoed all around them as he sucked her clit.

Cal loved eating pussy. Oh, he knew a lot of straight men didn't. But they were wrong. There was little he found sexier than a desire-swollen cunt, just waiting for his mouth. Like this one was. Slick with desire, her clit was hard, nearly begging against the flat of his tongue as he slid it across.

Her fingers caught in his hair and held him to her.

That was another thing he loved. The way Jules took what she wanted. Demanded it if she didn't think it was happening fast enough.

He slid two fingers up into her gate and her inner walls hugged him.

She rocked her hips, brushing herself against his mouth, setting her own pace. Her upper body was propped against the tiles behind her, the water cascading all around them. It was steamy and warm and all he cared about was the woman there with him. All he wanted was to bring her pleasure.

"Yes."

A whisper.

He gave her more, increasing the pressure against her clit and she came hard and fast, her fingers tangled in his hair, urging him up to kiss her. He wallowed in her taste, in the feel of her body against hers.

He liked his shower a whole lot too.

After he broke the kiss he stepped out and grabbed her a towel. "Let's dry off. I'll make you coffee if you make me pancakes."

She licked her lips as her desire-blurred gaze focused on him. "Yes, all right. After a blow job like that, I'll make bacon too."

"This is my favorite way to spend a Sunday, ever." Cal grinned at her as she puttered around his living room, picking things up, folding his tossed-aside sweaters and jackets. "The cleaning goddess will be here tomorrow, you know."

She smiled up at him. "Yes, yes, I know." She wore her hair in two braids. A T-shirt and jeans looked simple enough, but she looked like a princess in them anyway.

He went back to watching, pretending to read occasionally. His business line had rung several times because he often did work on Sundays, but he let the calls go to voice mail. If it was really important, they'd call his cell phone. But only a few people had that number, thank God.

On the surface it wasn't that different than the hundreds of other times he'd spent with her. But it *was* different. He could look his fill without the longing he'd had before. She was his. If he wanted to touch her, he could. If he wanted to kiss her, he could. It was no longer a fantasy—he knew what she looked like when she came. Knew what her skin tasted like. He'd known her pretty much their entire lives, but he *knew* her in a way that made those dreams he'd had before pale.

"What should we do later today?"

She gave him a look over her shoulder and he laughed.

"Well, that's a given. I pretty much want to sex you up every waking moment. But around our vigorous fucking schedule, we should do something else."

He liked having her all to himself for a little while. He and Gideon had convinced her to take off Sunday mornings and this was her first one. She'd called Tart twice and her assistant had told her everything was fine and hung up.

"We could go for a hike. It's a pretty day."

"That's not a bad idea."

"Let's see what Gideon thinks. If he's spent the whole day digging post holes or something like that he may want to choose a more sedate activity." She joined him, cradling her coffee in her hands.

"I'm clearly going to need to up my coffee purchases now that you're here more often."

Her smile was wry. "I'm a fiend, I know. I'll bring some from Tart."

She was, indeed a caffeine fiend, drinking four or five cups a day. Then again, now that he got woken up at four thirty in the morning a few days a week, he understood the need. Still, she was chipper in the mornings. Getting up easily before she got off to work. He admired that, not being anything near chipper.

Her phone rang and she answered. "Hey, Mom."

It'd been years since Cal had seen Jules's mother. She rarely came back to Washington and when she did, it seemed she was just around briefly before she left again.

Jules looked up at him before ducking her head down and Cal's interest sharpened. They'd been friends so long, he knew when she was hiding something. But the glimpse he got was filled with sadness.

He knew things had become strained between them in the years since her parents' divorce. The more her mother traveled, the less she came back. She'd often joked about how Cal and Mary's mother was more of a mother to her than her own.

And now, looking at her expression, he wondered just how much of a joke it was.

Jules moved from the room to hear better and to take the call in private. She had a feeling she knew what was coming.

"Darling, we're in Tahiti!"

"A great stop on your way here. I can't wait to see the pictures." Her mother had taken up photography as a hobby and was really good at it. She had a great eye.

Her mother paused, and Jules had been right.

"About that . . . We're going to Italy instead. Connor won't remember it one way or the other and some friends we met a few months ago have offered their home for us. A house-sitting sort of thing."

Anger made Jules's head hurt. She reined it in, wanting to see if she could guilt her mother into coming home before she headed off to Italy. Her nephew would start remembering his grandmother wasn't around much on his big days. "He's not a baby anymore. He remembers all sorts of things. Why not come back for a few days before you head off to Italy? That way you can see the kids and Ethan and me too. I miss you." *Please, please come.*

"I've sent him something fun. It'll get there before his birthday. I'll be back at the end of summer. I'll spend some time with Ethan then."

Jules hesitated, weighing her words, hating that she second-guessed herself so much with her mother. "You said that four months ago. About being back here for the birthday party weekend. Connor is four. He notices more than you think. And even if he doesn't, Ethan will. You're going to disappoint him if you don't come. Especially once he knows you're off to Italy instead. He misses you, Mom. I miss you. They only have one Nana, you know?"

"You're too sensitive, Julie. Ethan has a wife and kids. I did that already. You're both grown. You can't let other people's shit get in your way. Or you'll end up old and having wasted your life."

Well. *That hurt.* Also, her father had called her Julie. Her mother had always stuck with Juliet. It was like she just tossed it out there to fill space. Like it didn't matter that Jules was her daughter anymore. Jules felt a hell of a lot like a dependent and that sucked.

Jules tried to make herself cold, to ignore the hurt feelings and stick to anger. It was easier. "I'm sorry you feel like raising a family was a waste of your life. I'm busy just now; were you just calling me to tell me you're going to Italy?"

"Can you tell Ethan, please? It's hard to get phone signals here sometimes."

Then the anger wasn't so hard to keep. "No. You know he

gets upset when you don't come to his kids' stuff. I'm not play-ing your messenger here because you know he'll be mad."

"Really, I had no idea you'd grow up to be so difficult. I'm sure your father won't be there. But as usual there's a double standard."

"I can't imagine why you'd want us to feel about you the way we do about him." Jules hadn't meant to snap, but it happened anyway and she despaired at the loss of the close mother/daugh-ter connection they once had.

"I have to go. Tell Ethan, please, and let Connor know I love him." And she did hang up. Just like that.

Jules stood there, the phone in her hand. Wondering what the hell she was going to do.

"Hey. Everything all right?" Cal came into the room shortly after that.

Shame washed over her. Cal had great parents. His mother and father were involved and appeared to want to be so. How could she begin to explain what this thing with her mother was? Hell, Jules didn't even know what it was. Which only made her feel worse.

"I have to call Ethan to tell him my mother is going to Italy instead of Connor's birthday next weekend."

"Italy? And why are you doing it instead of her?"

Her mouth tightened a little and Cal homed in. He knew human nature and he most especially knew Jules. She was upset. "Yes. All I can hope is that she's at the very least sent something like she claimed. I want the day to be good for Connor."

Goddamnit, what the fuck was it with her parents anyway?

"And you're doing it why?" He needed to repeat that.

Jules sucked in a breath. "She says she has a hard time getting a signal."

"Really? But she called you."

"Look, I know. Okay?" He could see the strain on her face. She was holding it together. Every protective instinct he had rose in defense.

"Do you want to talk about it?"

Her normal open, beautiful smile shut down as she shook her head. "I have to call Ethan. I'll be done in a few."

He didn't leave the room though, instead settling in on the love seat near where she'd been standing. He had a feeling she'd be needing him when this was over.

Jules eyed him. He had that look. The one he got in court sometimes, or when Mary was pissing him off. He wasn't going anywhere and she got the feeling he'd be wanting more information about the whole thing with her mother.

She couldn't deal with that just then. And maybe part of her needed that. Needed to know he cared.

She dialed Ethan's place and her sister-in-law answered.

"Hey, Marci."

Her sister-in-law was good for Ethan. She was also a damned good mother. She'd never been anything but warm and welcoming to Jules, insisting Jules stay with them when she visited. Invited her to all major holiday celebrations. She was pretty sure it was Marci who'd been pushing her brother to keep in contact with Jules over the years.

"Heya, Jules. You looking for Ethan? He's out back with the boys."

"Yeah, if I'm not interrupting."

Marci laughed. "Of course not. Though you know you have to talk to both boys because they'll hear your name and go wild if they don't."

A burst of love broke through her. Her nephews were very important in her life.

"I just did FaceTime with H. Jack a few days ago." H. Jack was two-year-old Henry's nickname. His maternal grandfather's name was Jack so his full name was Henry Jack and it'd morphed into H. Jack.

"Thank you for that. I know they love being able to see you when they talk to you." In the background she heard Marci slide the patio door open and then the swell of noise from her brother playing with his sons. Laughter and squeals of joy made Jules wish fiercely that she'd told her mother off better.

"Jules!"

She laughed when she heard her nephews call her name and her brother tell them to quiet down so he could hear.

"Listen, I'm sorry to do this to you."

"Let me get in the house. Marci, can you take the boys?" His voice was serious all of a sudden and she knew he'd most likely figured out she was calling about something bad.

Some moments later he got someplace quieter. "All right. Tell me."

"I just got a call from Mom. She's not coming home next weekend."

"What the fuck? She promised. Connor is excited. And why are *you* calling about it? You'll be here, right?"

"Damn right I'll be there. I'm making the cake! I'll be in Friday afternoon with a fully packed car."

"All right, well, good. He's been talking of nothing but that. Why are you telling me this instead of her?"

"She said she couldn't get good signals and asked me to tell you."

"Funny how her signal worked just fine to tell you. She wanted you to tell me because she knew I'd be mad."

"Probably."

"What's so fascinating about Bali? She's been there months now." The sadness in Ethan's voice broke her heart.

"She's going to Italy to house-sit for someone."

Her brother got very quiet.

"I know. I'm sorry."

"Don't you dare apologize for her shitty behavior. You do it all the time. It's not your fault. Let her own her shit for once. She's always trying to hide behind what Dad did to her. As if she's the only woman on the planet who got cheated on."

He ranted on for some time and she nodded and said *uh-huh* in all the right places. He needed to share and she was the best person he could do so with.

When she hung up after talking to her nephews, Cal waited, his face sad.

"I didn't catch it all, but I think I got the gist. I'm sorry I had no idea it was this bad. Please share with me."

Because he said please, because he was her friend and because she needed to say it all out loud, she joined him on the couch. "I don't know if it's bad or good. It's just how things are now. It was all right when they first broke up and she traveled. She came back regularly that first year or two and then, slowly, she's just sort of disappeared from our lives."

He took her hand and it made her feel better. "I guess I figured she'd be a super-involved grandmother. I'm sorry to hear that's not the case."

"I don't know if it's that she doesn't understand the importance of this stuff, or what. My grandparents were a big part of our lives when I was growing up. Heck, I learned to bake from my grandmother! I assumed she'd get over this wanderlust when Connor came along. She came back when he was born, stayed a while. But she was gone again six months later. Wasn't back for Henry's birth or even his first Christmas. She comes back less and less." *She said she'd wasted her life.* The sting of it still had tears threatening to come.

He stroked a hand over her hair and she put her head on his shoulder.

"Hell, maybe I'm imagining things, wanting a better childhood than I really had. It hurts Ethan so much that she doesn't pay much attention to the kids. He blames my dad for it. She's doing damage now. I don't know if their relationship will ever recover."

"I'm not sure it should. As for your recollections being accurate? I was around for your childhood, baby. From the outside it sure did look like your recollections are correct. Do *you* blame your father for this?"

Did she? "I think he's certainly got his share of blame in the whole mess. But you know, no, I don't think it's about him at this point. I get it. She spent her whole life taking care of people. She wants something for herself. She clearly enjoys travel and her time with my aunt. It fills some need she has."

"But what about you?"

"I . . . As a woman, I get it. Or I try to. It had to have sucked to be traded in for a newer model after she invested her entire adult life in her family. I can imagine she's got a lot of resentment and she feels like she's missed out. But as her daughter, as Connor's aunt and Ethan's sister, I get mad at her for not wanting us much."

He knew it made her sad, but he'd missed just how sad. He heard it in her voice. The loss. He wanted to ask her more. Wanted to help her see this mess didn't belong to her in any way. But this wasn't a client. This was Jules and he didn't want her hurting.

"It's been this bad how long now?"

"Years at this point. Certainly all of Ethan's marriage. He misses her. I miss her too. But you can't make someone want you."

He collared her throat a moment, the excitement at the intake of breath and the widening of her eyes roared through him.

"How could anyone not want you, Juliet? Hm?" He kissed her and made himself let her go and back off. "It's more than that. She's got kids and she's just walked away. That has to hurt, even if you can understand she needed to find herself. She's being selfish." Cal couldn't imagine, not even in his wildest dreams, that his parents wouldn't be great grandparents. They were totally involved in their childrens' lives.

Jules was loving, clearly drawing strength and happiness from her friends, who were a great deal like family. To know she'd not only had her father disappear from her life but her mother too broke his heart. He wondered what his mother thought about this mess. He'd have to find a way to bring it up. She had a way about her, his mother. She knew people and Cal bet she'd have some great advice.

"She deserves this time. She raised her kids, ran a family business, worked hard for decades. She never put herself first in all that time."

How could she actually believe any of this was acceptable? Maybe she didn't. It certainly wasn't a very convincing tone she had. She sounded . . . lost.

He hugged her tight, not saying anything for a while. "You deserve to be loved and treated as special as you are. It's not selfish to want a relationship with your mother." No. It was selfish of her mother to not want to have a relationship with her kids.

Family law made up about half of his small three-attorney office. He'd seen more than his fair share of fucked-up families. But it was Jules who was so very sad. Jules who tried hard not to cry as he held her.

He loved this woman with everything he was.

The knowledge of it didn't shock him, but it did rush through him, warm and so very good. He took a deep breath, taking her in to his lungs.

"I love you, Jules. So much it hurts me to see you this way. You have family. You're being a good sister and aunt. That's not going to change. Maybe your mother will come back around in a few years. Maybe she'll settle back in. Or maybe not. But what I do know is that you've got to stop carrying the weight of what she does. You do not need to be guilty about her missing Connor's birthday party. *You're* not missing it. You're baking him a dinosaur cake and dozens of dinosaur cupcakes." He paused to snort a laugh. The theme had been her idea and she'd been working on the perfect dinosaur design for the last month.

"He loves dinosaurs, duh. Anyway, with my mother . . . I know. I just want to be supportive to her too. But she won't let me. Or maybe I'm not trying hard enough. I'm trying to understand."

"Sometimes people do stuff you can't understand. You're a good person. Loving. Loyal. You'd give up a kidney for your friends in a hot second. But not everyone is that way. Your mother is making a choice here, it seems to me. She's staying away of her own free will. It hurts you, and of course it does because you have a big heart and would never do anything like that to your loved ones. Hell, to anyone. You have to find a way to let this go or it'll eat you alive. You deserve more than that."

She was quiet a long time. Her body relaxed as she remained in his lap, wrapped in his arms. Letting him comfort her. Because she knew he needed it. Even in that moment thinking of others.

Despite the subject matter, it was good to just be with her, close and easy, their connection solid and strong. He'd worried after their fight the weekend before. He shouldn't have really; they'd had spats before and had always come out the other side closer. And this time, with Gideon in between them, it hadn't been difficult to move forward, the three of them in better sync than before.

"Thank you," she said quietly some time later.

"Anytime." He kissed the top of her head. "I've always got your back, you know that, right?"

She smirked. "I may have noticed."

"Good. I'm sorry, Jules. I'm sorry you're hurting."

Her smile was sad, but at least it reached her eyes this time. "Me too. But it comes with the territory, I guess."

"And you have me. Me and Gideon. Mary. Gillian, Daisy. Ryan. And that's just for starters."

"I'm lucky for it,"

He hugged her tight. "We're the lucky ones."

15

······················

She woke up and stretched. Nothing to do that day but the engagement party. She'd spent pretty much every moment of the last week preparing for it, which was good because it kept her mind off what had happened when she'd gone down for her nephew's birthday weekend.

In the two weeks since she'd confessed the situation with her mother to Cal so much had happened. Thank goodness for him and Gideon to help her work past the bloody strips Ethan's words had cut into her heart.

They'd all stayed over at Cal's place. She loved it there. So big and bright. Always a total mess, especially when the three of them were there so often. But his bed was more than large enough for everyone and she felt at home. Her stuff was in his bathroom. That made her smile.

How long had she fantasized about this? He was still sleeping, his dark lashes against the olive tones of his skin. He held her tight, an arm wrapped around her. Gideon snuggled behind, warm and solid, holding her quite like Cal did.

She knew Gideon was awake, given the cock pressing into the flesh of her backside. She smiled and started to turn, but Cal woke up. His eyes snapped open and focused on her.

"Hello, what have we here? There's a golden goddess in my bed." He kissed her bare shoulder and looked over it. "A golden god and a golden goddess. I must have done some mighty good shit in a previous life."

"I'll be right back and you can show me the proper obeisance." She scampered to the bathroom to clean up. She had plans for both of them. Once they left Cal's place she'd be caught up in all the prep for Gillian's party. This time belonged to the three of them and she had every intention of making the most of it.

When she came back out. Gideon was kissing his way over Cal's chest. She stood in the doorway, watching. They were unbelievable together. That fear that Cal would suddenly remember he liked penis best eased away a little more each time they'd all had sex. Each time they kissed or held hands. The normalcy of this not very usual situation had settled and she liked it.

"Don't just stand there like a deviant. Come over here and spread it around." Cal held a hand out and she jumped back into bed, meaning to get behind Cal, but he plopped her right back in the middle. "Where do you think you're going?"

"It's a lot easier to watch you two if I'm off to the side." Which was totally true. And as it had turned out, they all liked to watch.

Gideon laughed as he bent to lick across one of her nipples.

"We don't want you off to the side. I can get at everything I need with you right here."

Cal kissed his way over her belly. "Agreed. Access to this sweet cunt and to that cock too. You're right where we want you."

"Mmm. Promise to ravish me then?"

Cal looked up her body, into her face. "A promise I gladly make."

Gideon got up. "I'll be right back. You can get started on the ravishing and I'll catch up. I'm a quick study."

She turned to Cal, grabbing his cock and squeezing until he made that sound that tightened things low in her belly.

"Morning."

"A good morning to you. I need to be in you."

She took his hand and put it over her pussy. "I'd like that."

"Wet. Perfect. You know how I like it."

She scrambled atop. Fisting his cock a few times because he felt so good in her hand. Hard and real. Ready to deliver whatever she wanted.

"That look on your face would scare a lesser man."

She smiled down at Cal. "Good thing you're not a lesser man. I have plans for you. And for this." She shifted, her back to Cal's front as he scooted up to lean on the pillows he'd tucked against the headboard.

Gideon came in just as she was sinking down onto Cal's cock. Cal had moved the mirror in his bedroom so Gideon could watch better. Gideon, who met her gaze as he came back into the room and headed toward the bed.

"Look at you," Gideon whispered it as he knelt next to them. "Watching his cock disappear into your pussy and come out all wet with you is the hottest thing I've ever seen."

She arched her back to get him deeper, bracing her hands on Cal's thighs as she did.

Jules watched in the mirror as Gideon fisted his cock a few times. His gaze roved over her and Cal both.

"I love this position. I like to watch your tits in the mirror."

She smiled at Cal's reflection.

"They do sway ever so nicely." Gideon straddled Cal's legs, his cock brushing against her thigh and apparently Cal's something because he sucked in a breath behind her.

Gideon palmed her breasts before tugging on her nipples until she squirmed at how good it felt.

"She gets so tight and hot when you do that," Cal gasped out.

Gideon got closer and Jules grabbed his cock, rubbing it against her pussy and Cal's cock. The head brushed against her clit, sending ripples of pleasure through her.

"Goddamn."

She laughed, moving that last inch forward to grab Gideon's bottom lip between her teeth and tug.

"Make yourself come with Gideon's cock. But don't make him come just yet. I have plans for you, Gideon."

When Cal took over, he really took over. All that genteel reserve fell away and he was utterly and totally dominant. He wanted what he wanted and when he wanted it. It never ceased to make her shiver with delight.

"Gonna be hard," Gideon spoke through a clenched jaw. "This is so fucking good."

She moaned, agreeing.

Her clit was slippery and hard against the sensitive head of his cock. Gideon had to think about calling the vet to come out and see to the goats to keep from coming all over that glistening pussy. Cal's balls and his rested together, the friction sending little bolts of electricity through him. She angled him so that their cocks also slid against each other each time she lifted a little. Even as she brushed his cock over her clit to make herself come.

What they had dizzied Gideon. He wanted more. Each time they touched it led to something deeper and more raw than before. That trust he had for them both only made it hotter.

Jules's head fell back on a soft sigh and Cal growled, grabbing her hips and holding her down as he fucked hard into her body. Gideon slapped the head of his cock against her clit and she squealed, grabbing his forearm, her nails digging in deep for the long moments of her climax until she went boneless with a sigh.

Finally Cal helped her back to the bed, kissing her soundly.

She opened those blue eyes, still slightly blurred. "You two go on without me. I'm just going to lay here like a puddle of well-satisfied goo and watch you two have sex. This is the best day ever."

Cal grinned and grabbed Gideon by the back of his neck and pulled him close for a kiss. "Wait here. Be right back."

Jules laughed. "I'm pretty sure that's a given, Calvin." She turned her head to see Gideon better. "Hello."

He lay back with her, kissing her lazily. "Hello to you too."

Cal came back to bed and after kissing Jules he turned to face Gideon. "I want to suck that cock."

Gideon raised a brow and grabbed his cock. "Come on and get it then. You know how I like it."

Indeed Cal did.

Jules moved a little so she could watch better and Gideon gave over to Cal as he saw how comfortable she was.

His fingers slid through Cal's hair and tugged. Cal grunted

and sucked him deeper. Gideon took a deep breath and simply enjoyed how good Cal was with that fucking beautiful mouth of his.

Between a grunt and a snarl, Gideon managed to speak. "Next time my cock is going in that sweet ass."

Cal groaned around a mouthful of cock as an image of just what that was like flashed through his mind. Gideon had little patience once he got himself worked in to Cal's ass. He wanted it fast and hard.

And Cal was totally all right with that. The edge of pain worked for him. The way Gideon's laid-back control shredded as he fucked Cal worked for him. The way Jules watched them both hungrily only made the experience hotter.

He'd worried. He knew Gideon had as well. They frequently took cues from Jules as to how far to go, how fast. Neither wanting to hurt her. Neither wanting to give her reason to doubt.

True to her words though, each time they'd all been together it had been easier. There were no shadows in her gaze, only desire. Only love.

He took Gideon deep, breathing through his nose. Cal palmed Gideon's balls, fingertips pressing just behind. Gideon's grunt told him he was doing just fine.

Wet. He kept Gideon's cock nice and wet as he sucked him off. Gideon's fingers in Cal's hair tightened as he began to thrust, fucking Cal's face.

It was Cal's turn to groan then as shivers worked up and down his body.

"Fuck, fuck, fuck," Gideon nearly snarled as he came, his taste washing through Cal. Beside them, Jules expelled a breath she'd probably been holding as she watched the two of them.

"Again, I repeat. Best. Day. Ever."

Gideon bent and kissed Cal before he lay back down between them. "I totally agree."

"I'm stunned."

Gillian stood in the middle of the area they'd set up for the engagement party, her eyes alight with joy, a big smile on her face.

"You like?"

She hugged Jules tight. "It's perfect. *You made it perfect.* Thank you."

Grinning, Jules hugged her right back. "I had a lot of help, obviously. It was a group effort. Daisy handled all the table coverings and accessories. She made all the votives hanging from the trees herself."

"You made dulce de leche cupcakes."

"I did. But really it was for Adrian. He asked."

Gillian laughed. "You're incorrigible. You know how much I love them. I won't let you downplay your part in this. Who else would know how much I'd love that deep red? And the flowers! How'd you get those?"

Jules shrugged, flattered and so pleased she'd made her friend so happy. "I can't take credit for the flowers. I mentioned how much you like peonies and Erin made it happen. I have no idea where she got them."

"She's magic. I've ceased questioning how she makes things happen. But you, well, I know you have a busy life. We need to talk about all sorts of stuff. I feel like we haven't had a good long chat in forever."

Jules hugged her friend. "We did just two weeks ago. And you're planning a wedding, which is pretty stressful for a control freak like you."

Gillian laughed and squeezed Jules's hands. "Takes one to know one, my darlin'. How did the party go at your brother's place? Did Connor like his cake?"

She tried very hard not to let it show just how that went.

Those pretty eyes narrowed. Gillian missed nothing, damn it. "I know that look. Tell me."

She wasn't going to bring any of that ugliness into Gillian's special day. "Not tonight. Tonight is for happy stuff. And yes, he loved the cake."

"Of course right now. Jules Lamprey, tell me."

She hugged Gillian again. "You look beautiful. You got your hair done even. You smell delightfully ladylike and your makeup is perfect. This is your party, and your night and I've been planning this shindig for some time now. So, no, it's not for tonight. Tonight is for joy only. I forbid anything else."

Gillian frowned. "I'm coming to Tart tomorrow. You will tell me then."

"All right. Come near closing and we'll have lunch." Jules caught sight of Adrian. "There's your man; he's looking for you. Go on and get him."

"Thank you." Gillian waved to Adrian before turning her attention back to Jules. "There have been more times than I can count in my life when you saved me. Tonight is perfect because you planned it. And you love me."

"Course I do. Also, Erin helped. I've gotten to know her better through that, so really, I win all around."

Gideon came out, looking for her. When he caught sight of

Jules there, his smile totally changed his face. "Still gives me butterflies when he looks at me like that."

Gillian sent a grin Jules's way. "Gives *me* butterflies just to watch. There's literally no one else out here that matters to him once he sees you. It's breathtaking."

The two men ambled over, Adrian telling Gideon some story that made Gideon laugh.

"And you have two of them. Lucky you. We need to talk about that too." Gillian raised a brow and then turned to Adrian. "Hello there, Mister Brown."

"There's my lady. This is amazing." Adrian pulled Gillian to his side and shifted his attention to Jules. "This is more than I could have ever imagined. It's perfect. Thank you for being such a good friend to Gillian and me."

"I was just telling Gillian it was a group effort. Your brother and sister did a whole lot. Delicious worked their butts off as well."

"She does have trouble taking compliments." Gideon took her hand, smiling. "You look beautiful."

As did he. She'd never seen him in a suit and it totally worked. "You clean up damned nice." Jules tiptoed up and stole a kiss and turned back to Adrian and Gillian. "Now, you two go on and greet your guests. People are arriving. You can thank me with some great tickets to your next show."

Adrian hugged Jules. "Hell no, *you* get backstage."

She grinned. "Score."

They left and Gideon sighed happily. "You did good, Juliet."

"I keep telling you, it wasn't just me. Hell, you guys made this lawn look magical. I had nothing to do with it."

Gideon rolled his eyes. "Except for those detailed drawings you gave."

She laughed, blushing. "I couldn't leave it up to chance, now could I?"

"Not you."

"Thank you for helping so much."

"They're important to you. Hell, by this point they're all my friends too. So course I did." Gideon meant that. These people were her family, and if for no other reason he'd support her in anything to help them. But he liked them all too. They'd accepted him and their less-than-usual situation with such warmth and openheartedness, he'd been very touched.

He hadn't been sure how they'd respond. Cal had been part of their group since childhood. Gideon was an outsider, even though he'd been around a few times a year.

But he should have realized anyone Jules loved so much would be fine with anything that made her happy. And they were.

"This DJ is going to do some slow stuff, right? Because I need to dance with you tonight."

"You're on. I even got my hair done. I want to get everything I can out of tonight."

She was beautiful there, the fairy lights all around them casting a pretty yellow glow. Her hair had been done, yes. Swept up with a deep red rose tucked right at the base of her left ear. She wore more makeup than usual, shiny red lips, her eyes lined in a way that made them seem bluer and even bigger. Her dress was deep blue. It swept over her figure perfectly, highlighting those breasts of hers. Showing enough to make him want to bend his head and kiss each sweet mound showcased at the neckline. The shoes were peep toe. High enough that she didn't have to strain so much to give him a smooch and he had no complaints about that. They thrust her ass back, her tits forward and she swayed beguilingly as she walked.

Cal would lose it when he saw her like this. A shiver washed over Gideon when he thought about what he planned to do to them both when they got home later on that night.

Cal sat next to Patrick Carter, listening to a really great story about the ways Bainbridge Island had changed over the years. The man was a font of knowledge about so many things. Cal loved his stories and his asides. But what he loved more than that was the way the man simply accepted his grandson and his grandson's two lovers. Without blinking an eye.

Cal hadn't told his family yet. He was still working out a way to say it to communicate to them just how important Jules and Gideon were to him without making it sound like it was all about the sex or whatever. But Patrick, at eighty-four, didn't seem bothered by it at all. If he was in town and saw Cal, he waved and always made the time to talk to him. He stopped in at Tart all the time as well, Cal knew.

Gideon was fortunate to have this man in his life, and Cal supposed he and Jules were too.

He glanced around the area for her. She'd been slightly off over the last week. At first he'd chalked it up to stress over the party. Jules had wanted it to be perfect for Gillian and Adrian and the need to control every last detail had consumed much of her time.

But after she'd been back a day or two it had become clear to Cal that something had gone down the weekend before when she'd gone down to Portland to her brother's place. When Cal or

Gideon had asked about it, Jules had been full of descriptions about the party and her nephews' reactions to the things she'd done. But she'd avoided talking about anything else.

He and Gideon figured she'd had some sort of spat with Ethan regarding their mother. She had tomorrow morning off so he and Gideon would push her then. Damn her mother.

"Your girl sure looks fetching tonight." Patrick nodded toward where Jules stood with a plate of food in one hand, the other on Miles's forearm. The boy clearly adored his godmother. His grin was huge and he leaned toward her.

"She sure is, Patrick."

"First time I saw her she was not more than four or five. We used to eat in her parents' diner a few times a month and she'd be there. Over the years she waited tables or cooked there. Grew up fine, that one. Better'n her folks I wager." He shook his head. "Gideon came out of that damned marriage of his lucky. What he has now is better than what he had. I figure it takes the both of you to manage that woman of yours. But . . . with you too."

Cal choked out a laugh.

"I'm an old man, Calvin, I don't bother to beat around the bush. I don't much care for judging what people get up to in the bedroom, long as everyone there is on board. But I can see your heart. You wear it on your sleeve. You love my grandson and he loves you right back. And her too. So what difference does it make to me that there's three of you instead of two? Or that two of you have the same equipment? I'm going to die soon enough; I don't need to carry anyone else's choices. I just need to love my family. If you were bad for him, I'd show you just how well I can still throw a punch to the face. But you're all right. For a lawyer."

Cal just bet Patrick could throw a punch. The man was hale

and had fists the size of small hams. He worked outside every day. Cal had no doubts at all that should Patrick get to feeling someone was out to harm his family he'd do what was needed to set things right.

"I'm glad you approve. I never . . . well, I didn't set out to end up here. But I'm glad I have." Not that it was easy. But it was worth the struggle to get things right.

"Good. Take care of them and you'll never be sorry. I had that kind of love for my entire adult life. I met Clara when I was sixteen. She was fourteen then. Too young for me. So I waited for her and once she'd turned seventeen I went to her daddy to ask his permission to take her on a date. They invited me to dinner. We had dinner at her family's house for a good six months before they agreed to let me take her out. I never dated another since that first dinner and I never regretted it either."

That gave Cal hope.

"I've lived a long time. Seen things change a lot. But one thing that hasn't changed is that love is love, no matter how you cut it. And when you find it, you need to grab it with all your might."

Cal stood. "You're right. I'm off to go do that right now."

Patrick chuckled. "You do that, boy. She's too pretty not to snap up."

Jules glanced in Cal's direction, pausing to smile as he approached. He felt like the only person in the world, his heart swelling.

"Miles, are you trying to steal my woman?"

Miles looked up at Cal, horrified. "Ew. No. I mean . . ." He blushed furiously and Jules hugged him one-handed. "She's great and all, but she's my godmother!"

Jules's eyes danced with humor. "I did change lots of your diapers."

"Ew." Miles looked like he wished a hole would open up and swallow him.

Jules laughed. "Go on. You're free." She handed Miles the plate and he took it, rushing back to the table where the other kids were.

Cal pulled her to him and began to sway. "I haven't danced with you yet."

"What a neglected girl I am! You need to remedy that."

"Goddamn, you make me happy." He kissed her quickly and she settled in close, letting him lead. "I like these heels. Makes you nearly as tall as me so I can steal kisses easier."

"Glad you like them because they hurt like hell."

"Beauty is pain, darlin'."

"So men like to say."

He laughed but kept hold of her as the music changed. It didn't matter what song was on, she was in his arms, all his. He liked it that way.

"You and the rest of Delicious should look into party planning. I don't know that I've seen Gillian happier. Ever."

"No one I know deserves a happy ending more than Gillian." Jules turned her head to look at Gillian, sitting next to Adrian, his arm around the back of her chair. Her eyes widened. "Who's that dude with them? Holy shit, is that Damien Hurley?"

Cal took a closer look even has he tightened his grip around her waist. "Yes, I think it is. It's weird to know Erin and Adrian. They're both so down-to-earth it's easy to forget this is their peer group."

His sister Mary sat with them as well. A glass of champagne

in her hand and one of those mysterious woman smiles on her face. Cal frowned as the Damien guy looked at Mary like he wanted to eat her up.

"Isn't he one of those man-whores?"

Jules grinned up at him. "I don't know, but he's sex on legs, for totally sure."

He must have had some facial expression because she caught it and let her head fall back, laughing. "You're such a big brother right now. It's adorable. But I shouldn't have to remind you how smart your sister is. If she gets some, it'll be because she knows exactly what that guy is and wants a slice."

"I don't want to talk about that. Or about how hot he is. You have two men who can't get enough of you. That's your concern, missy."

"Well, sure. But we're not talking about me. She's a gorgeous woman, your sister. Of course some hot rock star wants to get into her knickers. Hello. But she's smart. No cookies will be given out unless she wants it that way."

"You killed my hard-on."

She laughed again, hugging him tight. "I can't even take how cute you are sometimes."

"Will it get me laid?"

"Hello, didn't you just say I killed your hard-on? Also, who was with me this morning if not you?"

Oh yes, that. "Well, really, I'd have to be dead to forget this morning. I think it tops our personal best if I do say so myself."

The three of them, spilled out in a mass of legs and arms, mouths and hands. He'd been in her, he'd been in Gideon, it had left his knees rubbery for hours after and just right then the memory made other parts of him distinctly less rubbery.

"Seems like you're recovering right now."

"You do have a way about you."

Gideon came out to the dance floor and instead of waiting his turn, he just put his arms around them both. They could do that here, in this safe space. And as it happened they weren't the only ones.

Ben, Erin and Todd, tanned and relaxed and freshly returned from a solo, romantic holiday, sat just beyond, Erin's head on Todd's shoulder, her feet in Ben's lap.

Gideon kissed Jules briefly and then Cal. "Hey there."

"Hey yourself."

They swayed under the stars, their woman between them and everything was just right.

16

....

Gillian poured them both a cup of tea as Jules brought out the plates for the huge bag of to-go Thai food they'd procured before coming back to Jules's place.

"Thank you again for the party. I'm going to remember it for as long as I live." Gillian grinned. "So, spill."

"You're not even going to wade in and pussyfoot around for a while? Man, you're brutal."

Gillian waved that away. "I don't need that artifice with you. Now, tell me."

Jules filled her in on some of the stuff about her mother and the way she'd dumped it on Jules to tell Ethan she wasn't coming. Gillian thought very little of that and for whatever reason, it helped Jules relax and remember of all people in the world, the woman across from her was her sister in every way but biological.

"So Ethan was mad at you about it?"

"No. He's got a lot of anger in general, but he went out of his way to let me know he didn't hold me responsible for the crap our parents pull. So one night we stayed up late and got to talking about our lives. I . . . I told him about Cal and Gideon."

Suddenly not hungry, Jules pushed her plate away and avoided the frown she knew Gillian would be wearing.

"What did he say?"

"He said . . . he said that he didn't want me around the boys anymore."

Cold and hot flashed through her at the memory of how she'd felt when he'd said that.

"He said wha?" Gillian grew up in London's East End and when she got very angry or excited, her English got up and she began to lose the end sounds of certain words.

"He said I wasn't fit to be around kids. That he couldn't trust me. I stayed in a hotel that night and didn't come home until late that next day. You can't tell Cal or Gideon. Promise me."

"You're taking the piss! You didn't tell them?"

Back when she first heard Gillian say that she was horrified. But then she'd learned it was a Britishism about playing a joke on someone.

"I wish I was. How can I tell them, Gillian? Huh? How do I manage to get that out of my mouth to them?"

"Well, I'm not telling anyone. I'm going down there myself and kicking the shit out of that great bloody git of a brother of yours. What on earth can he be thinking? This is insanity. How can he think to take those boys away from you this way?"

The tears were flowing now, no chance to stop them. She'd been in a haze for the last week, sick just to think of it. Sick at the loss of not just her brother but those two boys she loved so fiercely.

"I didn't take either of them with me. I went alone. I know it's not usual and that some people might be offended. It's not like I shoved it down his throat. I love those babies. I've never done anything to hurt them. I never, ever would."

Gillian was there, hugging her tight, smoothing a hand over her hair. "Shhh. You're not the bad guy here. He's wrong. So, so wrong."

"I don't know what to do. I tried to talk to him more, to work things out. I said I'd keep that part of my life totally separate from the boys. He said . . . he told me I was going to hell, that I was a whore and he kicked me out of his house."

Her shoulders shook as she kept crying. And then . . . she heard a tap on the front door. Gideon's tap.

"I can't. Oh my god, he can't see me this way." She stood up and Gillian shook her head, her hands on her hips.

"He knows you're here. Your car is out front. He's your boyfriend for heaven's sake. You have to tell them both."

"I can't!" Panicked and ashamed, she glanced toward the door and then back to Gillian, who shook her head.

"I'm not going to. Sweetheart, you have to. This is not your fault."

It was too late as he let himself in. The smile fell away from his features as he came into the kitchen and saw her. "What? Baby, what is it?"

Gillian moved out of the way as he rushed to Jules's side.

"Is everyone all right? What is it? What's wrong?"

Gillian said nothing and Jules knew she'd have to share.

"I was just telling her something about my brother. I need to clean up. I'll be right back out." Jules skirted past and into her bathroom.

Gideon turned to Gillian. "I'm about to have a heart attack. What's wrong?"

"She'll tell you. Just . . . be there for her. I'm going to go."

"Don't leave without telling her. She'll be more upset that you left."

Gillian took his hand. "You're perfect for her. Thank you for that. She deserves someone who loves her like you do. Anyway, she'll want to be alone when she tells you. Can you tell her I'll be calling later and to not even try screening?"

With a kiss to Gideon's cheek, Gillian was gone.

Gideon grabbed his phone from his back pocket. Should he call Cal? He decided yes, that in Cal's place, he'd want to be there too.

"Something is up with Jules. I stopped by her place and she was with Gillian. Crying her eyes out. She's cleaning up now."

"Is she physically hurt?" Cal's voice had gone sharp.

"Not that I can tell. Gillian would have said."

"I'm on my way."

Gideon hung up but before he could get down the hall to where she was, she came out.

"Cal's on his way."

Her eyes widened. "I didn't say it was okay to call him. I don't want to make a big deal out of this."

Gideon snorted and pointed to the bedroom. "Get in there. I'll be in in a moment with some tea. We'll snuggle and you'll tell me and Cal what's wrong. I'm not going to let you wall us out."

She sighed, sounding so very tired, but turned to go into her bedroom. Satisfied for the moment, Gideon put away the food and grabbed the tea Gillian had already made before going to her.

Before Gideon had even reached the door, he heard Cal letting himself in.

"Where is she?" Cal moved to Gideon, pausing to kiss him quickly.

Gideon jerked his head toward the bedroom. "She hasn't said anything yet. I'm bringing in tea."

They headed to her and found her propped on her bed, her feet tucked beneath her body.

Jules held a hand up. "Before you start in, I'm not walling anyone out. But wouldn't it be nice if I didn't have an issue? Just once? Don't you get tired of it?"

Gideon handed her a mug and joined her on the bed. Cal came in, one brow raised.

"What's going on, pretty? Hmm?" Cal settled on one side and Gideon the other.

"Stop trying to fix me." She frowned and Gideon couldn't help but laugh. As if they'd let her hurt without trying to help.

Gideon shook his head. "Juliet, sweetness, if you wanted men who didn't meddle, you chose the wrong ones."

"Oh, I like your cocks and all. The nosy part is annoying."

Cal leaned in and kissed her soundly. "You're stuck with us. Now, tell."

And when she'd finished and was fighting tears, all Gideon could see was red. That she'd carried this a week without telling them. That her brother could be so thoughtlessly cruel to stop her from seeing those boys she loved so dearly for something that had absolutely nothing to do with him.

"Why the fuck didn't you tell us this before today?" Cal's jaw was clenched tight.

"What can you do about it? Nothing. Am I giving you up?

Hell no. There is nothing to be done. I can't force my way into his life if he doesn't want me there. They're his children. It's his job to raise them how he sees fit. All telling you would do was make you sad and angry." She shrugged.

Cal sighed heavily. "We *can* do something, Jules. We can love you and support you. We can share your burden. Why won't you let us?"

"Some things can't be fixed. He kicked me out of his home at nearly midnight. I'm just grateful it was after the party so I got to share that one last thing . . ." She broke off, tears in her voice.

Cal looked at Gideon over her head, anger and anguish in his gaze. They both ached for her.

Gideon was fortunate in his grandfather. Patrick knew what was going on and was totally supportive of Gideon's life. He loved Jules and enjoyed Cal as well. He'd said whatever went on between them behind closed doors was none of his business as long as they all respected each other.

He hadn't told his parents yet though.

And as far as he knew, neither had Cal, though certainly Ryan and Mary knew about the three of them.

"Why would you hide this? God, I feel like an idiot. All this week it's felt like something was wrong but I told myself it was the hectic lead-up to the party last night."

She took Gideon's hands. "No. I just . . . When I said it out loud it became real and now I can't avoid it. I wasn't ready to say it just yet. It's not about you. It's about me. I've lost my mother and now Ethan and those boys." She shook her head. "I just needed the time to work it through."

"I understand that you needed some space, but I want you to come to us. I want you to share with me and Cal. You were hurting and you never said. Every time I touched you, you didn't let me help."

She smiled softly. "Every time you touch me you do help. Don't you see? It doesn't matter. It hurts and I'm devastated to imagine I won't have any relationship with Connor or H. Jack. But I can't live my life for my brother's morals. I have to live my own life in my own way. It hurts. It still hurts today that my brother has rejected me. But what can be done? Nothing. And so you move on because that's all you can do. I have so many people who love and accept me. It's important to remember family isn't about biology, but love."

Gideon thought for a while and realized for the most part she was right.

After a bit, Jules spoke again. "We can't get around the basic fact here. Our relationship *isn't* usual. People—some people— will be offended. Hell, have *you* told people? I mean we're fine with friends, which is more than a lot of people have. And I know Patrick is fine with us. But what about your parents, Cal? Have you told them yet?"

Cal sighed. "I can't lie, I'm concerned about this. I'm worried this will impact your business. I'm worried this will hurt the farm."

Gideon waved it away. "And your practice?"

Cal shrugged. "Nah, I don't think so. It's not like the judges I go before are going to care even if they did find out. And if they don't, clients most likely won't. My private life has always been private. I've never discussed my romantic life with clients anyway. But you, baby, you have a bakery. People want to feel good about that. What happens when this gets out?"

Jules snorted. "This isn't 1950, for god's sake. Mainly people won't know. And those who do aren't going to care. Some might, I suppose, but I'm not worried about that."

Gideon blew out a breath. "My granddad knows, but I haven't told my parents yet. They know I'm seeing Jules, but not about Cal. I've been waiting until I go down there in August so I can tell them face-to-face."

Jules nodded. "I think face-to-face is good. And it's not a requirement that you confess this relationship like it was a dirty secret. But we can't avoid reality. We know there will be people who react badly. People like Ethan who are not bigots and jerks in their daily life. But this pushed his buttons. He couldn't handle it. He was . . . well, I've never seen him so angry. I was a little scared for a moment. Marci tried to intervene, but he was outraged. Some people will be. Maybe even those we aren't worried about just yet. I just . . . look, I'll understand if you two don't want that."

"I need to tell you how much it makes me want to punch Ethan for scaring you. Did he hit you? Touch you in any way?" Gideon narrowed his gaze.

"He didn't. He was threatening and I was nervous about it. But I can't believe he'd ever hit me. He's being an asshole, but he's not that guy."

Gideon shook his head. "Beg to differ. Of course he's that guy. He did and said all that stuff. It's not like he was on medication or anything. If he so much as makes you jump in the future, he and I are going to have a one-on-one."

Cal snorted. "Let's go back to your comment for a moment, shall we, Jules? So you're fine if I just dump you or Gideon so I can avoid some random dick being uncomfortable. That pisses me off. If I can live as an out bisexual man, I can have a girlfriend and a boyfriend too. I *have* been avoiding telling my parents, but that's just a matter of not wanting to rock the boat when things between the three of us have been going so well. But even if they disowned me, I'm not going anywhere. I knew, going in, that this would be complicated. But it's worth it." He turned Jules to face him. "You're worth it. You and Gideon are what I want, what I need. I know my sister and brother think you're both wonderful. I know Patrick does. We know all our friends are fine. The rest we'll have to work through."

Jules shook her head. "It's easy to sit there and say everything would be fine if they disowned you. But you don't really know what it feels like." Her voice caught. "It sucks. I don't want that for you. I don't want that for Gideon either."

Cal hugged her. "I don't want that. None of us do. But as you point out, it's bound to happen with some people and we need to either break up or deal with it. I know my preference."

She smiled and Gideon relaxed a little. "Next time you'll tell us right away."

"Maybe."

Cal snorted. "No *maybe*. You have to share. How can this work if we don't share?"

She put on a sunny smile. "Seems to me we share just fine."

Gideon was charmed but he didn't want to show her that right then. "No jokes. Cal's right, look, this thing we have? It's not for slackers. It's not going to work if we don't all put all we have into it."

"You're right." She took his hand and then Cal's. "You're both right. Don't get used to hearing that, by the way. I'll try harder to share."

17

....

Daisy flitted around Tart, talking to customers, straightening things. She'd put up a new piece of art and had stayed to help out and visit afterward. Gillian had also wandered in and was currently sitting at the counter, drinking tea and eating a scone.

Jules loved that Tart was a place their friends often gravitated to during the day.

She cruised over to Gillian, kissing her cheek. "In like ten days, darlin', you're gonna be Mrs. Rock Star. Can we help with anything?"

Gillian smiled. "I'm remarkably calm. This is what Adrian told Erin yesterday. I'm still laughing about that. Everything I can do I've done. I have the dress. The food is in place, the flowers are taken care of. I have the best cake in the world, obviously.

All the tux fittings are done. Ben has sort of taken over keeping everyone of the male persuasion on task. He's adorable, that one. Erin gave us a trip to Fiji for a wedding gift. I told her people normally give things like gravy boats and vases. She reminded me she wasn't normal."

Everyone laughed.

"Speak of the devil!" Jules paused as Erin and Raven walked into Tart.

"My ears were burning." Erin grinned as she came in, filling every inch of the place.

Jules put her hands on her hips, pleased to see them. "You should have a doctor look at that. You do know you're not supposed to be putting anything in there. Not cotton swabs or penises. I worry about you."

Erin barked a laugh. "Ha! Oops. Who knew ear sex was a no-no."

Gillian spun on her stool to take them in. "I was just telling Jules about your present."

Erin winked at Jules and then looked back to Gillian. "She knew anyway. I told her back in May."

"She's quite good at keeping secrets." Gillian sipped her tea and held a smile back.

"I do my best." Jules waggled her brows. "Come in and sit down. What would you both like?"

Jules got started on the drinks and Daisy grabbed them some pastries.

"What brings you two over here today?" Jules asked over her shoulder.

"I needed to deliver this stuff to the house. But no one was there. So I went over to the new house and Blue was there with

Adrian so I dropped stuff off and Raven and I figured we needed to stop in here to eat and fuel up before we went back over to Seattle."

"What are you spoiling my son with now?" Gillian asked, shaking her head. Erin, as Miles's aunt, spoiled him rotten. As Miles was a great kid, he didn't take advantage. Even just six months before it might have been an issue with Gillian, who really took the time to raise her son to appreciate and earn what he had. But she'd come a long way, accepting the way Erin showered those she loved with gifts.

Erin laughed, not chagrined at all. "I had an extra case. It was cluttering up my office. I figured he could use a new one so I brought it by."

"With a new bass and strap," Raven added as she sipped her latte and pretended she wasn't stirring shit.

"God, you're a tattletale!" Erin poked Raven's side.

"She's scarier than you are." Raven tipped her head in Gillian's direction.

"Oy! He has three bass guitars already. He doesn't need another."

Erin rolled her eyes. "Of course he does. Plus at the new house the studio is full of instruments. He'll keep it there. Don't begrudge me, Gillian. I love that he plays bass. He's such a great kid. I like giving him things."

Gillian snorted. "As if I had a choice."

Erin took her hand. "You do. If it truly bothers you, I'll stop. Most of it."

Gillian smiled and Jules was so pleased to see the ease between the two of them. Gillian didn't love easily. She took a while to warm up to people. And Erin, a lot like Jules had, just sort of made it impossible to not be friends. Gillian would have said if it bothered her. She had in the past, Jules knew. But she'd come to a place where it was easier to let the Browns do more for Miles and that was a wonderful thing to behold.

Gillian sniffed, all prim and proper again. "You're all right. I suppose this is the family business. He wants to be like you and his dad so much. I'm absolutely sure he was thrilled. He already thinks you're magic."

"That's 'cause I am." Erin fluffed her hair, streaked with blue. "And you know I love your kid like crazy. Thank you for letting me spoil him."

Jules wiped the counter down. "Speaking of kids, where's Alexander? Also, you have Cookie Monster hair. I love that."

"It was Alexander's idea. I'm edging him toward Elmo next time. He's out for a day with Todd's mother. She took him to the zoo, I think. He loves his nana. Which is nice because she adores him right back."

They chatted a long while, laughing and talking about the wedding and the place where Erin was sending Gillian and Adrian for their honeymoon. Jules was reminded at times like this that her life was so full of people who cared about her. Not about who was in her bed, or how much she could do for them. But they cared about *her*.

Reminders like that were important. She needed to always remember that.

Cal strolled in to Tart, pausing at the door to take them all in. The place was full of beautiful women. He loved women. Loved being around them. Loved the way they talked, the way they smelled. He'd grown up around many of the women in this room. All lovely in their own way.

But it was Jules he couldn't keep his gaze from. Jules with all that pretty golden hair and the big, wide smile. Damn she was like a dream come to life.

Jules caught sight of him and made her way over, coming into his arms and turning her face up for a kiss. "Why, hello there, gorgeous."

It felt good, the way she came right to him, the way she offered herself, giving affection.

"Right back atcha." He kept an arm around her as he looked to the others. "Good afternoon, all you lovely ladies."

They all said their hellos and he turned back to Jules. "I'm just making a quick stop. I have a client meeting in twenty minutes. What are you up to tonight? I thought we could have some dinner. Maybe go to a movie? We'll keep it early. I'll be at your place at five?"

"Works for me. A date sounds like just the thing."

Gideon was away for two days, dealing with some business over in Eastern Washington, so it would be just the two of them.

She packed him up a latte and some tarts before he got back to work. "Walk with me?"

"Totally." She linked her arm with his and they strolled back to his car.

"I have very fond feelings about this alley now."

"The first place you kissed me."

"Ah, ah, ah. The second. The first place I kissed you was in the parking lot at the high school."

She'd been fifteen to his eighteen. So sweet and sexy. He'd

known then that she was beautiful and funny. And wanted so desperately to be kissed.

She stepped close as he bent to put the drink and pastry box in the passenger seat.

"I wanted to be kissed and you said not to waste my time with boys my age who didn't know what to do."

He banded an arm around her waist. "And you said no one else seemed to want to kiss you because they were all afraid of your brother."

She smiled. "I told you I was going to throw myself at some cute counselor at summer camp if that was the case and then you kissed me."

He had. The idea of her getting her first kiss from some college guy sniffing around younger girls had pushed all reason from his head. He'd simply leaned in and gave her a kiss. Intending it to be fast, but his tongue had found its way into her mouth, her taste a total tease.

It had been so good he'd backed way off and never did it again, afraid of what might happen. Never wanting to lose her friendship. Older girls went farther and God knew he was horny all the damned time back then. Ha. Now as well. But times were different.

"You're not fifteen now. And I can have you as often as I can manage."

"Lucky me."

"You took the words right out of my mouth." He leaned in to kiss her again, the memories of that time so long ago sweetening the moment.

"I'll see you at five."

She stepped back with a wave. "Drive safe."

• • •

"Damn he's pretty." Raven tipped her head toward the door as Jules came back.

"I know. It's nearly criminal. He looks way better naked than I do."

Raven laughed. "You're not so bad yourself. But I've seen him in shorts and a T-shirt and that was a nice preview. And the cowboy too? It's the manners, am I right?" She looked to Erin and Daisy, who both nodded eagerly.

Jules blushed. "Not even gonna lie. All that please-and-thank-you-ma'am stuff makes me tingly. He stands up when a woman enters a room. He can do it without being patronizing. You should see what he looks like on a horse. Or when he's sweaty from working outside all day. Good lord." When she saw him like that, she wanted to lick him like an ice cream cone.

Raven sighed. "Thanks for that image. I'm not actually seeing anyone right now and you're a hot-man hog. You and Erin both. It's selfish."

Jules liked Raven, though she wasn't always easy to like. One of those people who often said exactly what she thought. With no filters. Sometimes it was too much. Other times, most of the time, Jules believed she did it to keep people back. Jules saw how Raven was with Erin and knew of her friendship with Gillian. The woman had a big heart and tried to hide that behind a bunch of bitchy chatter. Sometimes she succeeded, but Jules trusted Gillian's instincts.

Erin snorted in Raven's direction. "Bitch, please. You need two men to handle you. Or even better, one super-hard, super-badass alpha male who won't take any of your shit."

"I'm not sure I've met the man who can tame Raven." Gillian patted Raven's hand. "But it would be fun to watch."

"You're all very mean to me." Raven sniffed dramatically.

Jules rolled her eyes.

Gillian told them all about something or other going on at the new house as Erin edged closer to Jules.

"Looks like you guys are working stuff out pretty well."

Jules hesitated for a moment but decided to share with Erin what had happened when she went to her brother's house.

Erin took both of her hands, distress on her features. "I'm so sorry! That's awful. Ben has had some pretty bad problems with his family since he told them about us. His father is . . . well, I'd hoped for several years that he'd get his act together, at least for the sake of his grandson. It's very ugly and it hurts Ben so much. Frankly I'd love to punch the guy in the face and be done forever. His mother is the sweetest woman ever, I don't get it."

Jules sighed.

Erin continued. "It's not easy. And it's really not easy for Ben and Todd. It's funny, they get more negative attention for showing each other affection than when the three of us do. Not everyone deals with what they don't like or understand in a positive way. Some people are going to judge you. Sometimes it's someone you really love and being rejected by them is incredibly painful. I'm sorry. I wish I could say it didn't hurt or never mattered. But you're a person with a big heart. Of course it hurts and of course it matters sometimes."

"Cal is worried that if people find out there'll be negative impact on Tart, or on the farm."

Erin shrugged. "It could be. But really, most people just want to eat something sweet with a cup of coffee. They don't care that you're in love with two men. This isn't to say I don't think you need to be discreet. We might all hold hands or give each other a quick kiss, but it's really not something we call attention to outside our family and friends. It sucks to have to play that game with bigots, but it keeps my kid safe and I don't have to deal with drama that way."

"I really don't know what I'd do without you to talk to."

Erin smiled. "That's a wonderful compliment. Thank you. I'm glad to have you to talk to as well. I'm not the only one out there now. It feels good. And it feels good that Alexander will be around other families like his. Um, not that you're going out and having babies next week or anything. But you know what I mean."

Kids was a whole 'nother thing Jules had been thinking about. One step at a time, though. There was time for that. One *giant* step at a time.

Cal had been so deeply involved in his work that he'd nearly jumped from his seat at the sound of the tap on his door.

Beautiful Jules stood in the doorway, looking annoyed. "You're working very late. This vexes me as I had plans with you."

Cal looked at the clock and then back to Jules with a cringe. "Shit. I'm sorry." He stood and moved to her. The look on her face made his cock hard and his heart swell. That summed up what she was to him. Everything. Hotness and sweetness at the same time.

"You move me, sugar."

Her annoyance slid away as she smirked and let him hug up on her. "Hm."

"You do. I'm sorry, the time got away from me. I did check the clock, but it felt like just an hour ago."

"I suppose I have to get used to being with an attorney."

"You look so pretty. I'm really sorry I stood you up." This wasn't unusual. He did have a tendency to get wrapped up in his work. But in the past he just didn't pay as much attention. Sometimes whoever he was dating would get annoyed, but he always made clear that his job was his priority.

But now . . . now he had better priorities. He had Jules and Gideon and suddenly working all the time seemed far less attractive.

"So." She grabbed the bag she'd left at the door. "I'm here to bring you something to eat and *also* to say that I know you sometimes have to work late. However, if you and I have a date, I expect you to call or text if you're going to be late. Otherwise I sit around waiting for you and then I do not feel very much like letting you touch my boobies at all."

"We can't have that, now can we? You know how much I like and admire your boobies. Being on the outs with them would be a damned shame."

She handed him a bag. "Sandwiches and fruit. I saved you a cinnamon roll." She kissed him. "I'll see you tomorrow."

"Can I come over later?" He liked waking up with her. Liked the scent of her skin on his.

He'd never actually lived with someone before. Oh sure, he spent the night or they spent time with him. But when it came down to it, his previous boyfriends and girlfriends were visitors to his life.

Jules was *part* of his life. Had been before they'd taken things to a new level. Jules was different. On every single level. How he reacted to her was different.

He should have been scared, should have been spooked that things were so serious. But he wasn't scared. At all. He was more sure of her than of anything else he'd ever known.

"Yes, you can come over. I might be sleeping. You know how I get if I'm not asleep by ten." She fought a smile and he enjoyed that too.

"I'll let myself in and be quiet. I'll even refrain from feeling you up."

She grinned. "You'd better not. Now, eat and finish your work. Come to me when you finish. I'll be there."

He kissed her long and slow, enjoying her taste so very much. "I'm always ready for you. I've got another hour or so but I'll come to you."

"Good." She kissed him quickly and left.

And he hurried up, needing to be with her.

18

. . . .

D ust the board. Just a little flour. The dough can get
sticky."

Gideon pushed his sleeves up and she tried not to get
ensorcelled by the sight of his forearms.

"I flour the rolling pin too. Just on my hands and I rub it over
the surface. You don't need a lot. Too much and the dough gets
rubbery."

"This is way more complicated than I ever thought. I have
new appreciation for what you do." Gideon said this as if he
weren't actually pretty awesome at everything she'd ever seen
him do.

"You're doing fine. I'm not grading you."

He followed along.

"What are you two making?" Cal wandered into the farmhouse

kitchen from the living room where they'd been watching movies all day.

"It's all Jules. She already made a cobbler and three pies."

Cal's features lit. "Pie?"

"I don't think you've met a baked good you didn't get all hot for." Jules snorted as she worked.

"It's good fortune, don't you think? Being in love with a pastry goddess is very fine luck indeed."

Already weak-kneed at the sight of Gideon and those gorgeous forearms, Jules fell into Cal as he entered the room.

Calvin Whaley was simply beautiful. At six feet and change, he was already imposing, but the broad shoulders stretched under olive-toned skin, taut with just the right amount of muscle. A narrow waist, a high, tight ass and long, powerful legs. Add the black hair, cut flawlessly and therefore framing his face to highlight his gorgeous features, and the blue eyes and you didn't even need the fact that he had an incredible sense of style so the package was always attractively dressed in clothes that fit him perfectly.

Breathless as she rolled out the dough, she couldn't take her gaze from him.

He kissed her on his way past. His gaze moved around the room as he took in the pies cooling on racks. His mouth curved upward a bit. Over to the stove where she'd just placed the finished cobbler to cool. Over to Gideon and up his legs and to his face. Sexy half smile this time.

Jules gulped, not even able to brace herself for his attention and when his gaze lighted on her face, she licked her lips.

"No one looks at me the way you do."

She blushed. "*Everyone* looks at you. All the time. You're one of those people other people want to watch on account of you being so pretty and all."

Gideon laughed, leaning to kiss the top of her head. "You're right."

Cal shook his head. "Not that. Though it's nice when you look like you want to spoon me up and take a bite." He paused. "I don't know if I can put it into words and do it justice. Everything you feel about me is written all over your face when you look at me."

His words filled her with so much emotion she nearly drowned. "You fluster me. No one flusters me. I'm pretty stone cold and all that jazz and you . . . well, you look at me and I get all stuttery and nervous and it's delicious." And scary.

"It's one of the things I love most about you. Now bake me something, woman. You know how hot it makes me to watch you in the kitchen."

She did, actually. Gideon said it was hot to watch a strong woman bake stuff for him. Cal had agreed.

"One of those pies is for Patrick so don't either of you touch it," she admonished lazily as she scanned the shelves until she found a juice glass she needed to cut the biscuits.

She returned to Gideon's side and continued her lesson. "And then you cut the shapes like this." She pressed the rim of the glass down through the dough with a slight twist and then pulled up again. "You might have to flour the rim a little here and there. And then just put the biscuit on the baking sheet."

Cal breathed deep as he kept his attention on her as she worked. The kitchen smelled fabulous. She wore a high ponytail and a sundress. In her bare feet, she padded here and there around the room. To the oven where she bent, giving him a fabulous view as her breasts heaved up. To the table where she'd been working with Gideon.

She looked like an ad for soap, or something else equally wholesome. But she was so dirty just beneath it drove him crazy. He'd had *no* idea what lay just beneath the surface until he'd drawn the curtains and she'd gotten naked with him.

"I like that dress." An innocent enough compliment, but he teased and she knew it.

She twirled and creamy skin up to her mid thigh flashed. On purpose as she teased back. "Do you?"

Playful.

Cal leaned back, his lids dropping a little. "Are you teasing? I think you might know what happens when you do that."

"I know. Why else would I do it?" She looked him up and down. Slow and sexy. He wanted to preen.

Of course Patrick would be back shortly and they'd have to savor that want a few more hours until they could be alone again.

"Christ, when you're like this it makes me want to bend you over something." Gideon came up behind her and hauled her to him, back to front.

Cal's cock ached, he was so fucking hard. When easy, laid-back Gideon got all dominant it worked all the fucking way.

"When is Patrick back?" Jules swayed a little against Gideon. Cal knew the feel of her ass as it brushed over his cock and he stepped to them both.

Gideon groaned. "Any minute now."

Jules sighed and moved away, fanning her face. "The wait will only make it hotter when we finally do get alone."

"Until then I'll be planning. I hope you have Epsom salts in your cabinet because I plan to make you very, very sore." Cal smiled, totally meaning it.

Jules blushed. "Now you're making a challenge. You know how I hate to lose, Calvin."

Cal grinned. "Oh, but we all win this challenge."

Gideon laughed and then they heard a car door slam outside, signaling Patrick's return.

"I'll hold you to your promise," Gideon said on his way past.

"You'd better, or what's the point?"

Cal paused just outside his parents' back door and took a deep breath before he went inside. Once he was there he relaxed. This was his home. He'd grown up in this house and everything would be fine.

"Hey, Calvin." His mother waved to him from where she sat, putting a puzzle together at the kitchen table.

He kissed her cheek and sat next to her, looking over the pieces and all the space she hadn't filled yet. They'd been putting puzzles together for as long as Cal could remember.

"Mary's in the den with your dad. He's on the computer again and I swear he opens up every link all and sundry send him. Like a bird with something shiny. He can't resist. We've got a virus again."

"Tell him to stop looking at porn." Ryan, his younger brother, came into the room.

"Language, Ryan." But it was an offhand scold. Jeanne Whaley could get going if she got mad enough. And Cal should know. He and his siblings had kept their mother very busy as they'd grown up. She could simultaneously grab the back of a shirt and haul a child to her all while brushing hair with her free hand, or washing a face, correcting math, whatever.

Cal tried not to laugh, but it was a losing battle and soon he and his brother were nearly choking at the thought of their dad clogging up the computer with viruses from porn sites.

"If you two are done?" She looked at them over her glasses and they calmed a bit.

"When's dinner?"

"In half an hour. Mary and your dad are grilling something or other. God only knows. I just know it'll taste good. There's beer in the fridge and some tea as well. I see a pastry box over on the counter. What did Juliet send to us today?"

Cal shrugged. "I don't know. Some walnut cherry thing. Bars of some kind." She'd made it specifically for them though, he got that much when Jules had handed him the pastry box.

"Your father will gobble up everything that isn't nailed down. You know how much he loves walnuts."

Cal only remembered right then. But Jules had known. "Actually, I just recalled that."

"Jules would know. She remembers things like that. So when are you planning to tell me you're finally dating her?"

He looked to Ryan, who shrugged.

"I wanted to be sure first."

"You've been sure . . . *ah*!" She fit a piece in a sea of green. "Little bugger. I've been working on that part for days now. Anyway, you've been sure for years now. Why you've wasted your time with anyone else is beyond me. You're lucky she didn't find someone else."

Ryan made a ha-ha-ha face where their mother couldn't see. "Well, it's kind of complicated."

His mother was no fool, even on her worst day. Her gaze snapped up. "How so?"

Ryan stayed where he was and Cal was grateful for it. He knew his brother would get his back if necessary.

"Well, I'm not only dating Jules, but I love her. That's the first part and I suppose you may have guessed that. The second part is . . . do you remember Gideon Carter?"

"Sure. You and he ran around every summer. Tall and blond like his dad. I think he slept over here dozens of times." She sat back, a smile on her face. "He's back in town now, right? Helping Patrick run the place?"

"Yeah. So. I'm with Jules but Jules was with Gideon first. I mean, she did get snapped up by someone else. And then I realized it was go time and I told her how I felt and . . ." He looked to Ryan, who shook his head. He didn't know how to tell their mother either apparently.

"You're not going around with her behind his back? Or, him around hers? If you are, I'll knock some sense into you faster than you can run for that door."

Ryan barked a laugh but they both knew enough to be damned sure she meant it.

"No! Of course not. I'd never do that to her, or to him. No. I mean, I'm with them both. They know it. We're all together."

"So you're all dating around? Like a soap opera love triangle? Calvin Whaley, that never works. It's always an episode of *Snapped* when that story comes to play."

He couldn't help it; he burst out laughing. "No. No, I promise.

I mean, we're all together. As like a set. A unit? A triad? I don't know the right word for it. I'm in love with them both."

She stared at him for several long moments before she expelled a huff of breath. "Ryan, bring me my emergency cigarette. Cal, shut the door so your dad won't smell the smoke. Boy oh boy, just once I'd like for you damned kids to do something minor."

Ryan got up and brought out the stool to grab her emergency kit. Some booze, chocolate, a hundred bucks in cash and a pack of cigarettes Cal had seen precisely three times in his life. None of them were his high points.

She lit up and sucked in a lungful of smoke. He cringed. She then took a shot of whiskey and sat back in her chair and examined him carefully.

"Let me get this straight. The three of you are in a relationship together. You're all, um, romantically involved."

"Yes."

"How's that workin' out for you?" She kept smoking.

"Actually, it's, um, really good. I've known them both most of my life. Jules is everything I could ever want. Gideon . . . well, he was unexpected, but that works too."

"Christamighty. How on Earth am I supposed to explain this? And they treat you well? You're happy?"

"I am. Gideon has a successful business. Jules has a successful business. They're adults who have real lives. No one is depending on the other, but if I needed either of them, they'd drop everything to help. It's not usual. Maybe not even normal. But I'm so *happy*. I've never been so at ease and comfortable in my own skin."

"One of you had better give me some grandbabies. I swear."

Steps sounded on the stairs up from the den.

"Leave your father to me. Ryan, put this all away before he gets here." She waved a hand around, opening and closing the back door to get the air moving. "And Calvin? I expect them both at dinner tomorrow night."

And that was that.

19

Gideon saw Cal long before Cal had noticed his approach. He liked that his granddad and his man had taken to each other so well. Right then the two of them sat up on the porch, laughing and talking.

Jules had been right when she'd said that Cal was the kind of person people looked at. He was, indeed, beautiful.

Cal turned his head and caught sight of Gideon as he walked up the short path and a smile appeared, just for Gideon. "Hey, you."

Gideon lifted a hand in greeting. "Nice surprise. What brings you my way today?" He tapped his boots against the bottom step to get rid of the dirt.

"I had some business with Patrick here and figured I'd do a house call. That way I could see you too."

It was nice being able to be open about their relationship

around his granddad. With the trouble Jules had had with her family, Patrick's loving, straightforward acceptance of his grandson's life was a relief.

Once Gideon reached the porch he dropped onto the small love seat where Cal sat and leaned over for a kiss before turning to his granddad again. "We had to order a new part for the hose connector. The old one is cracked beyond anything I can fix. It'll be three days."

The system to get water to the crops was imperative, but fortunately, they'd had a good, soaking rain the day before so if the part came in when it was supposed to, they'd be able to have everything up and running again before there was cause for alarm.

His granddad nodded and pushed a cup of coffee his way. "I suppose I should tell you Jules sent over some turnovers. I left you one. Cal made me."

Gideon burst out laughing. "Thanks for getting my back."

Patrick shrugged. "She'll bring me more. She loves me that way."

Jules had taken to afternoon rides with Patrick several times a week. She'd close up Tart and show up at the farm. At first Patrick pleaded that he was too tired after being up all day, but he'd yet met anyone with a heart who could resist her charm. She simply kept showing up and finally Patrick accepted it and now he was ready when she arrived.

Sometimes Gideon went along, others it was just the two of them. It got Patrick out and about. It was good for him to be active; especially because of the turnovers he loved so much. And he liked that both Cal and Jules were so good to his granddad.

"Smart move having a baker and a lawyer in the family, Gideon."

"I think so too."

"You're invited to dinner at my parents' house tomorrow night, by the way." Cal paused. "Invited is a pale word, really. You're *expected*. As in my mother will hunt you down if you don't come. Take it from me, she's really fast for someone so small."

Pleased that Cal had not only told his family but that they'd apparently reacted well, Gideon sipped his coffee. "Can't have that. Your mother is scary."

"She took the news that I was dating you both pretty well, all things considered."

"Leastwise she didn't kick you out of the house and call you names." That still burned in Gideon's gut. To see Jules so devastated by her brother's behavior tore him up. He wished it was something he could fix but knew he couldn't.

"Some people don't have the sense God gave a goose, boy. That whole damned family is a mess of selfish shitheads." Patrick sat back, ready to go off on a rant if he had to.

When Gideon had told him about what Jules's brother had done, his granddad had nearly lost a gasket. He'd paced back and forth in the living room, going on about self-righteous assholes and people who should know better. He'd been ready to get in the car and drive down to Ethan's house to punch him in the nose. Gideon had told him to get in line.

Cal nodded, a sour look on his face. "Truth, Patrick. But Jules has a family here. We just have to keep on loving her and supporting her. The people she was born to don't matter a damned bit if they don't love her like they should. I feel for those little boys because their dad is tearing her away from them when she adores them both so much. They'll lose out, not knowing her.

But the rest of them, well, they can keep the hell away from our Jules. She's better off without them."

Patrick gave Cal an approving head nod, as if he'd passed a test.

"I need to get back to the office. I just wanted to stop in and deliver the turnovers and hang out a bit." Cal brushed the crumbs from his pants. "Patrick, I'll get the papers back to you once I file them so you have a copy. They'll also be at the office, of course."

"Thanks, Calvin. Appreciate it."

"I'll walk you out." Gideon stood up and walked with Cal down the steps and toward his car. "Are we doing anything tonight?"

"I stopped by Tart earlier, she's all right. But it's some sort of preschool event this week. One she'd planned on attending. And now she can't. It's going to be a while, I know, before she can truly let go of what's happened with her family. It's one hit after the next with them. But I think we should just keep doing our normal stuff. She'll be pissy if we push too hard. And while that's often the stuff for spectacular make-up sex, I'd prefer not to poke at her about it for a while."

"She is pretty astonishing when she's mad." Gideon grinned.

"It's the way she's all girl-next-door sweet one moment and then bam, her eyes narrow and her mouth flattens out and she's a fury. I used to poke at her, back when I was dumb and with other people. I'd poke at her just to see her get mad and then work to get her to forgive me."

Gideon found this confession hilarious and yet sweet. He touched Cal's cheek. "You knew what you needed all along. It just took you a while to grab it."

"My mother claims I'm too stubborn. She's probably right. I had no idea about you though." Cal turned enough to kiss Gideon's hand. "Without you, well, she'd be with you and I'd hate it."

"But now you can have us both. And we have you. It's really a good deal when you think about it."

Cal brushed his lips over Gideon's. A hint at all that heat beneath the designer suit. "I do think about it. A lot. How about we make her dinner for a change? You two show up at my place at say, six? I'll grill some steaks. And yes, I won't be late."

"See you later then."

"Love you, Gideon."

Love filled him. "I love you too, Cal."

Patrick looked him over when he came back to the porch after Cal had driven away. "I wanted to wait until after Cal left, but you have a message inside. From Alana."

"My ex-wife? What the hell does she want?"

"Don't know. She was impatient as always. Just left her number and then made sure I knew how voice mail was really quite easy to use."

Gideon sighed and went inside. Whatever Alana wanted, it would be a pain in his ass, he was sure.

He called her back on the house phone. She didn't have his cell number and he liked it that way.

"It's Gideon, what's up?" he said when she answered.

"I'm doing well, thank you. And you?"

"I'm annoyed you're not getting to the point."

"You used to want to hear about my day."

"What do you need?"

"I'm going to be in Seattle next week and I thought we could have dinner like civilized divorced people."

For a long time he'd tried to remain on friendly terms with her. He'd let go of the cheating stuff. Had tried to live in the same place and run the ranch, but she had played games with him. He didn't hate her, but he was glad not to have her in his life and he sure as hell wasn't going to waste his precious free time having dinner with her.

"I hope you have a good trip. But dinner isn't going to happen."

"Why not? It's been years since we've seen each other. We've both grown up a lot, I'm sure. Maybe we could, you know, get together after that too. Just for the night; I'm not leading you on or anything."

"Sorry to hear you're lonely, Alana. I'm not. I wish you nothing but the best, honestly. But I'm not interested." He hung up and left the room.

For a long time he'd felt like a failure for the breakup of his marriage. He wondered if he'd tried hard enough, if he'd worked too hard at the ranch and ignored her into all her bad behavior.

Even as he'd traveled and enjoyed having sex with other people, he'd wondered. He hadn't connected with anyone else really, not emotionally, not apart from business.

But then he'd come back and Jules had shown up at the farm. The way they worked together had underlined that it didn't matter at that point whether he had or hadn't tried hard enough. It mattered that he had something real and lasting with someone he deserved to be with.

What he had with Jules and Cal was so totally different from what he'd had when he was married that he'd realized the most important lesson. He was capable of a real, lasting love with someone without hurting all the time. When he was with Jules they clicked. She didn't need his attention every moment. She didn't need to be taken care of. So much that it annoyed him sometimes when he wanted to fix her and she insisted on doing it herself.

When he spoke, she listened. When he needed her, she was there. Cal was the same.

It wasn't important, whatever he'd done, or not done. What was important was that he'd found people who completed his life without trying to take it over. And the love he had now was so much stronger and better; he could tell the difference from day one.

"What's she want?" Patrick came inside to put the coffee mugs in the sink.

"Doesn't matter. I've got what I need and she's got nothing to do with my life anymore."

"That's the truth. Glad you see it."

Jules had eaten dinner at the Whaleys' kitchen table countless times. Jeanne had been a lot more like a mother to her since the divorce than her own mother had been on several occasions. She adored the woman and her quirky and sweet husband.

And yet this time was different. She wasn't there as Mary's friend, she was there as Cal's girlfriend. Sitting next to Cal's boyfriend. The whole thing was surreal.

Jules sucked it up and knocked and then a thought occurred to her. She'd planned to bring something sweet, but occasionally Jeanne liked to bake so she didn't want to step on toes. And then she got a little panicked, thinking maybe they expected her to bring something. After all, she usually did. But before she could run back to Tart, Jeanne answered with a big smile and a genuine, warm hug once she'd finished pulling Jules inside.

"Juliet! You look so pretty." Jeanne stood back after the hug to look her up and down.

"Thank you. Gillian actually *made* this dress for me a few years ago."

"That woman, I tell you. She's good at everything. Well, come on in. Calvin isn't here yet. He was nearly a month past my due date too. I hope you won't hold all that tardiness against him. That and his messiness. You'd never know to look at him that he can't hang a shirt up to save his life."

She relaxed a little. "He's picking Gideon up. Gideon's truck is in the shop."

Mary came into the room and hugged Jules. "Hey you. You need a drink."

"Do I look that nervous?"

Mary laughed. "You look like you're about to run out the door."

"Nervous? What on earth for?" Cal's mother said it like she truly had no idea why.

"Well, not everyone's family responds so positively to the news Cal gave you. I . . . I don't want you to think poorly of me."

Jeanne snorted and waved a hand. "Poorly? Whatever for? Honey, you're like one of my own kids. We already love you. I'm Cal's mom, it's my job to kick his butt when he's being dumb, but also to support him when he's being smart. Picking you at long last is smart. As for the other stuff, don't hurt my boy and we're fine." She linked her arm through Jules's and strolled her through to the kitchen. "Now, Mary, get Jules here a beer. I'm having one too, you know, just to be a good hostess."

Mary handed them both a beer. "She is selfless that way." She winked at her mother and Jules felt a lot better just for the banter. Jeanne Whaley was an imposing woman who loved her family fiercely. If she'd been opposed to the relationship Jules had with Gideon and Cal, she'd have said so. Cal reminded her of this only that morning. She certainly wouldn't be having dinner at the Whaley house otherwise.

"So I take it from your comment about family responses that yours is having some trouble?"

She gave Jeanne and Mary an edited version of what had happened with her brother. "I haven't told my parents yet. My mom is in Italy for a month and my dad has two young kids; it's not like I have to tell them right now anyway." Though it had entered her mind that perhaps Ethan might tell them himself, but that wasn't something she could worry about right then. There was only so much she could deal with at once. Two bossy men and a business to run meant drama fell to the bottom of the list.

Jeanne sighed, tipping the beer back to take a drink. "Worthless as a tit on a boar, the both of them."

"Mom!" Mary put her hand over her mother's mouth.

Jeanne took the hand away. "Someone's got to say it. Anyway, Jules, dollbaby, you're always welcome in this house. I think you have very good taste, as it happens, to have been in love with my son for so long, even before he figured out how much he loved you too."

Jules grinned. "It's actually pretty easy to love Cal."

"That's what a man likes to enter a room and hear." Cal swooped into the room and kissed Jules soundly.

Gideon came in, a little more hesitantly. "Hello, Mrs. Whaley."

Jeanne got up and pulled Gideon into a hug. "I've told you a million times you can call me Jeanne. Now, we were just having a beer. You two want one?"

"I'll get them. Sit down, Gideon. Where's Dad?" Cal looked around as he got the bottles and popped the tops.

"He ran to the market to get some wine. He'll be back in a few minutes."

Jules knew he'd come to Cal's workplace and had talked with him a long time about Gideon and Jules and their relationship. Cal just told her they'd worked through a lot and that his father supported him. Which was the important part.

"He's been marinating the chicken and prawns all day. Made potato salad, pasta salad and roasted some vegetables too. He only does that for family. So you're all right." Mary patted Jules's arm.

Cal's dad was a big griller. He didn't care much about the kitchen, but the barbecue was his domain. All spring and into the fall he'd grilled every single weekend when they were kids.

Gideon sat next to her and she put her head on his shoulder a moment, both of them nervous, she knew.

"I like that dress." He nodded at her.

"Thank you. It was a gift from Gillian, the sewing queen. How's the truck?"

"Fuel pump is out and they don't have the part."

"You can borrow my car if you need to."

He smiled at her and Cal came to sit on her other side. "That's a mighty fine offer, ma'am, thank you. I should be all right. Granddad has a car if I need to run errands and it can't wait."

"So how is this going to work? Where is it you're all going to live? I imagine you won't all three keep your own places."

"Here's my mom! She's very shy." Ryan came in with his dad and paused to give Jeanne a kiss. "Hey, Jules, Gideon."

Jules laughed.

Mike Whaley came through the door, his arms full. Jeanne gave him the eye. "What on earth did you buy? I thought you were only getting wine."

"We needed ice cream." He put things away and Jules saw some chips and crackers too.

"He's supposed to be cutting out junk. But every time I turn my back he's shoving Doritos into a hidey-hole he thinks I don't know about."

Jules liked the two of them together. Mike was a man of few words, but he loved his family and he'd always been good to Jules.

"Evening, Ms. Juliet. How are you tonight?" He ignored his wife's poke about potato chips.

"Not bad. Even better now that I know there's ice cream."

Jeanne laughed. "I made pineapple upside-down cake; it'll go well."

"Really? It's my favorite."

"I know, that's why I made it."

"Oh and thank you, Jules, for the cherry walnut bars. They were mighty fine with my hot tea last night."

She knew it had been a way to hopefully soften the news that their son had gotten himself involved with two other people, but it never hurt to butter people up with something sweet.

"Glad you liked them."

They all adjourned to the huge back deck where the table had been set for dinner. The evening was warm, especially for late June. It was perfect out. The flowers in bloom in the garden just below scented the air.

"You asked us about our living situation earlier. My grand-dad asked me the same question today, Mrs. Whaley, I mean

Jeanne." Gideon blushed. "Turns out he's signed the farm and the farmhouse over to me and he wants me to make myself at home and live in it. With Cal and Jules."

Wow. Wasn't that something you said to your girlfriend in private before you announced it to all and sundry at a backyard barbecue?

It was clear Cal already knew of this as well, which only annoyed her more. Of course she wanted to live with them. She loved that old farmhouse, especially the kitchen. But she wanted to be asked, for goodness sake. It felt like they'd done all this planning, patting her on the head and not remembering she liked to know things like that before a decision had been made.

Mary gave her a look that told Jules she wasn't alone in her thinking.

There was silence for long moments until Cal spoke. "There's actually a mother-in-law suite on the basement level at the house. It's a daylight basement with its own entrance, kitchen and all that. Patrick wants to live down there in exchange for all the cherry turnovers Jules can make him."

Which was a lovely story and all, but when had all these discussions taken place and why was she hearing about them this way?

Gideon turned to look at her and jerked a little when he saw the look on her face.

"What's wrong?" he asked quietly as Cal continued to blather on and on about the farmhouse.

"I don't want to do this here." She kept a smile pasted on her face while she spoke in an undertone. She didn't want to ruin the evening with a spat.

"Are you mad?" Gideon asked, as if he was totally clueless.

"Yes."

Apparently he was. "About what?"

"What part of *I don't want to do this here* was confusing? We've shared enough with Cal's family for one day, don't you think?"

"Hey, have you seen the new water feature?" Mary spoke up, interrupting this little moment between Jules and Gideon.

"Oh!" Jeanne nearly beamed. "I did it all myself. Bought a kit and everything. Cal, go show it to them. I'll be over here drinking beer and awaiting your compliments."

"She's smooth," Cal said under his breath as they followed him down the steps out into the yard.

"Why do you have that gleam in your eye? You make me nervous when you look that way." Gideon glanced at her as they took a path to the left.

"Your mother is an amazing gardener. I can never get my roses like this."

Cal started to speak, stopped himself and then tried again. "It's the exposure here. Great sun all day. She does this custom mix for the soil too. You should tell her you like them, she's insanely proud of her roses."

"I will."

The water feature was quite lovely. Wide, flat stones rimmed a pool, probably about two feet deep or so. Two little waterfalls made lovely music as well.

Gideon watched her carefully. She was clearly pissed off so he gave her space.

"Spit it out, Juliet." Cal was clearly less patient. Gideon sighed. No finesse. It never worked to go straight at her like that. It only made her dig her heels in more.

Sweet Juliet Lamprey with her soft fabrics and gourmet coffee could totally be stubborn. She could out-stubborn most anyone else he knew. Even Cal, the second most stubborn person he knew.

And Cal was so intensely focused on her, had such a long history with her that he still spoke to her like he did when they were just friends. But Jules knew the difference and Cal did too when he wasn't agitated.

She raised a brow at him.

"If this was in my yard, I'd sit out here with my feet in the water on hot days. Maybe add a margarita to make it perfect." She looked up at them both. "Just because I don't like deep water doesn't mean I can't dip my toes."

Cal started to speak again and Gideon reached out to pinch his side and shut him up. Cal glared and Gideon glared right back.

"So when was it you two planned to include me in all this moving-in-together stuff? Patrick knows. Cal's entire family knows. You two have talked about home office space for Cal and yet no one bothered to run any of this by me."

Oh. Shit.

Cal sucked in a breath. "Christ. I'm sorry. It wasn't that we talked about it behind your back. Not together. I went out there yesterday to have him sign the final paperwork. He and I had been discussing it. I didn't tell you because he's a client and it was his to share or not. When I went to pick Gideon up just a while ago, Patrick told me he'd discussed things with Gideon. We all chatted a little. That's all."

"And I was so excited about it and we'd just talked it over with Granddad so I got excited to share it with Cal's family, you know to let them know we were serious and it was . . . I'm sorry. We should have talked with you."

She might be a fury when she was mad, but she never stayed that way long. She shook her head and sighed. "Lordamighty, you two are an awful lot of work. It's a really lucky thing you're both so handsome and good in bed. In the future, excited or not, I want you to talk to me first, before you announce big stuff to the world. What if I'd said no?"

Cal, bless his heart, gave a look as if the very concept of such a thing was inconceivable. "Do you want to say no?"

"Probably not. But the point remains, Calvin. Does it not?" She stuck her chin out and Cal's spine lost its rigidity and he sighed.

"Yes, it does, baby. I promise to try my very hardest."

"Such a lawyer answer. But it'll do."

20

....

Jules lit her candles and sat quietly, trying to breathe through monster cramps and a lot of general crankiness.

There was a knock on her door and she kept her eyes closed, ignoring it. But then Cal just let himself in and called out.

"Oh, I'm sorry." He jolted to a stop when he caught sight of her meditating. "I just wanted to see you. It's been three days."

She'd been insanely busy this week. Gillian's wedding was that upcoming weekend. They'd had a dinner the night before and people had begun to filter in from out of town. She'd made two hundred cupcakes for some thing Adrian had hosted and had made a full mock-up of the wedding cake that day, her second. At least that part was something she could control. And it was delicious too.

But she was worn out and had given so much to everyone else

that she barely had enough left and she needed some muscle relaxants and time alone.

"Are you getting sick?" Cal put a hand on her forehead.

Normally that would have charmed her, but just then it made her cringe and that made her even crankier because he was just trying to be sweet and she knew that. But she really wanted to be left alone.

"No. Thanks for asking." She forced herself to remain patient. "I'm just tired and cranky and on my dot."

He took a step back and she laughed. "Don't worry, it's not catching."

"I hear orgasms are great for cramp relief."

"I admire your ability to work orgasms into just about any topic."

"It's true! Look it up on the Internet."

"The Internet. Well then, if it's on the Internet, it must be true." She knew it was true actually, but it was fun to tease him.

"You do know it only makes me hotter for you when you're this way? God, you used to torture me when we were younger. You'd lecture me or be condescending and I'd jerk off to you for weeks after."

"Honestly, no one I know gives compliments like you do. Which is actually a compliment in and of itself. I'm not good company though. Go to Gideon's. You two give each other orgasms. Think of me and I'll see you tomorrow."

"I want to have orgasms with you."

"You're very charming and normally I'd say if you were down with it, let's go. But you can't possibly understand just how little I want to be touched right now. I'm bloated, sore and really bitchy. Let me eat too much ice cream and go to bed early with a heating pad. Go have hot gay sex with our man."

He smiled at her. "There's really no one like you in the world."

"Ha. There isn't, so don't forget it."

"You sure I can't help?"

"Dude, please, don't manage me right now. I'm telling you, I'm on my period and I want to cut someone. Just begone."

He got close enough to risk a kiss. "I'm going to have hot gay sex with Gideon and, yes, we'll think of you. Feel better. I love you, Juliet."

She let herself be charmed. "I love you too, Calvin."

He left and she closed her eyes, this time finding her center a little more easily.

Three months she'd been with Gideon. Nearly that long with Cal. Her whole life had changed. Nearly totally for the good. Business was outstanding. She'd hired extra staff so she had two days a week off now for the first time ever. Mary's catering business was also similarly prospering and Daisy's gallery had not only provided sales for her but a platform for other artists in the area. She saw less of Gillian now than she had before. And that was natural. Gillian had Adrian, who lived on Bainbridge full time now. Daisy was busy too with Levi. Watching the two of them build a relationship was pretty cool.

She, Cal and Gideon were growing together, learning each other. Gideon was that bridge between Cal's fiery intensity and Jules's sometimes uptight reluctance. Ah well, her total bitchiness. Since this was an internal conversation and she was currently nearly doubled over with pain, she could admit it. Sometimes she was just a bitch and she was too old to try not to be. It was good to soften herself for them, with them. But her base personality wasn't easygoing and sweet.

She and Cal had poked at each other a long time, but things were different now and so when they clashed, Gideon was that space between them. But she didn't mistake that temperament as him being too soft.

Of the three, it was Gideon who was most dominant. Not that she was complaining. Gideon getting all in charge with Cal was mind-numbingly sexy. Gideon cleaved himself to them both. He was a good man. Protective. Bossy as hell. But usually about things she understood. Good with his hands. He made her feel beautiful and smart and totally capable all while also making her feel precious and cherished. In short, he was pretty much everything a person could wish for.

And Cal, gorgeous, hot-as-sin Cal, who made her laugh. Who knew her so well and loved her anyway. Cal, who seduced her every moment he was with her. Cal, who brought her presents, usually gorgeous and expensive lingerie that she'd find tucked into a drawer so she'd wear it for him later. Intense. He might be looking around at other things, but when he was with her, she was his focus. It made her fluttery and sort of giggly at times. He was also intelligent and knew people better than most. She was one lucky woman. No doubt.

She loved them both. Of this she had no doubt. But moving in together was a huge step and while she was willing to think about it, it scared the hell out of her. It wasn't that she didn't trust Cal and Gideon, she did. She trusted that they loved her too.

But Cal had been a serial monogamist and Gideon had been married before. She hadn't been in a serious relationship. Ever. They were better than she was at it by a million times.

And the inescapable truth of it was, she knew she wasn't easy to live with. She was cranky sometimes. Aside from baking, she was not a patient person. Gideon and Cal were so much more easygoing about the day-to-day stuff than she was.

What if living with her ruined it and they really saw all her flaws and couldn't stand her? She'd been on her own since she moved out at nineteen. She needed to do stuff for herself and they tended to be very pushy where she was concerned. Which did, on the other hand, make the sex really hot because they liked it when she pushed back. But they took a lot of energy to manage.

Hell, she meditated every night because she was trying to be less bitchy and the god's honest truth was that she was probably just holding off the more scary side of the bitch spectrum.

What if it was why her relationship with her family was so messed up? What if she was simply incapable of maintaining a long-term romantic relationship?

Would she just move in with them and then fuck everything up? Would it wear off in three years? And if so, what did that mean anyway? Would she rather walk away from them and miss the happiness they could have to avoid the potential of pain?

She pushed out a breath. They just needed to get past the wedding. There was so much going on that they'd decided to shelve the planning and discussion about moving in together until afterward.

But she knew she had to face it and make a choice. Gideon was patient for now, but he wouldn't always be, and neither man was the type to not get what he wanted.

She just had to figure out if she could do it and make it work. But right then a heating pad and some ice cream waited.

. . .

Cal wanted *her*, damn it. With the wedding coming up so fast, he knew she'd be busy, but it had been three fucking days and he wanted to touch her and fuck her and be with her naked and sweaty. There was something about her, about being with her that filled him just the right way. It was a Jules-shaped spot and no one but her would do.

He should have known when he came in and she was wearing those sweats and that shapeless shirt. But no, he had to poke at her because it thrilled him like a dumbass and then of course she told him to go fuck Gideon and let her eat ice cream.

She wanted to eat ice cream instead of having sex with him. Though she did shoo him toward Gideon, who probably didn't want to eat ice cream instead of having sex.

He knocked on Gideon's door and when Gideon opened, once he was sure Patrick wasn't down visiting, Cal came in, slammed and locked the door behind him and looked Gideon over.

Gideon's surprise melted into something else. Heat rose between them.

"I was just at Jules's where she kicked me out and told me to come have hot gay sex with you."

"She's in a mood. I tried to coax her to come over tonight too. She told me she was feeling stabbity and to go away. A woman says she's feeling stabbity or anything related to stabbing and you give her space. As for hot gay sex . . ." He'd been wearing loose pants and he pulled them down, until his cock sprang free, hard. Cal's mouth watered as Gideon reached down and fisted himself a few times. "Bring it."

Cal dragged his shirt up and over his head and stepped from

his shoes, shoving his pants and shorts down, all before they met at Gideon's bedroom doorway in a gnash of mouths, a frantic shove and pull as they kissed, falling down onto the bed.

"I want you face-to-face." Gideon leaned down and grabbed Cal's bottom lip between his teeth and sucked it into his mouth a moment. Cal could barely think much less speak. Need raced over his skin like fire. He wanted more. More.

Gideon rolled over and riffled through a drawer until he pulled out the lube. He snapped open the cap as he raked his teeth over Cal's nipples. Then he poured some lube over Cal's dick, letting it run down his balls and to his asshole.

They slid against each other, cock to cock, teasing and stroking as they kissed. Gideon was an amazing kisser. He teased and tormented, tasted and took whatever he wanted. Truly, to be kissed by Gideon was to be kissed senseless.

Gideon got to his knees and rested as he rolled a condom on. "Spread your legs and jerk your cock."

Cal made a sound and he wasn't even sure where it came from or how he did it. Gideon moved his thumb back and forth over Cal's asshole, slowly working it in and stretching him. Cal didn't fuck men face-to-face. He generally preferred to be the one fucking and to fuck from behind. But Gideon was different and it was so intimate it shook him as Gideon stretched him and then pulled back a little, pushing Cal's legs up and apart before he began to press inside.

"Yes, god, yes. So tight." Gideon swallowed hard, sweat dripping off his neck as he kept it slow, not wanting to hurt Cal. "You're not stroking your cock."

Cal fisted himself and began to work his cock at the same pace Gideon fucked him.

He gusted out a breath. "You're so gorgeous there beneath me. I'm a lucky man."

Cal smiled in his way and as always, it shot straight to Gideon's cock. "You're about to get even luckier. Fuck me. I won't break."

Gideon pushed all the way in and then pulled out, pressing back. "I don't want to hurt you."

"A little pain is part of why it's so good." Cal groaned, deep and low and Gideon repeated that thrust, brushing the head of his cock against Cal's sweet spot over and over. Cal had started jerking himself slow and easy, but he'd sped his pace, so Gideon did as well.

"Yes, yes, like that."

Gideon thrust harder, deeper, over and over. One-handed, Cal stroked his cock, hard and fast just like Gideon fucked him. The other hand was tangled in Gideon's hair, pulling him close. Those big brown eyes seemed to look straight into him, and Cal gave over to it, letting himself fall totally, giving up that last bit of reserve he'd been keeping.

"Now, damn it, I need you to, Gideon." Cal's voice was hoarse, desperate, and Gideon swiveled once, twice, and then once more and began to blow. The warmth on his belly told him Cal had tipped over as well.

Cal smiled up at him. "I feel much better."

Gideon laughed as he got up. "Me too. Next time," he said, handing Cal a towel, "we should try taking our time. But whenever I see you naked, I lose all my control."

"Jules was right to send me over here." Cal stretched. "I needed that."

Gideon came back to bed, dropping to the mattress next to

Cal. "I miss her too. She's run ragged with the wedding stuff. She wants it to be perfect for Gillian. We'll have the day after the wedding to recuperate. Jules has the day off, I took the day off, you'll be off."

"Let's go wild and sleep until eight." Cal laughed.

"Mmm, we might sleep till noon. I expect we'll be at the wedding until late. We'll wake up late, go out to breakfast maybe. Or lunch. And have sex. Lots and lots of sex." And push her into making a commitment on moving into the house.

"I don't know how I lived without sleeping with Jules and you. I miss fucking her when she wakes up." Cal got up and went into the bathroom, returning a few minutes later. "I've gotten used to her. She makes me happy. I'm grumpy when she's not around." Cal jumped back to the bed next to Gideon.

"Good to know I'm not the only one. She fills my life up with, well with a certain level of Jules-ish-ness. Or whatever. She makes me laugh and I like to fuck her. Oh and she can bake." Gideon thought the combination pretty much rendered her perfect.

"She doesn't take any shit. And she's not helpless."

Gideon smiled a moment before it fell away. "She sees being upset about her family as a weakness. Or a personal flaw."

"For as long as I can remember, Jules took care of people. She wants to take care of her mother and her brother and those kids and they won't let her, and it's them, not her, but she doesn't see that clearly."

"She's scared to move in with us." Gideon sighed.

Cal snorted. "Not because she doesn't love you and me. She does. She can't hide it and she sucks at lying anyway."

"Do you think she's still worried about the gay thing?"

"She sent me over here tonight. Not as an afterthought, not as a way to get rid of me, but because she knew I needed to be loved and touched and she wasn't up to it. I've seen her watch us together. There's no fear there. No anger or sadness. I think she's telling the truth when she says she's not feeling worried anymore."

"So maybe she's afraid to fail? Afraid we will? I don't think she gives a damn what anyone in town thinks about our relationship. I don't think she's worried about the backlash, though she is for us, but that's how she is."

"Sunday, after the wedding, we'll work it all out." Cal turned to face Gideon, kissing him. "For now, let's have a glass of wine and then you can suck my cock later."

Gideon slapped his ass as he stood up. "Deal."

21

The night before the wedding all the men stayed at Gillian's old house and the women stayed at the brand-new one. Gillian led them through the place, giving the first official tour since the very final touches had been applied.

The house was set up on a sloping hill from the water. Adrian had purchased a boat recently and it sat at their dock. The views were insanely beautiful and there was one from pretty much every single window in the house.

Gillian practically glowed with happiness. "Brody and Elise gave us the landscaping out back as a wedding gift."

"God, all I got you was a vibrator and some silver crap." Jules threw a look over her shoulder at Elise and raised a brow. "Some of us just like to show off."

Elise, Adrian's sister-in-law, who was also a former principal ballet dancer, burst out laughing. "Haters gonna hate, Jules."

It was beautiful work. The path down to the dock was bordered by butterfly bushes and a riot of flowers of all types. Halfway down there was a little deck carved out of the hillside with some tables and chairs.

The studio was in a separate building, across a breezeway from the main house. Adrian had been working there for a few months and had just finished recording his next record. They'd be leaving to go on tour right after they got back from the honeymoon. Erin, Ben, Todd and Alexander would go along, as well as Gillian and Miles. A Brown family rock-and-roll tour. Jules liked that a lot, even though she'd miss Gillian and Miles fiercely.

The master suite took up half of the second floor and Miles was on the first level. Gorgeous bedrooms and common spaces. The house was large and totally swank, but at the same time, it was comfortable. The furniture invited you to stay and visit. Gillian's touch was everywhere and kept it elegant but comfortable rather than impersonal and so spotless you couldn't sit down anywhere.

A home theater where they'd watch all the horror movies they wanted. A big playground area to the front of the house, fenced and away from the water so all the various little ones could come and play. And maybe when and if Adrian and Gillian decided to expand their own family too.

The kitchen was a dream. Jules wanted to marry the giant oven and Gillian had assured her she was welcome to come and bake things there anytime she wanted.

"You're getting married tomorrow." Jules took Gillian's hand as they looked out over the area they were setting up for the wedding. They'd do more the following day, but they'd put up the structure for the tent. Though it was already July, it was still the Northwest. Rain was a given all year long, and quite often near July Fourth, so they didn't want to take a chance. It'd be open on the sides though if the weather stayed nice so people could wander all around.

Jules avoided any mention of the security and how they'd had to set up artful flower and drape displays to block paparazzi. There was no way around that necessity, but she knew Gillian hated it and Jules just wanted everything to go off without a hitch.

"I really never thought I'd marry at all, much less someone like Adrian. I had Miles. I was content to wait until he was out of high school and then maybe date. And here I am, marrying his father. A rock star who buys me boats and builds me dream houses before he packs us up on tour with him."

"Not a sedate life, for sure." Jules winked.

"Says the woman with two boyfriends." Gillian winked back.

"Oh! I didn't even tell you. Wait, we need drinks and something to eat for this."

They got settled in the family room with a few trays of margaritas and the appetizers Mary brought with her. The room was full of awesome women, and Jules took a moment to admire them all.

Erin was there along with Raven. Elise, who was married to Adrian's brother Brody. Ella, who was married to Ben's brother and was Erin's sister-in-law and an old family friend. Ella drank juice instead of a margarita because she was expecting. Then all of Delicious. Daisy, looking adorable in some sort of retro sailor dress thing that anyone else would look ridiculous in but that Daisy made look stylish. Gillian of course and Mary, who clucked over the food.

"Don't worry everyone, these are totally different appetizers than the ones we'll be serving tomorrow."

Jules patted Mary's hand. "Good, because I was totally judging you for it in my head." She rolled her eyes. "None of us would have cared. We would have eaten just as many tomorrow, only we'd have advance notice of our favorites."

Gillian laughed. "Good point. Now, what happened?"

"Well, Mary knows because she was there, but Cal told his family and they're totally fine, thank goodness. But in the middle of dinner Gideon just up and starts talking about how we're all going to live in the farmhouse. Cal chimes in and they're planning and talking about all this stuff I have no idea about."

Mary snorted. "You should have seen her face. You know the one she gets where it's sort of placid on the outside but her mouth flattens out and she gets very stiff? Took them a few minutes to get it. Boys can be so clueless."

Gillian shook her head. "Is everything all right now?"

"Yes, it's fine. I told them why I was pissed. We made up. We've shelved the moving-in talk until after the wedding."

Gillian sniffed and then sipped her margarita. "Are you excited about it?"

"Yes. And scared. The usual. But it's not about me right now. I told my story. Let's talk wedding!"

Gillian frowned and waved a hand. "Ugh, let's not. It feels like it's all I've been talking about for months now. Let's talk about you."

Raven nodded. "Agreed. We know about Gillian and the man who should thank his lucky stars to have her. He loves her. She's moony for him. Blah, blah. We got that. We want to talk about you and your two dudes."

Jules rolled her eyes. "Nothing to tell really."

"Do you want to move in with them? Patrick is all right with all this?" Gillian asked.

"Patrick is beyond wonderful. He's supportive of Gideon. He's sweet to me and he loves Cal too. It's really beyond anything I ever expected. He deeded the farm over to Gideon, including the house. He wants us all there, he says. There's a whole mother-in-law apartment in the main house. He wants to live down there. Part of me thinks it would be good because we can keep an eye on him better. He's in good shape, but he's got some chronic health issues. He and Gideon can clash when Gideon gets too pushy with Patrick about taking care of himself. He's nicer to me."

"Because you spoil him with cherry turnovers." Daisy winked. "Damn, Mary, these little cheesy ham things are made of win. I would eat an entire tray of them. Hell, I may just do that right now. But look, we're all with pushy dudes. It seems to be a trend with us. Levi, good lord, he's so bossy. Which you know, works in the bedroom and stuff. But outside he likes to be in charge too. It's work but really, I can't imagine being with some guy who just sort of let stuff happen without worrying about it."

"And you have two of them. I imagine the sex is pretty fabulous though, to make up for the work of fending them off when they get to be too bossy," Ella spoke from where she sat. "And I also vote for eating an entire tray of those ham things."

Mary beamed.

Raven tucked her feet beneath herself. "Yes, let's talk about the sex. Erin should too."

"Raven, you clearly haven't gotten any of late. You've got a one-track mind." Erin sent her friend a look. Raven shrugged.

"Oh, are we supposed to pretend none of us thinks about it? 'Cause you know we do."

Jules laughed; she couldn't help it. In truth she was totally curious about Erin and her dudes before she had a threesome of her own. Leave it to Raven to just say it out loud.

"The sex is . . . well, I can't lie, it's fucking spectacular. They're both, um, really accomplished. And when they team up on me, it's unbelievable."

"I'd totally be smirking if I were you." Raven raised her glass in a salute.

"I am in my head. All the time pretty much. And the two of them together? At first I did worry. You know, what if Cal decided a woman wasn't what he needed and then you know, they left me. But after a while?" She shrugged. "It doesn't worry me any-more. They're grown men. They can make their own choices and they've chosen me as well as each other. And it's hot as hell to watch them have sex." She realized the way she sent Cal to Gideon earlier that week had been a sign that she really didn't worry over it any longer.

Erin laughed. "Yes, gurl, yes."

"But you're avoiding the moving-in stuff." Gillian of course missed nothing.

"Not avoiding. Precisely anyway. I like being with them. They're not helpless. I don't need to pick up after them or man-age their lives. Though Cal is a messy man, so I imagine he'll have to find a way to deal with that. I do pick up around his place when I'm there, but as a sort of absentminded thing as we're there. I don't want to do that full time."

Gillian gave Jules a look over her glass. "Really? Your key issue is Cal's beard hairs in the sink? Pull the other one, Jules. I know your game."

"Damn you, Gillian." She frowned and Gillian pretended not to notice and circled her finger in a go-on movement. "They're better at this stuff than I am. I've never lived with anyone before. They've both been in long-term relationships and I never have. They have a lot more experience than I do. Plus, well, you may not be aware, because I'm so ladylike and all, but I'm not always easy to be around. I want to be left the fuck alone when I have cramps and I want to eat ice cream instead. I don't want to have to apologize for my moods. And when you live with people, you have to take that into account. Or you'd be a dick, and I'm not a dick. Just sort of a bitch."

"Your bitchiness isn't a secret, sweetheart." Gillian patted her knee. "They know it's part of you, just like you know their moods too. Anyway, it's a whole different experience living with people you're involved with. Living with Miles was not really an adequate primer on what it's like to live with Adrian. I just think it's one of those things you can't prepare for. You just have to do. Of course they'll piss you off. That's what men do. And you have two of them. But I'm not worried about you. You're totally capable. If you want to do it."

"And I think you do," Mary added. "Look, I've seen Cal with people over the years. Some of them nice enough. He was good to them all, but he never really, I don't know, he never really let himself be with anyone. You know, just let it be natural. He's not putting on his company manners around you. Or Gideon. You're the real deal for Cal, and I think that's been true for a long time. He's totally spoiled. Look at him! But he doesn't really take that for granted with you the way he might have with the others. And he'll just have the cleaning lady come to the farmhouse. He's a slob, that's just how he is. I'm biased because he's my brother, but this is real, Jules, and you should do it."

"I agree with Mary." Daisy nodded.

Gillian tipped her chin toward Erin. "And you don't even have to do this blind. It's sort of awesome to have two triads in our group. Erin can be your ménage mentor."

Jules snickered. "We should get her a shirt with that on it. Anyway, she makes it look easy."

Erin guffawed. "It's not easy. But nothing worth doing ever is. I do know I've got more love in my life than I ever thought possible. I know those two love you. You can see it on their faces. I watch the way the three of you work together and that's the foundation for everything. But yes, Ben and Todd team up against me all the time. It's sort of hot, even when it's annoying."

"You're happy, Jules. Things are going well in your life. The business is doing great. You're in love. Let yourself be happy."

22

The morning of the wedding was clear and bright. Jules thanked the weather goddess and hoped it would continue to stay clear as she made her way over to Tart to handle all the cake details.

She'd finished it all the day before and all that needed to happen was to get the levels put together and delivered to the house.

"So I want this brought up to the reception tent. I've marked the table exactly how I want it."

Alison, Jules's assistant, nodded and heroically didn't roll her eyes at Jules's going over the same things repeatedly.

"You mean where you showed me yesterday?"

"Yes, okay, we all know I'm anal retentive. But this is my best friend's wedding. She deserves a totally perfect day."

"The cake is gorgeous. You know it tastes awesome. It'll be

fine." Alison had been in wedding catering for a few years before she came on at Tart. She knew her stuff.

"All right, all right. I get it. And it totally is a yummy cake. I'll check in with you once the ceremony is over."

"I've got the checklist. I'll talk with you then. Go on. You've been here two hours already and I know you want to get back to Gillian."

"First she needs to get back to me."

Jules turned to catch sight of Gideon standing in the doorway, looking all delicious and distracting.

"I totally do." She turned back to Alison. "You know where I am if you need me. Thank you so much for all your help!"

Alison hugged her. "Go!"

Jules took Gideon's hand and went out the back door with him. "Hi there."

He bent and kissed her. "Hey yourself. Cake looks beautiful, by the way."

"Thank you. I made the frosting this morning. Thank God it worked out. The caramel was being a little . . . Never mind, I can see your eyes glazing over. What brings you here? Is everything okay? Do they need anything at the house?'

"Nope. A lot of people aren't even up yet. But Brody is in charge at the house so everything is on track. Gillian seems very calm, which is her normal setting so that's good. They've got the tents up and the chairs are being set up now. Adrian made Gillian eat break-fast and I figured I needed to do the same. Cal is waiting for us."

"You're good to me."

"Course I am." He opened her door and she got in. She and Mary had driven in together and Mary had been going back and forth, making sure everything was exactly how it was supposed to be. She'd hired extra staff as well, but of course they wanted the day to be perfect for Gillian.

The breakfast place was one of Gideon's favorites. Big, hearty plates of food. They were open at five, which meant he could work for a while, come to town and get breakfast with her or Cal and still get back to his day.

Cal waited at a table already and she slid into the booth next to him.

"Coffee is on the way. I said to bring the whole pot."

She grinned and Gideon just looked at her a while. No makeup on, hair in a messy bun, she was still gorgeous.

She patted her hair. "I know. I'm getting dolled up later. Raven is doing everyone's makeup. She told me exactly when to show up. I'm better with concrete details."

Gideon rolled his eyes. "I was just thinking how beautiful you looked right now with no makeup and a messy knot in your hair. Also, we're aware of how much you like concrete details."

"Oh. Well. Thank you." She blushed and he liked that. He liked the way her face had totally lit when she'd turned to see him standing there in her doorway. Every time that happened he felt as if he were ten feet tall. No one made him feel so fearless and in charge as Jules did. Just by looking at him.

"How was the boys' night last night?"

The coffee arrived and she gave the server her order as she poured coffee for each of them.

"I drank too much." Cal sipped his coffee. "Miles and Alexander were there so of course it was mellow until they went to bed. And then we somehow got involved in an epic quarters game and there were shots. I don't think I've had this much to drink since I was in law school."

She kissed his temple. "Sorry. Were there strippers?"

Gideon snorted. "No. That would have interrupted the quarters game. Really, there was drinking and laughing. Smoking cigars. Sharing stories. Nothing wild about any of it."

Cal popped some pain reliever. "I think we're all getting too old for it. Though we did talk about all our pretty ladies."

"Well, that's good. We talked about you guys too." The way she blushed made Gideon wonder just what it was they said.

"I've only woken up next to you twice this last week. This is not a trend I like." Gideon frowned as he salted the hash browns on the plate of food that had just been delivered.

Jules slathered jam on her toast. "It seems like so much in my life has been focused on this wedding and now it's finally here. Gillian is so happy. God, it thrills me to see her this way. She and Adrian are so opposite on the outside and yet they're perfect for each other. And Miles is such a great kid, I'm happy for him too."

Cal grabbed the hot sauce for his eggs. "It's hard to share him. I remember at first, when I met Adrian, I was like, dude, back off, that's our Miles! Can't deny the kid is thriving through."

Gideon knew Jules was a little hurt that Miles was staying with Erin while Adrian and Gillian were on their honeymoon. Oh sure, she understood Miles was Erin's nephew and he loved his aunt. But she'd been his aunt longer. She'd never say any of it out loud though.

"Do you want kids?" He hadn't meant to ask it out loud. Not yet anyway.

Her head came up. "That's a random question."

"Not really." Just because he hadn't meant to ask didn't mean he wasn't interested in her answer.

She held his gaze several moments before answering. "Yes. I do."

"Okay, good. Cal?"

"What's not to like? I don't have to do anything but have lots of sex. She does all the grunt work like gestating and breast-feeding."

Her brows rose slowly. "I'd most assuredly expect you two to change diapers."

Gideon smiled, imagining her pregnant with their baby. Oh yes, he knew it would be complicated. He'd actually had a discussion the night before with Ben about it.

Ben was a good guy and they'd struck up a friendship. It was a bonus having Ben as a sort of resource for what they were all doing. So they'd been drinking beer out on the back deck of the house and he'd just asked.

"Can I ask you something? About your relationship I mean."

Ben leaned back and nodded. "Yeah, of course."

"I know it's doable to have the three of us living together. The farmhouse has plenty of room. We love each other and have a supportive group around us. But . . . well, I'd like to have kids. How do you work it out?"

"Well, I think you know the nuts and bolts of how we made Alexander work out." Ben laughed. "But we talked a lot about it before we made the decision to go forward. We decided not to put any emphasis on which of us was the biological father. I mean should anything happen health-wise and we need to know, we can find out easily enough. But for us, it was important that Alexander be our baby."

"Fair enough. It makes sense."

"It's easy now. He's not old enough to be around kids outside the family. No one is going to make fun of him. We don't have to explain much to him. Later on it'll be something we have to work on as we go. The path we're on." He tipped his beer at Gideon. "The path you're on too, it's complicated. Most of the time no one gives a shit that you have a man and a woman in your life. This is a group of artists and funky people. What we both have isn't usual, but we're surrounded by people who only care that we're good to each other. But sometimes out there in the world you'll go on your way and suddenly get slapped in the face with it. Someone will take issue with you holding hands with both of them. We've gotten grief for sitting together at the movies and me having both my arms on the backs of Todd's and Erin's seats."

"And sometimes it's your family who disappoint you most." Gideon thought of Jules's brother.

Ben snorted. "Tell me about it. My father doesn't speak to me. He's never even held Alexander. Some of Todd's siblings don't speak to him. What you have freaks some people out and it makes them react horribly. I don't know that I'll ever have a relationship with my father again and we were close before."

"I'm sorry, man. That's fucked up. What grandparent doesn't want to be around their grandchildren? I don't understand it. It's none of anyone else's business. If they don't want to be in a triad, they don't have to. Why does what we do matter if they're not involved?"

"I've made a lot of mistakes in my life. I'm old enough to have broken a few hearts by being careless. But being a father is the best thing I've ever done. Sharing this amazing experience with the two people I love most is, well, I've never had a moment

of regret. That's my boy. I get to watch him grow up. I can't imagine ever walking away from him. But my father did. And Jules's brother did. Sometimes love can't overcome fear. But it's not that way in my house."

Gideon's stomach clenched a little. He wanted that too. Had wanted it with Alana, but it was a good thing they never did. But Jules was a whole different story.

Jules and Cal were a whole different story.

First things first. They needed to settle in and work on their relationship for a while. He knew she was busy with her business just then and he was building the farm up to enter a new era. There was time.

23

·························

Jules stepped back to look Gillian up and down. "You're gorgeous. Oh my god." The emotion swept through her and she found herself fighting tears.

Gillian's eyes widened. "Don't you cry! I can't take it if you do. I'll cry too and my makeup will smudge."

"Don't ruin my work!" Raven called out as she put the finishing touches on Erin's face.

Gillian's dress was a gift from all her friends. Much like its wearer, it was classically beautiful. Elegant. Spaghetti straps with a lovely bit of beading on the bodice. The material seemed to float around her as she moved. A chapel-length train so nothing too hard to manage. And in a nod to her place in life, instead of white, she went with a pale green instead.

Her long, dark hair had been pinned up with roses tucked at the back. Instead of a bouquet, she'd opted for a single rose.

"I look all right then?"

Jules nodded. "Gillian, I've never seen you more beautiful. Adrian's socks will be knocked off."

Gillian smiled. "This dress makes me feel like a fairy princess."

"You totally are."

The day that'd started off perfect had continued that way. Jules really couldn't have asked for a better one for Gillian. There was a breeze and the sun had been out all day so it was still plenty warm without being too hot. The water glittered off in the distance. Music drifted up the stairs from the front lawn where the ceremony would be held.

Jules took a deep breath. "Are you ready? I'll go tell everyone if you are."

"Oh my god, what if I'm the most horrible wife ever? All these women who throw themselves at him. They're all so young and pretty."

Jules cocked her head and grabbed the panic attack by the throat and tossed it away in the only way she knew Gillian would respond to. "Sucks to be an old hag like you. Buck up, sister, it's time to get your wedding on. I'll be right back." She kissed her cheek and headed out to let them know Gillian was ready.

Cal stood leaning near the doors leading outside and perked up when he caught sight of her. "Looking mighty fine there, Miz Lamprey."

And she did. Her dress was deep green and it played against her hair and skin perfectly. It showcased a body he knew intimately. Her makeup was glamorous, with smoky eyelids and lush lips.

"Flattery will get you all sorts of places." She smoothed down the front of his suit. "Cripes, you're handsome."

"I like it when you pet me like this. We should play wayward rogue and stern governess later."

She laughed and he stole a quick kiss.

"You're very good at that. You didn't even smudge my lipstick. Gillian is all ready. Can you find Brody and let him know?"

He pushed to stand straight. "You got it."

"I'm off to find Miles. I'll see you in a bit." She paused. "I love you, Calvin."

Touched, he had to force himself not to haul her close for a real kiss but he resisted, not wanting to muck up her lips. Later he'd muck up more than her mouth with great enthusiasm.

"I love you too."

He heard her call Miles's name and his answer as Cal headed off to find Brody.

As Brody Brown, Adrian's brother, was so tall and broad shouldered, it was easy enough to locate him in a crowd.

"Jules just came down to let me know it's a go. She's got Miles too." Miles was walking his mother down the aisle.

Brody grinned. "Bet those ladies are looking fine."

Cal nodded. "I only saw Jules, but if they're wearing dresses like hers, it's going to be a nice evening."

Brody laughed. "Give me a few minutes. I've got to collect Adrian and get everyone on their marks."

Cal nodded and got himself seated. The wedding was small, which he knew Gillian wanted. There couldn't have been more than fifty people there, which meant he knew most everyone.

There was that dude who'd been at the engagement party. The one who'd been staring at his sister, most likely imagining her naked. Which Cal did not approve of. He gave the guy another look to underline that.

Instead the guy smiled and made his way over. "I'm Damien. You're with Gillian's friend Jules, right?"

Cal shook the guy's hand, not wanting to be rude to one of Adrian's friends. "Cal Whaley. And yes, Jules is with me." He looked around and caught sight of Gideon, waving him over. "Him too."

Damien turned and then looked back to Cal with one brow raised. "You too, huh? I knew about Erin. Well, more power to you. Oh and you're Mary's brother, aren't you?"

Gideon came to sit on Cal's other side and Cal had to admit he liked the way Gideon got close enough to make it clear he was taken.

"I'm Damien." He held a hand out and Gideon took it.

"Gideon."

The music came up and everyone got to their seats. Cal remained half turned in his seat, not wanting to miss any entrances.

A full string ensemble played the wedding party in. They were all musicians Gillian knew. Rennie, Adrian's niece, tossed flower petals as she walked down the aisle first. Alexander followed behind, picking the petals up and shoving them in a pocket. He had a ring pillow he clutched to his body tight as he motored his way toward the front where Adrian had knelt to get his attention. He ran full tilt the last few feet and jumped into his uncle's arms. Adrian kissed his cheeks and set him down. Rennie then kissed her uncle and took Alexander's hand as they moved into place.

Because of the size of their group of friends, all the brides-maids came out first. Cal surely did note that Damien seemed very interested in his sister when she walked past.

And then the groomsmen looking very dapper in their tuxedos. At last Brody came out with Jules.

"Damn, our woman is fine," Gideon said in his ear.

Cal agreed.

Miles walked his mother down the aisle and Cal could remember back to the days when the kid was only just walking and talking. He was growing into a good man and it was pretty much all down to what an amazing mother he had. Though Adrian had jumped right in when he'd learned of Miles's existence.

Adrian hugged his son, taking his face in his hands. "Love you, kid. Thanks for giving your mum away."

"Love you too, Dad. Don't break her."

Gillian hugged her son, who then went to stand next to Brody.

The ceremony was short, with vows the couple had written themselves. Cal caught sight of Jules dabbing her eyes discreetly a few times.

The minister held her hands up. "I'd like to introduce you all to Gillian and Adrian Brown."

A cheer went up as Gillian and Adrian faced the crowd, holding hands, grinning like lovesick fools.

Damn, Cal wanted forever with Jules so much it made him ache with it. She locked her gaze with him, a smile on her mouth. She wanted it too, he could see it in her face.

Adrian indicated everyone settle down so they did. "Right around the corner here we've got some cocktails and food waiting. Please help yourselves. Thank you all for coming!"

He led his new wife down the aisle as everyone followed.

"I'm going to go check on Jules. I saw her head to the left so I know she's going to check on the cake," Gideon said.

"Good idea. I'll save you and her a seat inside."

Gideon kissed him quickly. "Thank you, baby."

Miles rocketed over to him, a big grin on his face. "Cal!"

Cal couldn't help but grin right back. "Miles! Do you feel any different?"

"Nah, not really. I like this house though. Did you see it all?"

"Your mum gave me a tour a few days ago. You've got an awesome room."

"And a boat."

"Can't forget the boat." They walked toward the reception tent.

"I know Jules won't go out on it. I did tell Mum to be sure she had enough life jackets just in case Jules came along. I'd wear one too, you know, to make her feel better."

"Don't tell her that story today or she'll get tears and stuff all over you."

"Oh, good idea. Mum cried on me already. Did you know Damien Hurley was here? He's one of Dad's friends from the old days back in Hollywood. He did all the drum work in the studio for Dad's new CD."

If Adrian had the guy around his kid, chances were he wasn't a total deviant drug addict or anything.

Still, Cal watched as the guy sidled up to his sister and began to talk to her. Mary's face lit as she laughed at whatever he'd said.

But then he saw Jules. Watched Gideon take her hands to his mouth and kiss them. She wore a bemused, sweet expression as he did it.

"Let's go get some grub on, Miles." He squeezed Miles's shoulder and they picked up the pace.

• • •

The entire day had simply evaporated as she moved through it. Jules had loved every moment of it, from Gillian's gorgeous dress to the informal reception where everyone from schoolteachers to rock stars mixed and mingled, drinking champagne and eating too much.

The cake had been a huge hit and she'd actually given out more than a few business cards to people who wanted her to bake for holiday events and parties. It hadn't been something she'd really thought about, but she'd run some numbers that next week to see if it was viable.

The DJ had been great, but he'd gotten off stage and a whole bunch of activity took place as the stage was set for a band. Gillian didn't know about the song yet so Jules couldn't wait to see her reaction.

Adrian tapped the mic a few times. "Hey, everyone, if I could have your attention."

Cal and Gideon approached, bracketing her on either side and she snuggled back, putting an arm around each man's waist as they watched.

"Gillian and I are really thrilled we could share this day with you. Each and every one of you is important to us. Some people though, well, they get a special nod. Brody, my big brother who raised me. Thank you for all the advice. You've been there for me more times than I can count. I only hope I can be half the father you are. My sister Erin, who taught me my first guitar chords way back when. Thank you for driving over here to see Gillian that first day and thank you for coming to my house to tell me I had a son. My son Miles, who teaches me just how old and slow I am, thanks for being patient with all my mistakes. I love you more than I ever imagined was possible. Even if you are a bass player."

There was laughter as Adrian teased his son and sister at the same time.

He turned to Gillian, who said, "No, don't. You'll make me cry."

"You're supposed to, English. *My English*. Man, when I think about how I nearly messed it all up and sent you screaming the other way." He shook his head. "You are my everything. My partner in life and the other half of my heart. I love you. Thank you for loving me back and giving me a safe place to be. I have something for you. A little ditty I've been working on for a while. It'll be on the new CD; no one's heard it yet but those of us who were in the studio."

Erin got up onstage, along with Miles and Damien Hurley, and the song started. It was slow, with a wending, winding bass line. Erin, even in formal wear, rocked it, her head going forward and a spill of hair covered part of her face. Adrian held the mic in one hand, clearly used to being on stage, but he never took his eyes from Gillian as he sang to her about finding love you never knew you needed. About being whole and happy. About her and the love she brought to him.

By the time the song had finished, Jules simply handed Gillian a handkerchief.

"Wait, Mum. Uncle Brody's been helping me with something." Miles spoke up. "Hi, um, I'm Miles . . . um, Brown now, yeah. Adrian and Gillian are my parents. Mum is pretty awesome. She never gets mad when I bring home stray animals. She always helps me when I need it. She loves scary movies and lets me stay up late on Friday nights so we can all watch them together. She's the best mum ever. And because of that, she found Dad and took a chance by telling him about me. My song isn't as awesome as Dad's but it's my present to you both."

Jules pressed her fingers over her lips, trying hard not to lose it. Such a sweet boy. Gillian had given up, tears steaming down her face as she dabbed them away. Brody came to stand with her, whispering something in her ear, making her laugh.

Miles's song was sweet and simple. She knew he'd been practicing it like crazy over the last month. It didn't matter, it could have been the worst thing ever and they'd have loved it. But it was wonderful and easy to see where he came from. Music came down from both sides of his family.

When it was over there wasn't a dry eye in the house.

"You're a lucky mum." Jules hugged Gillian tight. "And a lucky wife."

Gillian turned to face Jules better. "And a lucky friend. I know you've put a lot of your life into all this planning."

"You're important to me. Of course I did. And it was worth it to watch you today. You deserved a special day."

Jules stood back and noted Mary ducking into the house with Damien Hurley, but said nothing about it. She'd hunt her friend down later and demand details.

"I have a little something for you." Gillian waved Adrian over.

He came to Gillian's side quickly, kissing her soundly.

"Thank you for that. I've never had anyone write songs for me before you came along. I quite like it."

"Good to know." Adrian looked at Gillian like there was no one else on the planet and it made Jules look back over her shoulder to Gideon and Cal, who stood with Brody, laughing about something or other.

Gillian's blush was visible even in the twilight of the reception. "I'm going to give Jules her present now."

"Ah, good. Hang on." He ducked around the stage and was back holding a pretty wrapped box, which he gave to Gillian, who handed it to Jules.

Jules took it with a smile, carefully peeled the paper away and then gasped when she saw the earrings tucked inside. "This is too much."

"No, it isn't. I'm capable of saving money, you know. And as I didn't have to buy a wedding dress, a house or much else of late." Gillian sent Adrian a look. "I had a few extra pennies. You're always there for me, Jules. You don't know what that's meant to me and to Miles."

The earrings were delicate flowers. Nothing big or showy. That wasn't Jules's style. It was totally clear Gillian had chosen them carefully and totally with Jules in mind. "These are gorgeous."

"They're forget-me-nots. Like you never forget me. Or Miles."

The tears were back as she ran a finger over the pale purple stones making the petals. They dangled just a tiny bit. Enough to really catch the light but not so much they'd get caught in her hair or make her nervous wearing them out and about.

"You're making me cry."

"Good, you've all done nothing but make me cry for months now. I'm glad to share the happy tears. You're happy, Jules. That's the best present you could ever give me. Be brave and let yourself accept the love right in front of you."

She nodded, hugging Gillian again as they both cried.

24

············

She looked so pretty there, asleep in the passenger seat, that Gideon hesitated before picking her up and taking her into the house. Cal ran ahead and unlocked the door.

She woke up then with a start, relaxing when she saw where she was. He put her down.

"Wow, I totally conked out."

Gideon bent to take first one shoe off and then the other, setting them side by side near the door.

The smile on her face shocked through him. Damn, he loved this woman.

"I liked that. Thank you."

"I like taking care of you." It was the total truth.

Cal came back inside with his arms full of stuff and she

laughed when she saw it all. "We don't have to leave the house at all tomorrow. Or I guess today." She looked to the clock. "Plenty of food. Cake. Even champagne. We should have champagne and cake for breakfast."

"Works for me." Cal put things in his fridge.

She unzipped the side of her dress and took it off before she meandered upstairs, both men watching. "I'm going to take a shower so if you want to see me with all this fancy makeup and hair you'd best do it now."

Cal looked back to Gideon and headed up after her. Gideon made sure the door was locked and followed.

He stood in the doorway and watched Cal push her against the bathroom counter and then fell to his knees, pressing his face against her pussy through her panties.

Her lids slid down halfway. "My, you're both awfully accommodating this evening. I've neglected you both terribly this week, I know."

Cal yanked her panties down and she stepped from them. "You have. And after I lick you and make you scream a little, you can make it up to me and Gideon."

"No need to ask twice."

Cal knelt there, with her legs spread, holding her pussy wide so he could kiss and lick her all over. She watched him, her fingers sliding through hair Gideon knew was soft and thick. Gideon knew the feel of that hair, knew the taste of her body, knew the taste of Cal's body as well.

As if she felt the weight of his gaze, she shifted to look in Gideon's direction, the connection there clicked into place. "Why . . . oooh." Her head fell back a moment before she looked to Gideon again, swallowing hard. "Why are you all the way over there? Only want to watch this pretty man lick me? Hmm?"

Cal hummed against her and she shivered. Gideon got closer. Close enough to see the gooseflesh on her arms.

"Do you like what he's doing to you?" Gideon flipped the strap of her bra down and slid the cup back to expose her breast.

"Mmm, yes. He's very good with his mouth."

Gideon stole a kiss, his fingers joining hers in Cal's hair.

From his angle, he looked down much as she did to watch Cal eat her pussy. She whimpered when he sucked her clit into his mouth over and over.

"He is." Gideon pinched the exposed nipple, not wanting this moment to end. Just Jules, Gideon and Cal. Nothing but skin and sex and ease between them. It felt good to be back together this way.

She started to answer but ended up on a strangled gasp, her eyes blurring as she came, one hand in Cal's hair, the other on Gideon's shoulder, trying to remain standing.

Cal sent her a coy look as he kissed her thigh and then stood.

"I missed this this week. I'm sorry I've been so busy with the wedding and all. I know I've neglected you both."

Gideon took her lips slowly and then backed away. "We missed you too. We've decided you can't be away from us for a whole week anymore. We don't like it."

Before she could say anything else, Cal moved in close for a kiss. She wrapped a leg around him to hold in him place as he meandered his way over her mouth and down her neck.

Gideon's mouth watered to taste her again.

"Now then. Shower and then lots of fucking," Cal said.

"Or"—she put her bra on the counter and turned the water on—"we could fuck in the shower. Whichever."

She stepped in after undoing all the shiny bits from her hair and groaned as the hot water hit her skin. Gideon shucked his clothes as quickly as he could and jumped in with her, followed closely by Cal.

Gideon didn't want to wait anymore. He spun her around. "Hands on the wall. Spread your feet apart."

She obeyed, getting on tiptoe as he bent his knees to get to the right height to slide his cock into her pussy.

She was so wet Gideon shivered at how good it felt. They'd decided two weeks before to stop using condoms after they'd all been tested. He had to admit this was a hundred million times better. The wet, hot embrace of her cunt, skin to skin, the slick of her honey against his cock and balls drove him close to the edge before he'd even gotten four or five strokes in.

Cal slid his soap-slicked hands over Gideon and then Jules. She turned her head and he kissed her, swallowing her cries.

Gideon banded her waist with his forearm and dug in deep, fucking her hard and fast, needing her after not having her for a week. Needing to be inside her after such an emotionally exhausting day.

He'd had a wedding already, but he wanted to belong to Jules the way Gillian and Adrian belonged to each other. He wanted to belong to Cal like Ben and Todd belonged to each other.

Orgasm hit him when she thrust back with a little twist of her hips. It sucked him under as he came so hard it stole his breath. For long moments after, he remained wrapped around her, gasping in air as his pounding heart slowed to normal.

"Christ, I needed that."

She turned in his arms and kissed him. "Me too."

Cal washed her hair as she soaped his cock. Gideon loved the two of them together. Cal unabashedly demanding to be touched and stroked. Jules responding, giving him everything.

"Not too much." Cal put his hands over hers. "It's been a week for me too. I want more than a hand job from you."

Jules laughed as she stepped back to rinse off one last time and get out. "Well, not a week. After all you and Gideon got down a few days ago at the very least."

Cal grinned and then looked to Gideon. "And that was hot. Not even going to lie about that. But as gorgeous and talented as our Gideon is, I need *you*."

"I'm all yours, Calvin."

"I know." He got out and stalked to her, picking her up and placing her on the edge of his counter. "This is the perfect height. And all these mirrors will please Gideon."

Gideon dried off as Cal teased her pussy with the head of his cock.

Cal tapped the head of his cock against her clit and she moaned. "Yes."

"Yes?" He tapped it a little harder and her moan went up an octave.

"Yes!"

"Just making sure. You're so wet and ready for me."

She nodded. "Now. Now. Now." She pulled him close and wrapped her legs around his waist as he laughed.

Cal slid into that slick heat and paused to really appreciate how damned good it was. Her skin warm and fragrant from her shower gel. Her cunt was swollen and wet all around his cock.

His woman.

"Too long."

He began to thrust, delighting in the way her tits bounced. She bent a little to put her arms behind herself, bracing against his movements.

"Mmm. You two have each other when I'm not around, you know."

"We do. And we did, believe me." Cal sent Gideon a smile that had the other man laughing in that knowing way. "But I need Jules in my life. Every day. I need to wake up with Jules snuggled down between me and Gideon." He thrust three times. "And I need to bury my cock in your cunt."

"Yes," Gideon added.

"I missed you too."

He picked up his pace and she walked her fingers down her belly. She was spread open, his body holding her thighs apart so he could easily see it when her middle finger brushed her clit. He certainly felt the squeeze around his cock.

"You're a dirty, dirty girl."

"I'm a stern governess, remember?"

He swore at the images in his head. They really did have to look into a little bit of role-play because now he really needed to be reprimanded and pay his penance with his mouth.

"Yes. Play with your clit, Jules. I want you to come again."

One arm behind herself, the other hand on her cunt, playing with her clit and Cal didn't know what the hell to look at first. So much to see. She was a visual buffet.

"N-now?" Her pussy spasmed around his cock and he knew she was right on the edge.

"Oh yes. Right now."

She sucked in a breath and began to come around him,

squeezing him so hard there was absolutely no way he could last another moment.

"Give it to me; we have time for more. Always more," she whispered.

And he came with one last thrust, growling her name.

Jules snuggled down into the bed, her eyes heavy. It had been a long day. A long week. The wedding had been a wonderful event, the sex had been amazing and now she needed to sleep.

Gideon got in on one side and Cal the other. "We should talk about the farmhouse now."

She pulled the blanket over her head. "I've been up nearly twenty-four hours. I've been eaten and fucked boneless. I need sleep. We can talk when we wake up."

Gideon kissed her temple and put an arm around her. "We can, indeed. I love you, Juliet."

"Mmm, love you too. Both of you."

Arms surrounded her as the heat of their bodies lulled her deeper into rest. Safe and loved.

And that's all she remembered until her ringing phone woke her up not even three hours later. She scrambled from bed and took it out into the hall before it woke them up.

The area code was 949. Her father lived there so she answered quickly.

"Hello?"

"Juliet? It's Donna. Donna Lamprey."

Everything in her went cold. Donna was her father's wife and she sounded freaked out.

"What's wrong?" She headed downstairs, grabbing a shirt Cal had tossed to the side.

"It's your father. He's had a stroke. He's in surgery right now. Can you come?"

There was no other answer. "I'm on my way. I'll get the first flight I can. I'll keep my phone on when I'm not in the air."

"Thank you." Donna told her the location of the hospital and Jules hung up, shoving her things in a bag and scrawling a note to them both. They'd been up as long as she had and she wanted them to rest. They couldn't help anyway. Not with this.

Gideon woke up and realized Jules's spot was empty and cold. She'd probably woken early and, not wanting to wake them, had gotten up. He pulled a pair of pants on and headed out. She wasn't in Cal's office or watching television, nor was there any detectible scent of coffee, which began to worry him. When Jules was around, there was always evidence of coffee.

He went downstairs and saw the note on the fridge right away. *Didn't want to wake you. Dad is in hospital. I'm on my way down. Will call to update you on location and his condition. Love you both. J*

He called her cell but it was off and went straight to voice mail. He had no idea when she'd even left. Whether it was an hour ago or four. He saw she'd left a voice mail on his phone, pretty much repeating what her note had said. Her voice was flat and emotionless. Brisk as she went over the details. She'd made a reservation at a hotel near the hospital and would call when she got settled. The last call had been three hours before. She must be on a plane right then.

He couldn't believe they'd slept through all that. Damn it.

He couldn't believe she hadn't woken them up either.

"Shit." He headed back upstairs to wake Cal.

Cal shot straight up when Gideon shook him gently. He smiled when he saw Gideon but then sobered at his expression. "What? Jules?" He patted the bed. "What's wrong?"

Gideon told him.

"I can't believe she fucking left without even waking us up. What kind of trust is that?"

Gideon shook his head. "No, I don't think it was a lack of trust. Check your voice mail."

Cal frowned but did it and then sighed as he hung up. "She's on autopilot."

"Sounds like it, yes. I don't like that she didn't wake us either. And if she'd been a little more together she would have, you know it. But you know how she is. She went into planning mode and so she just made it all happen while she thought about four thousand other things, all with the purpose of getting down there to a man who barely speaks to her. Hell, she probably also left us sleeping because she was worried we hadn't gotten enough rest."

That was most likely true as well. "If they treat her badly, I'm gonna burn shit down." Cal pulled his pants on.

Gideon nodded. "Get in line. Look, I've got to arrange for coverage at the farm. I'll go to her once that's done."

"I have two hearings tomorrow. I can't postpone at this point. I'll come right after that though."

"All right." Gideon kissed Cal hard. He knew Cal would be feeling guilty over having to work and he wanted to address that. Knew Jules would have too. "Do what you need to. She understands that. I understand that. I'll go first and you'll follow. We'll go to her. Be there when she needs us because that's what you do for people you love. She's going to need the support especially if Ethan is there."

"That fucker better keep his mouth shut or I'll punch it shut."

A flush of desire swept through him. Cal was normally so mellow that when he'd gotten vicious in her defense it touched Gideon. Oh and it made him hot too. "I like it when you get sort of violent. Makes me want to fuck you."

Cal grinned. "No teasing. Go on. I'll handle stuff on this end. Come back when you're done and I'll take you to the airport."

Gideon headed back home. His granddad was sympathetic, reminding him he'd run the damned farm before Gideon had decided to move back to Washington and he'd be just fine. He spoke with the foreman as well before packing a small bag and heading back to Cal's.

"Hey, take care of our girl. Give her love for me. I'll be down tomorrow night. I've already booked a flight."

Gideon leaned across the seat and kissed Cal. Savoring his taste. "Didn't even get any this morning. It's a crime."

"I'll miss you too. Call me when you get there and give Jules my love."

Gideon headed off to her.

He hated that she was alone facing her family. He hated that she hadn't woken them up, though he did understand it. He'd seen her like this back with the situation with her brother. She'd turned off her pain and had sunk into just getting through. But he wanted to be first in her mind when she had a problem. He wanted her to turn to him and Cal as an instinct.

He knew she was scared. He knew she'd been left behind and disappointed by a lot of people she should have been able to trust. But he wasn't any of those people. He'd do anything for her and it was high time they moved to the next step. She needed him and unlike those others, he was coming to her.

Jules was able to do a half-assed job on her makeup in the bathroom at Sea-Tac so when she arrived at John Wayne she was ready to hit the rental car counter and get on her way to Mission Viejo where her father's in-laws—did that make them her step-grandparents?—Donna's parents, both younger than her father, had built them a home just a mile from their place. Jules had been there once and though they had seven bedrooms, she'd stayed in a hotel.

Ugh. Not the time to think about that. Donna had called and asked for help. Jules would give it to her because it was her father after all. She wanted to hope things could get better. Coming down here and helping, hell, being *asked* to help could be something that would bring them all closer together.

She hooked her phone into the car's sound system and checked her voice mail.

Messages from Gideon and Cal wanting to know how she was. Messages from Mary, Erin and Daisy as well.

And one last one from Gideon.

"Juliet Lamprey, I'm on my way. My plane should arrive shortly after yours. I'm coming for you and you won't be alone. *Remember that.* Cal is coming tomorrow night. I love you."

Tears burst forth as she wiped her eyes with the back of her hand. Her chest hurt. She needed them so much and they were coming for her. The ice in her belly thawed a little. She wasn't going to be alone.

Truth was, she hadn't allowed herself to really think about it. She'd just gone into that place where she could bury all her emotions in planning and taking care of the details. But now she could admit to herself she'd needed to hear they were with her.

Once she'd gotten herself back under control, Jules called Cal, who answered right away.

"Hey, gorgeous, what's the status?"

"I'm just about at the hospital now. I don't know anything more than what I did before I left. I'm guessing Donna's phone is off because she's in the hospital."

"You should have woken us, Jules." His voice was gentle, but she heard the hurt there and it cut her deep.

"I'm sorry. I really am. I just went into planning mode. I had so much to do and I know you had work this week and Gideon has Patrick to keep an eye on. I just wanted to be doing something and I didn't want to wake you."

"Wake me? Do you think I'd prefer to be well rested or to fucking help when you get scary news? Don't be a pretty dumbass."

She sniffed back her tears and kept her eyes on the road. "I know it was wrong."

"Good. I accept your apology. I'll see you tomorrow night. I wish it could be earlier but I can't get out of this appearance."

"I understand. I really do. I promise. I just . . . thank you. I need you." She swallowed her emotion back.

"Thank the gods you finally fucking admit it."

She smiled. God, she loved Calvin Whaley. "You're full of bad words today. Are you hungover?"

"Smartass."

"I have to go. The exit is coming up. I'll talk with you soon. Calvin? I love you."

"I love you too. Take care of yourself. And Jules . . . don't let any of that bullshit get to you. Okay? You don't have to take any abuse. No one gets to hurt you or they'll have to deal with me."

"You're going to make me cry."

"All right. Remember what I said."

"I'll try," she said and hung up.

She managed to find the right building and lot. Once parked, she smoothed her hair back and touched up her makeup. And while she did that, she pulled herself together.

Donna was sitting in a waiting room near ICU when Jules came around the corner. "Donna?"

Her dad's wife sat up at the sound of her name. Jules recognized Donna's father, who was at her side, and she nodded to him.

They didn't hug. They didn't even really know one another. She was younger than Jules and had fucked Jules's father behind her mother's back. They weren't friends, but they both cared about her father and that was enough. "Any news?"

Donna didn't seem overly excited to see her, but Jules chalked it up to having her husband in intensive care. "He's in recovery. He had another stroke right before they got him into surgery. There's damage but they don't know how much yet. They're waiting for him to regain consciousness to do some more testing."

"All right. So tell me, what else?" She pulled out a notebook, needing to plan, needing to list and bullet point so she didn't have to think about the fact that even though the man recovering just a few doors down had walked out on her, he was still her father.

Donna's father took over the telling. Her dad had been complaining of a stomachache for a few days. He'd been at his in-laws, swimming with her brothers at their pool when he'd stood and then collapsed.

He'd had a small stroke six months before but they hadn't connected it to the stomachache.

"He had a stroke six months ago?" Jules had spoken to him once during that time and he'd never bothered to mention that. She shoved it away with the years of other such events.

"Yes. After the blood pressure problems we changed his diet and he went on medication. You know. He lost the weight and his blood pressure had come way down."

She sat there listening to this woman talk about her father and their life. His health problems he'd never shared with her, though she always did ask. She wasn't sure if he didn't feel like she cared or if it was he who didn't care.

"Can you call your brother to fill him in? I need to go call my mom. She's got the boys at home. We didn't want to upset them."

Jules was numb as she nodded and headed out to where she could use her phone.

She really, really didn't want to call Ethan, but he needed to know and what could she tell Donna anyway? Hopefully they could be adults and get past this silliness for their dad's sake.

Jules steeled herself and dialed her brother's number. It

was Marci who answered. "Jules, I'm sorry. Maybe in a few months . . ."

"I'm not calling about that. I'm here at the hospital so if you'd like an update you'll continue to listen." Even to her own ears, Jules sounded like a stranger. She'd always really liked Marci, but all she felt was numb that this situation with her brother was even happening.

It was stupid and a waste of time and really, none of Ethan's goddamned business. And then the numb began to heat into anger.

"Oh! Of course. How is he?"

Jules filled Marci in briefly and succinctly. She missed the boys. Wanted to ask about them. Wanted to hear them shouting her name in the background.

"Donna may be calling with more information, or it might be me. It's going to depend on whoever can do it. Unless Ethan wants me to let her know why he can't bear the thought of me calling his home to hear about his father, who is in ICU."

"It is stupid. I'm sorry. If it were up to me . . . but it's not. Give him time."

"No, I think I'm done doing that. I've been there for Ethan whenever he needed me. I had an active and loving relationship with your children. Those boys love me. I'm good for them. My brother had me as a guest in his home and he called me a whore and kicked me out at eleven at night after I'd driven three hours and three dozen cupcakes and a dinosaur cake down for his son. Because I'm there for those boys just like I have been for him. I've had it, Marci. I'm tired of being crapped on and taken for granted. It breaks my heart that I won't be able to watch your sons grow up. I love them very much. But I don't plan to take any more shit from anyone. I'm turning over a new leaf. Have a good day." She hung up and took a deep breath.

It wasn't that she'd never told anyone off before. But never her family. And it wasn't Marci's fault, she knew.

She wondered if she should call back to apologize but then decided not to. She was done with that.

25
·······················

The knot of tension in Gideon's stomach finally loosened when he pulled his rental into the hospital parking lot. Jules had left him a voice mail and had sounded so fragile it had taken all his control to not race to get there.

He found her by herself in a corner of the ICU waiting area. She'd been sitting sideways, her sweater balled up so she could rest her head on it. And she looked lost.

"Jules."

She looked up and when she saw it was him her bottom lip quavered and she got up, nearly tripping over her things to get to him. He hugged her tight, swallowing past the well of emotion at the way she'd greeted him.

"I'm here, baby. I'm here." He stroked a hand over her hair until she relaxed and stepped back to look up at him.

"He's conscious. Donna went in to see him a bit ago."

He guided her back to where she'd been sitting and joined her. "Now you can rest your head on my shoulder instead of the wall."

"That's the best offer I've had. Ever. Thank you. Thank you for coming."

"Are you all right? Is he going to be okay?" She worried him. He wasn't used to seeing her this way. She was normally spunky and vivacious. This Jules made him want to pull her into his lap and pet her.

"They are cautiously hopeful. That's what the surgeon said. Apparently there've been a series of strokes and a few years' history with dangerously high blood pressure."

He tried not to gape at her. "You didn't know?"

"Not until today, no. I yelled at Ethan's wife."

"You did?" He raised a brow, impressed.

"Well, not yelled. But I told Ethan off through her. I shouldn't have. It's not her fault. But I'm sick of being crapped on by people. I need to stay home where everyone loves me."

He hugged her to his side. "They do. We do. But I'm here now and I love you."

Her father's wife came out a few minutes later with a guy about ten years older than Gideon was. That they'd gone in and hadn't bothered to invite Jules burned in his gut, but she took it calmly so he let it go.

"There's nothing else to do for now. I'm coming back in the morning. I need to get home to the boys. Do you need a ride to the hotel?"

Jules whipped her head, just a little. "I'd like to see him before I leave."

The father-in-law shook his head. "He's already tired and needs his rest."

Jules pushed back. "I'm not going to play tennis with him. I just want him to know I'm here. I want to see him with my own eyes and know he's all right."

"You're going to make him worse. Is that really what you want? I thought you came down here for him, not for you."

Jules blinked at the father-in-law. "Excuse me? I've been here all day. I came down here because I was asked to. I resent your implication that I'd make him worse for kicks."

The new wife stepped in after tapping her father's arm. "Of course he didn't say that. Your father is tired. You can see him tomorrow. He's probably asleep by now anyway."

Gideon didn't hide his distaste. She'd rushed down here because this woman had begged her to and they hadn't bothered to even courtesy invite her to stay with them. Christ.

"I'll make sure she gets to the hotel."

Jules squeezed the hand he'd been holding. "Donna, Bart, this is my boyfriend, Gideon. Gideon, this is my dad's wife Donna and his father-in-law, Bart."

He nodded his head, not bothering to offer a hand.

"We'll see you in the morning." Bart guided Donna out.

"I'm going to stay a while." She looked to him. "It's okay if you want to go get settled at the hotel."

"Do you think I came all the way down here to leave you here on your own and go to a hotel?" He took her hand. "I'm here. Not going anywhere."

They got settled again.

"I'm glad you're here." She put her head on his shoulder and he put an arm around her.

"I'm glad too. I'm sorry it's under these circumstances though."

"I hate hospitals."

"Why?"

"When I was seven, I was in one for several days. And then afterward I had to come back for a lot of appointments. I hate the smell. I hate the carpet. I hate the muted and yet omnipresent noise." She shivered.

"What were you in the hospital for?"

She sat up a little. "I thought you knew." Her laugh was humorless. "I almost drowned. If the water hadn't been so cold I might have. Anyway, I had water in my lungs. When he threw me in the water, he missed the deepest part. I struck my head on a submerged log. Blah, blah, blah."

He hoped his horror didn't show on his face.

"He?"

"My dad. He's one of those believers in the 'throw the kid in deep water and they have to swim or else' school. Not so much."

He blew out a breath. "Your aversion to the ferry makes a hell of a lot more sense now. I'm sorry."

"It was a long time ago. But it did leave me with an intense dislike of hospitals and deep water. I still like to run through sprinklers though."

His parents hadn't been perfect, but he'd been loved. He tried to imagine this scene if his father had been in the hospital and he couldn't. They'd have all united instead of this nonsense.

He hoped anyway.

So he settled in with her, holding her close as the next hours ticked by.

It was getting into late evening when he finally stood up. "We're going to the hotel now."

"What if he wakes up?"

"You can't see him anyway. Visiting hours are over. You can't do anything. They know you're here. They've got your cell number at the nurse's station. Come on. You need a bath and to sleep for a while."

She allowed him to pull her to stand.

"I don't want you driving tonight. You're beat. You can get your car tomorrow."

The hotel wasn't far and thankfully it was out of the way and quiet. He took their bags up and pushed her into the bathroom to shower while he ordered up some food.

And then he called Cal.

"How is she?" Cal answered unceremoniously.

"So tired she's got circles under her eyes. She's alone down here. The wife didn't even invite her to stay at their house. Couldn't be bothered to have her talk with the surgeon and when they went in to see John they didn't even so much as look back to her much less ask if she wanted to see him too. Then they guilted her when she asked to see him before the new wife left. It's a wonder no one got punched. She's in the shower right now. I ordered some food and then I'm making her sleep."

"Why are you still there? If it's that screwed, bring her home. It sucks, but you can't pick your family. You can choose walking away when they shit on you so much though. We can't let this happen."

"I can't make her leave, Cal. I wish I could. I wish I could sweep her up and get her the hell away from these people. But she's scared for her dad. She needs to make the choice to leave if that's what she wants."

Cal huffed a breath. "I wish I was there right now."

"Me too. She does as well. But we'll see you tomorrow."

"Can't get here fast enough."

She came out of the bathroom, hair wrapped in a towel. He turned, smiling. "I'm on with Cal; you want to talk to him?"

She nodded and took the phone.

"Hey."

He let Cal work on her while he pulled the blankets on the bed back and fluffed the pillows.

He really did want to grab her and run for the hills. He didn't like these people at all. Didn't like the way they'd summoned her and she'd come and then been pretty much ignored.

She'd just finished the call by the time he'd finished washing up.

"Get in bed. Food should be here soon."

She nodded. "I don't have any big shirts or anything. I just packed day clothes."

He pulled the shirt he'd been wearing off and handed it her way. "Here. All warmed up."

She put it on and it swallowed her to her knees.

"Much better. Though I do like it when you sleep naked."

The food arrived and once they'd eaten, she'd snuggled down in the bed and he'd put his arms around her, holding her tight, and things felt better.

"Why are you staying?" he asked after they'd turned the lights off.

"What do you mean?"

Gideon weighed just exactly how to put it and decided she deserved blunt. "Here. Why are you staying here when clearly they don't give a crap? I'm sorry to say it. Mainly because it hurts you and I don't want that. Let's sleep and then tomorrow morning stop by the hospital, pick your car up and get the hell out of this place. Go home where people love you."

"She called me for help. I didn't think of saying 'oh hey, keep me updated.' I guess that's what Ethan did. I just got on a plane to get here because he's my father. I don't know why she'd have called and asked me to come if she hadn't wanted me to. I'm chalking her behavior today up to shock. If one of you guys was in the hospital I'd be a mess too."

"You make excuses for people's shitty manners too much."

"I know."

He hadn't expected that. "You'd never take this from me or Cal, or any of our friends. Why would you take it from your family?"

"Practice maybe. I don't know. I'm done with it though. Today when I was talking to Marci I just got mad. Like really, truly mad and I was short with her. It's not her, though. I needed to say it to Ethan. He should be here."

He sighed, burying his face in her hair.

"Or maybe not. Maybe he made the better choice."

"Baby, all you can control is what *you* do. Not what anyone else does. You did the right thing and came down here. Now, as to whether or not you stay? I can't tell you what you should do."

She laughed, turning to face him. "You tell me what to do all the time."

He kissed her soundly and she held on tight.

"And sometimes you listen. But that's different. I can't boss you around through this. You have to make your choices. I'll give you my opinion and support you no matter what you choose. But you need to be the one to choose it. Family is a completely different situation than driving around on an empty tank of gas."

She started to cry. He'd seen her cry with her friends. She was a woman who showed emotion, good and bad. But this was different. This was a way she cried only about her family and it tore him apart.

"I want to tell you to go. I want to tell you that I'll pack you into the car right now and get you to the airport so we can be in our bed by noon. I want to tell you that you've held the post of familial whipping boy far too long. You didn't cheat on your wife and break your family up. You didn't disconnect from your life and essentially abandon your children and you didn't throw a childish fit and insult your sibling. They do this to you too much. It makes me mad. It makes me want to punch people."

"And you're mad I didn't tell you before I left."

In the dark it was easier to be honest.

"I want it to be second nature for you to turn to me when you're in need. I *know* you're capable of handling this stuff yourself. I don't doubt your abilities. But you don't have to do it on your own. You've got me. And you've got Cal. I get that you were on autopilot and went with what you've had to do over the years. But I want to be your new habit."

"I've been on my own since I was nineteen. Living on my own anyway. I'm used to doing things myself. When I don't turn to you it's not about you, it's about me." She paused, thinking carefully over her words, he knew.

"Just say it. We'll work out the rest."

"I'm not sure how you always know what I'm thinking."

He kissed her forehead. "Because I love you. Because you're not that mysterious. Just a little scared and a lot sad."

She hugged him tight. "I love you, Gideon. So much it used to scare me. I'm sorry I didn't turn to you right away. It's not that I didn't trust you. Fuck, maybe I don't trust me. Or them." She shivered a moment, though it wasn't cold. "The whole thing is humiliating."

There it was. He breathed out, trying not to choke on his swallowed-back words of anger at her family.

"Why can't I be enough? I'm ashamed that they treat me this way. I'm ashamed that I take it. I'm ashamed of whatever it is that makes them reject me. It's not something I want to share. Which isn't about you, it's about me."

"You're more than enough, Juliet. You're everything. I'm here. Not because of them. Because of you. Right? It *is* humiliating, but not in the way you think. It's them who should be humiliated for acting the way they do. They take you for granted all without saying thank you or even realizing how wonderful you are. I hate that. But I love you. And so I will *always* get your back. I will *always* be at your side. Because when it comes right down to it, family is what you make. I'm your family. Cal is your family."

She let out a long, shaky breath and snuggled in closer. "I know. It means a lot to me."

"So bright and vivacious, my Juliet. You love so much, care so much. I wish I could make all this better for you."

"I've got broken pieces."

He laughed. "Baby, everyone has broken pieces."

"And yours are that you think you failed with Alana."

He froze, the pain—and the truth—of it was a little arresting.

"I guess that's true. I tried. I did. But in the end I wasn't what she needed."

"She's a blind, selfish bitch who couldn't see right in front of her damned face. Makes me want to punch her and then thank her for being so dumb that I got you instead. At least I know what to do with you."

He smiled in the dark. "You and Cal both have such a violent streak. It's hot."

She rolled him onto his back and scrambled atop.

"You're not wearing underpants, ma'am."

"Not even. It's a waste with you around anyway." She sighed.

"I worked hard at my marriage. Just not hard enough. I know that scares you, but all I can do is promise to do better this time. Moving in with me and Cal isn't a mistake. We won't fail you."

She bent to kiss him. "Is that what you think I'm worried about?"

"You're not?"

"Man, we need to work on our communication. No. I'm not worried. Because while I'm obviously biased, I don't think the failure of your marriage was your fault because you're a bad guy. I think part of it was your fault, just because it's a relationship and it has two people." She laughed. "Well, unless you're us, which you are now."

She moved around and he nearly shouted when she took his cock inside her body.

Above him, she threw her shirt off and all that loveliness was bare. Though he couldn't see her perfectly, he *knew* her. Knew the weight of her breasts, the dark pink of her nipples. He played his fingertips over them, knowing they'd tighten, knowing they'd darkened.

"What I think, when it comes to your marriage, is that you have more experience at this thing than I do. Cal does too. I don't know how to be in a relationship. I suck at it and you guys get mad. If we live together, you're going to see what a bitch I am. I'm horrible at sharing stuff."

"Because you're used to doing it alone."

She rose and fell, surrounding him. Her weight was perfect, her skin soft against his. Pleasure built slow and steady.

"It's not that I can't share. I can. I do. It's just my first instinct is to fix it myself because that's what needs to happen."

"I hate to burst your bubble, Jules, but Cal and I already know you have bitchy moments. Just like Cal and I have our too-bossy moments. You think you're the only one who has stuff to learn about being with someone? Neither Cal nor I know a fucking thing about making a go in a forever-type way. All those people he was with before? He never lived with any of them. This is new territory for all of us."

She hummed her pleasure when he skipped his fingertips up the line of her back, pulling her down to kiss him again.

It was the dark, she realized, that had enabled her to confess this way. She didn't have to watch every line on his face. Didn't have to worry about her expression. In the dark it was easier to be honest with the tough stuff.

"I'm not worried about your failing. I'm worried about my own."

He slid his palms up her thighs, up her sides and to her breasts to pull and roll her nipples until she writhed.

"Mmm, yes, that's so good. If you live with me, I'm going to wake you up with sex and French toast. I bought a better coffeemaker last week. Just for you."

She was so ridiculously lucky.

"Yeah?"

"Yeah. Let me in all the way, Jules. Live with me and Cal, be with me. We'll all learn together." He did some magical thing with his fingertip against her clit and she sucked in a breath at how good it was. "You'll have your own space. My grandmother's old sewing room would be a good place for you to meditate and be left alone when you want it. I can't promise we won't be up all over you, because as you may have noticed, Cal and I like to be up all over you. But I don't want your independence or every moment of your life. I just want to love you."

He said such good stuff. "All right."

He rolled her to her back and loomed over her. She tugged him down for a kiss as he began to thrust deep.

"Was it the new coffeemaker? Was that what sealed the deal?"

"You know me so well. Also it's because you make me come so hard and look good naked. And I like your grandpa."

He ground against her, sliding the line of his cock against her clit as he pulled out and shoved himself back in. Each stroke brought her closer and closer to the edge.

She rolled her hips and wrapped her legs around his waist. Her angle opened her up and he slid in impossibly deeper. She was so close.

He picked up the pace, fucking into her hard and deep until orgasm came and stole her breath, sucking her under.

He followed with a whisper of her name and she accepted it all, opened herself to him, flaws included.

26

Cal called once his plane had landed. He didn't want to complicate matters by showing up at the hospital when Gideon had already been there with her. He resented having to hide his relationship with her, but the ICU waiting room wasn't the time for any sort of big reveal.

Gideon answered. "I'm at baggage claim. We turned Jules's rental in so we can all ride together."

He moved steadily toward baggage claim once he'd made his way off the plane. "I'm on my way."

He saw her first. She wore sunglasses, her hair was tied back and she was in jeans and a T-shirt and was the best thing he'd ever seen. She looked in his direction and took off the glasses, smiling and moving to him and straight into his arms.

"That's the way to be **greeted**. Just sayin'." He brushed her hair back, kissing her.

"You're here."

"I am. I didn't expect to see you. I figured you'd be at the hospital."

"I made her take a break to come with me." Gideon approached, hugging them both. "Do you have anything checked?"

"No. But I'm starving."

"Me too and I know Jules is because she's barely eaten all day. There are several restaurants near the hospital."

"What's going on today?" Cal asked once they'd gotten on the freeway.

"He started the morning off a little shaky, but he's been showing some positive signs as the day has passed."

"Have you seen him yet?"

Things got quiet.

"What?"

"He can only see one person at a time for short period. So I haven't been in yet. I've asked several times and they keep putting me off."

"The new wife has been in there and when she hasn't the father-in-law or mother-in-law have been. No one has bothered to ask Jules, though when I asked about it they said it was best to just keep it to immediate family. You know, because his daughter isn't immediate enough. Not like his fucking in-laws."

Gideon's voice was so taut and filled with anger it took Cal aback. It wasn't a tone he heard from the other man very often.

"I'm going home." Jules spoke suddenly. "I've been thinking

all day long about it. Well, since last night actually when Gideon asked me why I was staying."

Cal sighed and leaned forward to squeeze her shoulder. "Baby, I'm sorry. We'll be here with you though. If you want to stay, we'll stay."

Gideon pulled off the freeway and into the parking lot of a nearby strip mall. "Let's get something to eat first. We can talk inside. Japanese all right with you two?"

She nodded and Cal got out to open her door.

He put his arm around her, hugging her to his side. "Goddamn, I've missed you. Just a day since I saw you last. I'm addicted."

She smiled, but it wasn't all the way to her eyes. He pulled her against him in the parking lot, breathing in the scent of her hair as she clung to him. He ached for her.

At last he let go and turned her gently. "Come on. You need to eat."

Once they'd ordered and the beers had been delivered, Cal turned his attention back to Jules. "Why do you want to leave? You dropped everything to come down here."

"I know. I'm sorry you two interrupted your lives to come down here with me. But I'm not wanted here. He hasn't asked to see me. She hasn't said more than ten words to me directly. Maybe she called me in a moment of panic. But whatever her deal is, she's made no effort to include me in anything going on. It's a waste of my time and emotional energy to be here."

She sipped her beer with shaky hands.

"I waited a bit. I mean, it's ICU, her husband could have died. They have young children. I figured she'd be scattered and freaked. And she is. She called me, which I appreciate."

"But?"

"He doesn't want me there. She doesn't really either."

Cal sure as hell hoped she'd finally get the gumption up to tell them all to fuck off and leave her alone. It was high time Jules disconnected herself from people who didn't appreciate her. Or worse, who made her feel bad on purpose.

"What about Ethan? Why isn't he here?"

"I have no idea. I've given up calling to try and update him because he's making Marci take the calls."

Gideon growled. "But you feel guilty about it. Stop that. Look, baby, you know Cal and I love you more than anything. I hate seeing them treat you like this. Sure it was a good idea to give her the benefit of the doubt. But they won't even let you see him. He didn't bother to tell you about any of this health stuff."

"Maybe he was trying to protect me." She sighed heavily. "I don't want to rush into judgment, but . . . I'm not sure how else to take the sum of all this stuff. So I think it's time for me to go."

"I think so too."

Cal nodded. "If that's how it is, let's do this. I'll get us on a plane later tonight and we'll get the fuck out of here and back home where we belong."

"I can tell her for you." Gideon pushed her plate closer. "Eat."

"God, you're bossy." But she picked her chopsticks up and popped a tuna roll into her mouth. "I appreciate the offer, but I'll tell her in person. It's something I have to do myself. I don't want to make a fuss. Not so much because I'm worried about pissing her off, but because she's got enough shit to shovel and I don't want to pile on. Not right now."

Cal looked to Gideon, who shrugged a little. He'd learn the whole story when they were alone.

•   •   •

They finished dinner and headed to the hospital after Cal had called to make the plane reservations for a few hours later.

"I'll wait down here. No use adding more to the situation." Cal indicated some couches in the main waiting area of the hospital.

"Are you sure? I don't want to hide you."

Cal smiled, pulling her close. "You wreck me, you know that? I don't feel hidden. Just go and tie that loose end and get back to me. We'll be in our own bed soon enough." He kissed her forehead.

"We'll be right back."

She turned to Gideon. "You don't have to."

He snorted. "Yes, yes, I do. I told you, we have your back." He held out a hand and she took it.

"I'll be here. Let Gideon kick anyone who fucks with you."

She smiled and this one went to her eyes.

"I don't want to make a scene," she said to Gideon as they got off the elevator. "I just want to say my good-byes and go."

"All right."

To be honest in her head and all, she sort of loved how protective he was over this mess. He'd been with her, at her side all day.

Donna was in the waiting room, alone for a change. Jules took the seat next to her. "I'm going to go back home. I don't think you need me here."

"I think that's probably best." Donna didn't bother to even meet Jules's eyes.

Well, that was unexpected.

"Okay then." She stood and started to leave before she changed her mind and sat back down. "No, not okay. Why did you call if you didn't want me to come down?"

"I was worried. He'll be fine. He's got a new life, Juliet. He doesn't need to think about what came before. I shouldn't have called. He's mad at me."

Gideon made a sound, but to his credit he didn't say anything. Jules nearly got up to leave again, but all the years of not saying what needed to be said had worn her down. *That* Jules took a lot. The Jules she wanted to be didn't.

"Say again?"

"He's been trying to keep you away for a few years. He did his duty. He remembers your birthday and Christmas. But we don't need you here. He has young children. You two had him and now our sons need his attention. We have a good life here; we don't need memories of the past. I'm just being honest. He's moved on. I called in a moment of weakness. My parents didn't pick up. I didn't expect you to come down here. They agree too. You and your brother drag up things best left alone."

She wanted to throw up. "Like the family you helped wreck?"

Donna's eyes widened and her mouth gaped a few times too.

"Yes, that's right. Since we're *just being honest* and all. It was bad enough that you did what you did. But people make mistakes. It wasn't enough that he left his wife and his family? Being in contact with us is unacceptable? What is wrong with you?"

"I can't believe—"

"Oh yes, you can. Cripes. I've gone out of my way to give you the benefit of the doubt. I've never pushed myself into your life. I tried to retain some sort of relationship with my father. And yes, he's my father and you're a shitty, heartless bitch of a mother if you think a man should just walk away from his kids. And he's a shithead for doing it. But what if it was your sons? What kind of person would find that acceptable?"

"He'd never do that to our sons!"

"You helped him do it to his oldest son already!"

"He's a man; he doesn't need John like my boys do. It's my sons who should have inherited that building you stole."

Jules laughed, but there was no humor there. "Look here, you. *Stolen?* You should look the word up. Better yet, look in the mirror." She stood. "Don't think you can come at me again. I've taken it for years, which may lead you to think I'm going to continue taking it. But I'm done now. I wish your children good luck; with parents like they've got, they'll need it. And if you want Ethan updated, call him yourself. Or not."

And she walked away.

27

....

Back at home, she found herself in her kitchen, rolling out dough, sucking down coffee and moving a little slow because both men's loving attention had left her sore. She smiled at that.

It was good, she realized as she sat on the plane on the way back, to just say it. All the stuff she'd shoved away because it was family and she hadn't wanted to rock the boat had only been clogging up her life. She didn't take shit from anyone else in her life, why should she from people she barely knew anymore, or who should have known better?

It was a new era for Jules on many different fronts. She and Gideon had needed that night back in the hotel room. They'd cleared the air and she felt as if she understood him a lot better afterward. Hell, she understood herself better too.

They'd be helping Patrick move into the apartment at the farmhouse that upcoming weekend. Cal had already put his house on the market, never being one to sit around once he'd made his mind up.

She had to call her landlord later that day to see if he'd let her out of her lease early. She'd been a tenant for years; hopefully he'd cut her a break.

Her phone rang and because it was not even five in the morning, she checked the caller ID and saw it was her mother of all people. She paused a moment. Did she want to do this?

She sighed and picked it up.

"Hello?"

"Jules, it's your mother. I've just had a phone call from Ethan. Do you want to explain to me why you've refused to share information about your father?"

Her nervousness washed aside, replaced by anger. "Are you telling me you're calling me about some business between me and Ethan?"

"You can't just refuse to talk with him about John's illness. That's selfish, Juliet; you should know better."

"Mother, you've picked the wrong day to do this. Take a step back. First of all, not that I owe you an explanation, but I'm not even in L.A. anymore. I'm back home. I've been back four days. If Ethan wants an update, he can call Donna. Marci knows why I stopped calling to update Ethan. And so does Ethan. Why he'd call you about it I don't know."

"What do you mean you left? He's still in ICU and you left?"

She slammed her hand down on the counter. "I told you you picked the wrong day. I gave you a warning. Yes, I left. For my own reasons. Why do you care anyway?"

"That's your father. We didn't raise you to choose your friends over your family. I'm disappointed in you."

"You're disappointed in *me*? Really? Does the irony of calling me from Italy instead of from your son's home miss you? Remember Connor's birthday? Remember choosing to swan off to Italy instead of fulfilling a promise to your family? Yeah, so really, if you want to call me out, you'd better come at me from a much better position because I'm all about some truth today. Want to keep going?"

"What's gotten into you?"

"You know, I don't take guff from anyone. In my day-to-day life I'm a strong woman who knows what she wants and goes after it. Except from my family. Which seems silly to me. I'm equalizing that. Now it's my resolution not to take anything from anyone. Including you. Including my father or his wife. I don't owe you explanations. You gave up that right when you just fell off the face of the planet and call me to tell me I was a waste of your life and to yell at me over some crap you don't know a thing about."

"I had no idea you felt this way."

"You should have known it. You're my mother. But I'm telling you now. I love you and I wish you the best. I want you to find whatever it is you've been missing. But I'm not a friend from high school you connect with every few months when you're feeling lonely or you need someone else to deliver news you don't have the guts to deliver yourself. The days of Jules running everyone's crappy errands are over. The days of me silently taking it are over. Now, if you're done yelling at me over something you don't understand, I have a business to run. By the way, I'm going to start using the apartment over Tart as business offices. That way you won't have to come back here because you feel like you have to."

"You've clearly been bothered by things for a while."

"I have. And it's not entirely fair for me to dump this all on you at once out of the blue."

Jules poured herself more coffee and then went back to fluting the edges of the tart dough.

"I used to have a mother who listened to me. Who liked being around me. Who I could talk to about most anything. I don't have her anymore and it breaks my heart. But I accept that you have a new direction. I can adapt, but you can't have it both ways. I'm not giving you a pass anymore."

Her mother was silent for long moments. "I don't think you or Ethan are wastes of my life. I'm sorry I said that. I'm sorry you've been hurting and I didn't look close enough to see it."

"I accept your apology. I'm sorry you're so sad and I wish I could make it better for you. But you don't need John anymore. He's regressed as a person. He's better off with Donna."

Her mother laughed. "There's a story with that one, I can tell."

"There is, but it doesn't need to be told because you don't need it. He's not yours anymore. Not your problem, not your burden. He's not a nice person. He's someone else's husband and someone else's father and he doesn't want any of us. And in the end, though it hurts, we're better off because he's not a real man."

"He isn't. But he was my man for thirty years. It's hard to be something for so long and then not anymore."

"I bet."

"Do you hate me?"

Jules snorted. "No. I love you. I miss you. I'm telling you to find your own path *because* I love you. But your self-imposed distance hurts. I can't lie about that and I don't want to. Our relationship has to change for me to be in it and not resent you."

"All right. I'd like it very much if you and I could meet somewhere. To visit and talk. We've got a lot to talk about."

"I can't go to Italy right now. I have . . . so much going on. Speaking of that, since I'm being honest and all, I'm in a relationship. It's not conventional, but I'm happy and it's good."

"You're a lesbian?"

She laughed. "No. I'm with two men. Cal Whaley and Gideon Carter. We're moving in together in a few weeks."

"Wow. Really? Two? And Cal looks just like his dad, which is a good thing because he's a handsome man. Two. I'm impressed."

"You are?" Relief washed through her.

"Juliet, I've made a lot of mistakes. I wasn't brave when I needed to be and I hurt you. I just needed to be away, I guess. But I took too long. I don't wish for you to be unhappy. If these two men make you happy, what's it to me that there are two instead of one?"

"I wish Ethan felt the same."

"Well take it from me, you can't live for other people's expectations. It never works. I can't . . . I can't be the woman I was before. I don't know if she's even inside me anymore. But I'd like to be who I am now and have a relationship with you. I'm coming back to the States in two months. Your aunt has some business she needs to deal with at home. Will you meet me in Chicago then? We can hit the city. Do some shopping. And talk."

"All right." She only hoped her mother kept the promise.

If she didn't, Jules would walk away once and for all.

. . .

Cal was waiting for her in the alley when she came out after work. He leaned against his pretty sports car, looking long and lean and handsome.

"Honestly, Calvin Whaley, can you stop being so delicious for a few minutes and give a girl a chance to breathe?"

He smiled but he was up to something, she could see it.

"Gideon called. He's going to be late coming back tonight. So how about you and I have a quiet night in? I've cleared my calendar and have turned off my phone."

"Will there be sex? Because I insist that if I make you dinner, you have sex with me."

"I think we can manage that, yes."

"I'll be at your place in forty-five minutes or so. I have to run home first."

He kissed her hard. "Wear that navy blue skirt I like so much."

"Who am I to refuse you?"

"Exactly, Jules. Just remember that."

Cal waited for her at his house. He poured them both a glass of wine as he checked on the prawns marinating in the fridge. He had her all to himself for a while and he wanted to take advantage of that.

She'd been . . . different since they got back from L.A. She always had been a confident person, but it was as if standing up for herself had thrown the doors wide open. She worked hard on putting the stuff with her family away. He believed she needed to confront her brother and mother, but that needed to come on her time and no one else's.

He put on some music and settled in to wait. But it wasn't very long until she showed up. Ever punctual, was his Juliet.

And she had a pastry box. Score.

"What'd you bring me?" He sidled up to her as she laughed.

"Nothing fancy. Just an apple cranberry tart. I heard someone I know liked them."

He peeked at the masterpiece she referred to as *nothing fancy*. "Looks pretty fancy to me. Almost as tasty to eat as you."

She blushed. "You're in a mood."

"I am. You make me that way. I poured you a glass of wine. The shrimp is marinating. Let's give it another half an hour or so. I picked up fresh ginger today so I want it to really get in there."

She sipped the wine. "Hits the spot." And then she told him about the call with her mother.

"Look at you, Jules. Grabbing all sorts of bulls by the horns and handing out Come-to-Jesus talks right and left. Sounds hopeful though."

She shrugged. "I think so. But I can't afford to totally trust it. I figure if I keep my expectations low she won't disappoint me. And if she does what she's supposed to, it's a big plus."

"I can't believe your shit of a brother called to tattle on you."

"He's being a dick. I can't fix that either. I can only refuse to let it in my life. Maybe one day he'll get his act together. I wanted to thank you." She put her wine down and walked to the windows to look out.

"For what?" He moved to stand behind her, his chin on her shoulder, arms around her waist.

"For being there. I was wrong to leave without talking to you both first. I told you on the phone and I told Gideon. But I needed to say it to you again. It wasn't that I didn't trust you, but I needed to fix it. To make it better and I just went into that mode. I should have turned to you first."

"I hated that you were alone for part of it. I hated that I wasn't there to hold you and protect you from whatever was going to happen. I know . . . I know it's hard for you to trust me. But I'm trying to prove myself to you."

She breathed in deep. "It's not hard to trust you at all. I've trusted you since we were kids. I'm sorry I made you feel that way."

"I've been with other people when I should have been with you."

She laughed then, putting her arms over his, leaning back into him. "We're dumb. Cal, you were with other people and you had a life before we got together, yes. But you shouldn't be sorry for that. I never wanted you to be unhappy. I just wanted you to be happy with me instead of Tom, Susie or Harry."

"I see what you did there." He kissed her cheek. "I don't want to fuck it up. You're the best thing in my life and I want to do right by you."

"You do. That's what I'm saying. I was the wrong one for not talking to you guys, not the other way around."

"None of them, the ones before, were near what we are. Do you understand that?"

"I do. You show me that every day."

"None of them ever had a key. I never wanted to pick out paint with any of them."

"Cal, you don't want to pick out paint with me either."

He laughed. "You're right. But that's about the tedious process of paint choosing, not the person choosing it. And while we're being so honest and all, are you still worried about me leaving you for Gideon?"

"I told you it was a stupid fear. A *small* stupid fear I had back at the start. I don't have that fear anymore."

"Good. I hated that you'd ever think that. I wouldn't. Not ever. I do love Gideon. But you're my heart, Jules. You're mine in a way no one else could ever be and while I do love that pussy of yours, the choice has nothing to do with your plumbing being indoor."

"You're so poetic."

"I am!" He stole a kiss. "You're with us then. All three of us."

"Yes. I've never been anyone else's. Surely you know that."

"I guess I did, but it can't hurt to hear it."

"I love you. Not just because you're handsome and well dressed. Not just because you make me dinner and seem to really enjoy eating pussy. There's no one else like you. No one else knows me the way you do."

He kissed her temple. "We're good now." It wasn't a question.

"We totally are."

"Glad you wore that skirt. You know I love it."

He pressed his cock into the luscious flesh of her ass.

"I do. Why is that? You really like blue, is that it?"

"It makes your legs look long and gorgeous."

She arched into him as he slid his palms down her thighs. He reversed, pulling the hem of the skirt up as he did. "It's short enough for me to get at your cunt whenever I want."

She was his to tease. She leaned back, affording him a great view in the glass of the window.

He let the skirt go, skimming his hands up her belly, to the hem of her shirt and he pulled it apart, sending her buttons flying. She gasped and the sound licked along his senses. Enticing.

She braced herself, palms to the window, watching him in the reflection of the glass, watching his hands on her breasts. Watching as he peeled the cups of her bra back, exposing her breasts.

He paused to admire them as he tugged and rolled her nipples until she made low, needy sounds.

"If you were my camp counselor, would you have kissed me?"

He groaned. "Yes. I shouldn't have kissed you the first time. You were my sister's friend. So young. God. But I had to. I couldn't bear the thought of any dumbass college dude kissing you."

"Fuck me." She paused, meeting his gaze in their reflection. "No one else is around. I won't tell." Her mouth tipped up on one side.

"Pull your skirt up for me. And be very quiet. We don't want anyone to hear us or I could get sent home from camp."

Her nipples hardened as he ground himself against her from behind. He slid his hand down the front of her panties and she widened her stance, giving him better access.

"I'll make it good for you. I promise."

She gasped as he slid her clit between thumb and forefinger, plumping it ever so gently. "Will it hurt?" She reached around and cupped his cock through his pants. "You feel so big."

Christ, she was going to kill him with this game.

He thrust into her hand. "Will you kiss it? After I make you come. You need to be ready first."

He fingered her pussy, watching her face in the window, knowing she was close as she made sounds low in her throat and began to roll her hips, stroking her cunt on his hand to get what she wanted.

"Yes, take what you want from me," he murmured in her ear as she gasped and came in a hot rush all over his fingers.

"Touch it," he said as he spun her and backed her to the nearby doorway. He planned to fuck the hell out of her and didn't want to break a damned window doing it.

She unbuttoned and unzipped his pants and pulled his cock out. Sending him a coy look through her lashes, she licked her lips. "Like this?" She gripped him, pumping her hand up and down a few times.

"Mmm, yes. Do you want to kiss it?"

"Really?" She fluttered her lashes.

"On your knees. Just a little kiss. You can stop if you don't like it."

She caught her bottom lip between her teeth for a moment before going to her knees. The first lick was a tease, but then she sucked the head of him into her mouth lightly, keeping him wet. No high school girl he'd ever met knew how to suck cock like that, though.

"Yes, god, yes, that's it. Touch my balls."

She looked up at him as she reached back to touch his sac, dragging her nails over him, sending a shiver up his thighs.

"For your first time, you're pretty good at this."

She pulled off his cock with a pop. "I'm an honors student."

She went back to work, taking him deep, all pretense dropped. She pushed him closer and closer to the edge until he grabbed her by the upper arms and hauled her to stand.

He stumbled back, resting his weight on the arm of the couch. He held his cock just so and she backed up, sliding her cunt down over him, sending him a thousandth of a second away from blowing.

"Hands at the small of your back."

She did and he grabbed her wrists, holding her exactly how

he wanted as he levered himself into a position where he could control the thrusts.

In the windows, the sun had begun to set and they were reflected, her skirt up high, blouse hanging open, her breasts exposed as he fucked her.

"No one else has ever come close to making me feel the way you do."

She sucked in a breath. "I'd totally have let you get to third base, Calvin."

He laughed even as he groaned when she tightened around him.

"I'm already running around the bases after this home run."

She laughed, reaching down, he saw, to rub one out. "Goddamn, when you do that, it fucks with my head. So sexy."

Greedy, she pushed herself over nearly immediately, which sent him hurtling over with her, unable to withstand the way she felt as she came.

He rested his forehead against her back.

"I love you, Juliet Lamprey."

"Thank God you do, Calvin Whaley."

Gideon came in, the scent of sex greeting him, speeding his steps. He paused in the doorway to watch a moment as Jules pulled herself up and off Cal's cock with a smile.

She turned, that smile shifting into one just for him.

"My, you have wonderful timing."

He put the bouquet of roses down on the counter and moved to them both. "I do. What'd I miss?" He pulled her close and kissed her long and slow, his hands cupping her ass as he tasted her mouth.

When he pulled back she licked her lips. "You jumped in just fine."

He stumbled back to the couch and sat and she scrambled on after him, pulling his cock free with greedy hands.

"We were just playing camp counselor and slutty camper." She winked and then laughed as Cal got on the couch on her other side and felt her up.

"Maybe we should add hot camper from the other side of the lake to the game." Cal leaned around her body to kiss Gideon, his fingers tangling with hers as they stroked Gideon's cock,

"Promise you won't tell?" Jules sent Gideon a coy smile. "We could get in so much trouble."

Gideon gulped. Never had he experienced anything so hot.

"I promise to make it worth your while." Cal got to his knees between Gideon's thighs, replacing his hand with his mouth.

Perfect suction. Nice and wet. He sucked the head and crown of Gideon's cock until it seemed his entire body throbbed.

Jules kissed his ear and neck, her nails abrading his nipples through his T-shirt. She stroked over Cal's hair as they both watched him suck Gideon's cock.

Cal kissed down to Gideon's balls, licking and kissing them and then back up to his cock again.

"He's dirty, isn't he?" Jules whispered.

"Y-yes." It wasn't a stretch to stutter it out.

"Her pussy is hot and wet." Cal kissed the head of Gideon's cock, licking through the slit.

"Yes. Yes, I want it."

Cal pulled back and helped Jules straddle Gideon, holding Gideon's cock straight for her to slide herself down over him.

Cal pulled her hair to the side, kissing down her neck as she began to fuck herself onto Gideon's cock. Over and over.

Hot. So totally hot he nearly sweated. Instead, Gideon watched as Cal pinched and rolled her nipples through her shirt, his gaze locked on Gideon.

"She's the prettiest thing I've ever seen. But your cock tastes fucking magnificent."

Jules made a sound and it vibrated through her body. That sound tore at him, tore at his control.

"If I wanted you . . . If I wanted you both, could I have you?"

Things were far beyond role-playing silliness now.

She opened her eyes, staring straight into his. "I'm yours already."

"Me too." Cal leaned in, pushing her closer, as he kissed Gideon.

He was so close. He danced right on the edge and having them both there, having her look at him like he was everything, having Cal with them on her other side, completing their union, only shredded his control further.

And in the end it was okay. Because there would always be more. Always be more love and desire. More commitment and connection.

Always.